C000128293

JARVISF

Gretta Curran Browne

SPI
Seanelle Publications Inc.

To UNA

*With much appreciation and thanks
for helping me to open locked doors.*

PART ONE

Chapter One

Island of Mull,
Scotland.

Early one afternoon in July 1826 the proprietor of the *Tobermory Inn*, Angus McLeod, was leaning on his wooden "Reception" counter with his head resting on his hand and his eyes closed in sleep.

There were no guests in residence, so no more work to be done, and the homemade remedy he had taken for his constant headaches, together with the humid summer heat, had sent him drooping into a doze.

Surprisingly, to all visitors to the island, Mull often enjoyed sub-tropical heat in the summer due to the Caledonian Forest of trees that sheltered it from the easterly winds.

The rickety old door to the inn was suddenly pushed open, bringing light into the dim entrance, followed by a boy's laughter.

Angus jerked awake, stared at the two figures in the doorway, and the comfortable expression on his face tightened.

Now the boy ... Angus didn't know who he was, nor cared ... but the man at his side, George Jarvis, always caused Angus a feeling of consternation.

There was nothing about him to dislike, and he wore the finely-tailored clothes and had the speech and manners of an educated gentleman, but he was still a *foreigner*, and many of the locals who

3

drank at the inn in the evenings found him a constant subject for curiosity, not only because he was different to anyone else they had ever known, but also because he had been brought up since boyhood by Lachlan Macquarie, a man who had been an acquaintance of the King; and George Jarvis too, it was said, had also spent time in the grand houses of the English aristocracy.

Angus narrowed his bushy eyebrows together as he looked at the tall, black-haired young man talking down to the boy at his side, noting the clean brown moulding of his face and the way his body had a strong and lithe grace.

The light from the open door illuminated his extraordinary physical attractiveness, and that alone made him very easy to like, along with his polite and agreeable manner. Only the older local men were blind to all but his race, yet none were sure what race that was exactly, except for the one thing they knew as a fact – he was definitely '*no*' *Scottish*' and definitely '*no*' one of us!'

But money was money and business was business. 'Good afternoon to you, Mr Jarvis,' Angus hailed cheerfully. 'Are ye in town to collect your post?'

'As always, Angus, as I do every Thursday,' George Jarvis smiled. 'Only today I have brought a helper who needs some refreshment.'

Angus looked down at the golden-haired boy beside him. 'And who might this laddie be?'

It was the first time young Lachlan had been allowed to travel up to Tobermory with George, but now that he was twelve years old, Elizabeth had finally given in to her son's pestering.

'This young man,' replied George, 'is Master Lachlan Macquarie Junior, the heir to the Jarvisfield Estate.'

George glanced down at young Lachlan to see how proud he might be of such a title, but the boy didn't look proud at all, just horrified ... his eyes staring in shock at the head of a small skull staring empty-eyed at him from the side of the wooden counter.

George Jarvis had seen the skull many times and thought it's display to be obscene, but he had never asked the reason why it was placed there.

The boy moved closer to George's side, silently letting him know that he did not like this place.

Angus half-laughed at the boy's fear. 'Ach, don't be afeared of my wee skull here, it canna harm ye.'

George decided to finally find out about the skull and asked, 'Did it belong to a relative of yours, Angus? Someone ... beloved ... that you couldn't bear to bury?'

'What? A relative o' mine?' Angus was insulted. 'I'll have you know Mr Jarvis that I'm a good Christian man and the entire Church of Scotland will back me up on that. But I suppose ye wouldn't know anything about that, our religious rules and laws ... ye not being a Christian.'

'I was married in a Christian church,' George informed Angus politely.

'Whaaa ... *were* ye now? Married in a Christian church?'

Angus looked shocked. Despite his fancy English name, everyone hereabouts knew that George

Jarvis was some sort of Arab from the Orient that Lachlan Macquarie Senior had adopted as a boy over in India or Egypt or somewhere. Well, fancy that now – him being a *Christian*!

Young Lachlan was still staring at the skull, and George knew the boy would pester him with questions all the way home if he did not find out the answer now.

'Is it from a hospital on the mainland then?' George asked, pointing to the skull.

'Nay, it came from a ship that sunk out there in the waters of Tobermory itself, A pay ship, carrying gold. *The Florencia* its name was, and they say that this here is the skull of a young blackie girl aged about twelve or thirteen who musta died somewhere down in the bowels of the ship, one of the galley slaves.'

It was not the explanation George had expected, and it disgusted him. His dark eyes fixed seriously on Angus as he said quietly, 'A young black girl, who drowned tragically in the slave-hold of a ship ... would it not be more fitting to take her away and give her a decent burial?'

'Take her away? Och nay, Mr Jarvis, she's been sitting on this counter for years. People from all over Mull come here to Tobermory just to see her, aye, they do, and from the mainland too. Brings me plenty of visitors she does.'

'How do you know she was black?' the boy asked curiously. 'The bones are white.'

'Well now ...' Angus leaned his forearms on the counter to answer the boy in the same way he had answered the same question by many another visitor. 'Those that found her said the skin on her wee face was as black as midnight, that's how I know.'

'And how do you know she was a girl?' the boy asked.

'Because when the sailors found her,' Angus replied, 'she still had a small ribbon knotted in her hair, tied in a girlish bow, that's how the sailors knew then, and that's how I know now. A girl with black skin, one of the slaves from the gold ship.'

'And you think that's a good enough reason to have part of her remains displayed here like an ornament?' George asked. 'Because her skin was black?'

'Aye, I do.' Angus nodded his head positively and went on. 'Even Minister Bannon said there was no wrongdoing in it, and by God – here he is now! Ask him yerself.'

The door of the inn had opened and a short barrel of a man had entered, his over-red face beaming as happily as a child's at Christmas.

'Good day to ye, Angus! Has that good woman of yours got any of that delicious grouse pie left?'

'She has, Minister, a good thick quarter of it was left the last I saw.'

'Oh, excellent, my stomach is rumbling like thunder. And how are those headaches of yours, Angus? Any improvement?'

'Nay, nay, still crushing me down,' Angus groaned. 'Betimes the pain is so bad I think one of these nights my skull will explode and that will be the end of me.'

'Pray, Angus, pray hard, and God will cure you.'

Minister Bannon turned to look roundly at George, his eyes widening. 'Oh, Mr Jarvis, well, indeed, it's not often we see you in here. And how is Mrs Macquarie these days?'

'She is well.'

'And the bonnie lad is here with you too? Hello young Lachlan, looking after your poor widowed mother are you?'

With a great effort the boy drew his eyes away from the small skull on the counter, his face still white from the shock of seeing such a sight.

'Minister ... ' Angus butted in apologetically, 'Mr Jarvis and the laddie seem to think there is something no' right with my wee skull sitting here, but you told me there was no wrongdoing in it, didna ye?'

'Nothing wrong in it at all, Angus. The owner of the skull was certainly a heathen and also black-skinned which means she was from the darkest part of the earth where the Devil himself abides'

'Minister Bannon,' George interposed coolly, 'such a view does not dignify your role as a pastor, and certainly not your high station.'

Bannon looked at him sharply, a sudden anger creeping into his tone. 'Such a view, you say? It is a *common view*, Mr Jarvis, so why do you oppose it?'

'I oppose anything that I consider to be ignorant, cruel and bigoted.'

Angus looked at George Jarvis with shock, then looked at Minister Bannon whose fat face had turned from its normal beetroot red to a deep purple and for a moment the Minister seemed unusually lost for words.

'She was a heathen!' Bannon burst out.

'God is the Father of all mankind,' George replied, 'and so respect should be given to all, including a small black girl who is long overdue a decent burial.'

'Respect, *respect* – you talk as if she is still with us,' Bannon expostulated, 'and not a skeleton long dead!'

George contemplated the minister with an expression of remote dislike, and then replied in the same quiet tone, 'Our bones may moulder, but our spirit issues forth and lives on high in a condition of glorious brightness ... with God who is the Father of *all* mankind.'

Bannon's temper got the better of him. He snapped sneeringly, 'Is that what your *pagan* God says, whoever *he* is!'

'No, I believe it was Saint Paul who said it.'

Bannon gaped at George like an astonished trout, sucked in his breath as if to speak, then changed his mind and abruptly turned and walked away without a word.

Angus leaned over the counter to watch him marching down the short narrow passage and then violently push open the door of the dining room.

Angus turned back to look at George reproachfully.

'You had me worried there for a minute, Mr Jarvis, fearing ye might have destroyed his appetite for that last quarter of grouse pie, but nay, nothing ever comes between Minister Bannon and his food. And mind, be prepared now ... he won't talk to you when ye go in there for your own food, Mr Jarvis, it's a cold face he'll show you.'

I don't want to eat in there,' the boy said quickly. 'I'm not hungry.'

Food was the last thing on George's mind now. He was looking at Angus with a fixed expression of grave concern. 'Those pains in your head, Angus, when did they start?'

'Oh, a long time ago ... let me see now ... just after I bought this place. Aye, a day or two after we moved in here is when the headaches started, mild at first, and then worse and worse they get with every year that goes past. Tormented I am, tormented.'

George looked at the small skull of the girl. 'Was she here when you moved in?'

'Oh, aye, right where she is now.'

'And why did the former owner sell this place? Do you know?'

'Well, before moving here I lived on the other end of Mull, down at Carsaig, so I didna know him at all, but he said he was selling because his health wasn't good, and he believed his wife was dying of some malady or other, so that's why – '

'Dying?' George interrupted. 'Of severe pains in her head perhaps? The same as the pains in your head?'

'Ach, I dunno, all he said was ... ' Angus looked into George's dark eyes which seemed to be suddenly illuminated with a glint of suspicion.

'Ach, ye canna be thinking...?' Angus turned his own eyes to the skull.

'Who knows,' George responded in an ominous

low tone. 'The girl has been done a great injustice, and maybe ... without a proper burial ... her spirit is unable to rest ... and so she has no other choice but continue to harm in some way those who continue to disrespect what is left of her earthly body.'

Angus stood looking at the skull with a frozen expression on his face.

George leaned closer across the counter and asked Angus in a conspirator's whisper:

'Does your wife get these fierce pains in her head also?'

Angus snapped out of his chilled stance. 'Nay, nay the skull canna be the cause. Ye're jesting with me, Mr Jarvis. Nay, my wife's headaches are due to those long pins she sticks in her hat ... And anyhows,' he added quickly, 'the Minister wouldn't hear of it, wouldn't do it – not a proper burial, not a Christian burial, nay – '

'But you could return her to the privacy of the depths of the sea, Angus, back down to the same place where the rest of her mortal remains lie. It would be a decent and respectful thing to do. Shield her from the stares of any more visitors. Do you know which part of the sea around Tobermory the ship went down?'

'Aye, I do ... ' Angus cleared his throat and pulled himself together. 'Many more lives have been lost since that ship went down ... Men diving down there searching for the lost gold, but none could go that deep, and those that did never came back up again.'

'So, will you do it?' George asked.

After another frozen silence, Angus shook his head and snapped, 'Nay! I canna do it! If you think it should be done then you do it, Mr Jarvis. Here ... 'Angus picked up the small skull and thrust it into George's hands.

'You do it ... you can take my wee fishing boat out there, it's moored at the very end, the one that's painted blue and white, and you do what needs to be done.'

Young Lachlan shrieked with jubilance. 'Yes, we'll do it! We're not scared of the sea, are we George?'

George Jarvis was looking down at the small skull of the girl in his hands.

'Yes, we'll do it,' he answered, and then looked at Angus. 'Do you have some kind of a cloth to cover her?'

Angus gave him a small towel, and then instructions as to which part of the sea the ship had sank, adding finally, 'I just hope this burial will be the cure for the torture of my headaches... But now, Mr Jarvis, how am I going to explain to all and everyone where and why the wee skull has gone? How am I going to spare myself from their criticism and complaints?'

George smiled, that calm and gentle smile which disarmed and charmed many an adversary and which Minister Bannon hated so much.

'You could say it was stolen, by a vagabond or a drunken sailor.'

Angus pursed his lips together nervously. 'I could say that, aye, I could ... but I reckon Minister Bannon will know the truth.'

Again George smiled, but cynically. 'Minister Bannon has never known the *truth* of anything, Angus, not even the truth of his own miserable ignorance.'

Chapter Two

As they walked along the waterfront, the crew of a small trading vessel was loading its cargo, barrel after barrel of what George suspected must be kegs of Tobermory's own malt whisky destined for the mainland. All the other boats were mainly fishing boats that ventured out every morning and night and George's eyes moved up beyond the row of shops and warehouses along the quayside to the rows of fishermen's houses on the hills beyond.

At the end of the quayside they found Angus's small boat, painted blue and white, with a few lobster pots inside it.

'Maybe we could try and catch a few lobsters,' young Lachlan said eagerly, but George shook his head.

'No. Angus gave us permission to use his boat to go out to sea to do one thing only, and that is all we will do.'

As soon as both were seated on the two small wooden planks opposite each other, George untied the rope, pushed away with an oar and began to row out towards the deeper waters of the Atlantic where the gold ship had gone down.

As the boat moved smoothly and silently further and further out, only the laughter and screeching of the sea birds broke the tranquillity of the deep waters of the ocean.

Young Lachlan Macquarie felt at home on the sea. He had been born in Sydney when his father was Governor-General of New South Wales and by the time he was five years old he had been given his own private cove next to Sydney Harbour which had been named '*Lachlan's Cove*.'

At first he had simply played down at the cove, sailing little boats which the convict-servants had made for him as birthday presents; but later, by the time he was seven, he had his own rowing boat taking him further out to sea, and always manning the oars, and ensuring his safety, was George Jarvis.

George paused in his rowing, his eyes scanning the sea that was glistening sharply under a golden sun.

'I think this it, or near enough,' George said, inserting the oars into their catches.

Lachlan sat silent as George lifted the small skull and removed the towel, pausing to look down at it in his hands. 'She was just a child,' he said softly.

'That's what everyone still calls me,' Lachlan said seriously, 'just a child.'

'Then you should say the prayers for her,' George replied. 'The prayers of one child for another.'

Lachlan nodded, and joined his palms together as he had been taught to do, and began to pray aloud, his eyes closed and directing all words to his "Father in Heaven" as he had been taught to do, by his mother.

George sat looking at the closed eyes of the golden-haired boy, his heart touched by his simple childish piety. His prayers for the young black girl were as heartfelt as any he would have said for a white child, because to young Lachlan there was no difference. Since his infancy he had played and had fun with the black Aboriginal children who had been his friends back in his homeland of Australia.

'Amen,' Lachlan said finally, and opened his eyes, waiting with a sombre expression for the next part of the ceremony, which would be done by George.

George sat motionless in thought for a long moment, then leaned over the side of the boat and gently placed the skull on the shimmering sea, watching it sliding downward under the surface of the water, while whispering his own prayer.

'*Khudaa Hafiz* ... God be with you.'

Chapter Three

Angus McLeod couldn't believe it – the constant pain in his head had suddenly disappeared!

'Vanished!' he cried in a daze of euphoria, rushing into the dining room where Minister Bannon was still eating. 'One minute it was there as ever and always, and then of a sudden it was gone! *Gone* I tell ye, clear gone! How do you explain it, Minister?'

Bannon pushed the last piece of suet-heavy pastry into his mouth and chomped irritably, 'Calm yourself, Angus. You are always losing things, are you not? So I am sure you'll find that whatever you have lost has not gone nor vanished, but has simply been misplaced somewhere.'

'Misplaced? 'How can you misplace a thumping great pain in the head?'

Mrs McLeod came in from the kitchen to see what all the loud talk was about. Fortyish and fat she moved like a wheel, round and rolling. 'What's to do, Angus?'

Angus looked at his wife and pointed to his head. 'It's gone. The torture of the pain in my head just stopped and vanished clean away.'

The eyes in Mrs McLeod's face shot wide in disbelief. 'Oh, bye, but how can that be? Ye've suffered that pain for nigh on ten years now, it canna have just *gone*!'

'It's a miracle!' Minister Bannon cried, his face suddenly beaming a triumphant smile. 'I told you,

Angus, I told you God would cure those headaches of yours one day; and now He in His glory has done just that! This calls for a celebratory drink! Mistress McLeod, if you would be so kind as to bring some malt?'

Mrs McLeod frowned. Minister Bannon was always calling for a drink for one reason or another but always forgot to pay for it.

'Nay, it was Mr Jarvis who done it!' Angus declared in his light-headed and pain-free excitement, looking at his wife. 'True as I'm alive, Lizzie, soon as he took that skull out of here to bury it, I felt a strange easing in my head, and now it's vanished altogether. I still canna believe it!'

'Mr Jarvis?' asked Minister Bannon, his face suddenly chilled.

'Mr Jarvis?' his wife also asked, a smile creeping on her lips. 'Mr *George* Jarvis?'

'I know no other,' Angus replied. 'But blow me down he came up quick as lightning with the answer to my affliction better than any doctor. Cured I am, Lizzie, cured at last!'

Minister Bannon sat back in his chair, his face stiff as stone as he glared at Angus.

'Are you trying to tell me, a representative on earth of Christ himself, that a heathen such as Mr George Jarvis took your skull away and thereby cured your headaches when all my prayers for you in my Kirk could not?'

'Och nay, sir,' Angus shook his head positively. 'He's not a heathen at all, he's a Christian.'

'He's a brown skinned Arab who has only once set foot inside my Kirk on a Sunday and that was to

18

accompany Mrs Macquarie at the time of her husband's death. One visit inside a Christian Kirk does not a Christian make!' Mark my words, Angus, he's one of the Devil's own.'

Lizzie McLeod had heard enough. She had a good few reasons for detesting Minister Bannon, but only one for liking George Jarvis. She rolled closer to the Minister's table, deciding to give him a reminder of his own religious teaching.

'He may be a brown-skinned Arab but so was Jesus himself, wasna he? From Palestine Jesus was, or so the Bible says. And as well that, Mr Jarvis has always seemed to us to be a nice man, a good man, and also very *handsome* in his looks. All the women hereabouts are in love with him, even old Widow Mickenchie says she'd marry him tomorrow if he'd have her and he was free. And me and Angus, well, to be honest, we don't think it's right that you should damn a man because – '

'Black magic,' Minister Bannon said thoughtfully, having stopped listening to Mrs McLeod after her first two sentences. 'So Mr Jarvis told you that if he took the skull of the blackie girl away, that would also take your headaches away?'

'Nay, he didn't say that,' Angus replied, 'but now ... aye, well ... now that I'm able to think straight and clear-headed ... well, I suppose he did *hint* at it, in a way.'

'In what way?'

Angus shook his head. 'I don't know ... I just knew he wanted the skull taken away to be buried, said it would be more respectful to the girl that had owned it, and well – '

'I knew it! Took the skull but you did not see him bury it, did you? He's probably going to use it to work some kind of heathen evil on us all. Something he probably learned from those black natives over in Botany Bay.'

'My Lord!' exclaimed Mrs McLeod with a laugh. 'I don't think it's a glass of malt whisky you need, Minister Bannon, I think it's something cold to calm your ravings, something like water.' I'll fetch you a glass will I?'

She turned and rolled out of the room without waiting for his answer, nudging her husband to follow her. 'You can carry it back out, Angus,' she said quietly.

'Oh, aye, aye ... '

As soon as she was back in her kitchen, Lizzie McLeod lifted the water jug and poured a good measure into a glass, then quickly added a big pinch of salt to it.

'There now, salt,' she muttered mischievously, 'they say a pinch of salt a day keeps the Devil himself away.'

When Angus appeared at the kitchen door she handed him the glass of water.

'That'll soon shift him,' she said, 'if not in one way then another.'

Chapter Four

In the Macquarie house on the Jarvisfield Estate, Elizabeth Macquarie and Mary Jarvis were aware of the late hour and wondering what was taking George and young Lachlan so long.

Mary was still not acclimatised to the fact that during the four months of summer, Mull had almost no night, just a couple of hours of darkness before the sun rose again. She looked at the clock – almost ten o'clock – and still broad daylight.

So different to Australia where the sun just disappeared in a fast drop at the same time every evening, winter and summer, around seven.

'George has never been this late before,' Mary said anxiously.

'Never this late,' Elizabeth agreed, although she was not in any way worried. She was too busy looking at the books of the estate, gratified to see that the rents from the tenants had always been paid on time, and there had been no problems or complaints from any of them.

And even more gratifying, was that they all seemed happy and satisfied with the man who had overseen and run the estate in the years they had been away in Australia, a Tobermory man named Robert Dewar.

Elizabeth looked up from the books to where Mary was sitting on the sofa.

'It will be Lachlan who has caused the delay today,' Elizabeth said with certainty. 'Before his father's death it was penny plain for all to see how much he loved George, but since that awful day Lachlan now follows George around like a puppy and he would stay out with him from dawn to dark if he could.'

'It's understandable though,' Mary said. 'From the day he was born George was always there, always near, a part of his family, and so he sees him as an older brother of sorts.'

'Yes, an older brother,' Elizabeth agreed, 'but that was *before* that awful day ... now he won't agree to do anything unless George tells him to do it, as if George has now taken the very high place of his father.'

Mary smiled sympathetically. 'He feels safe with George, that's all. In his heart, I'm sure that no one could take his father's place.'

'I should hope not.'

Mary slowly moved the sleeping child from her lap, laying her gently back on the sofa and stood up to walk over to the window, realising that for quite some time now it had become Elizabeth's habit to view every event and every action from how it had been before that awful day of her beloved husband's death, and how it was since then, every little change was noted with a tone of regret.

Gazing through the window, Mary suddenly jerked alert as she saw the horse and trap coming over the small hill in the distance.

'Here they come,' she said happily. 'George and Lachlan – home at last.'

*

As soon as George had stepped down from the trap Mary was in his arms, hugging him as if he had been away for years.

From the doorway, Elizabeth stood watching them: the slim and beautiful blonde-haired girl who was still so in love with her husband, and George who was as equally devoted to Mary – both smiling at each other as if in the first flush of romance instead of nearly five years of marriage.

But oh ... they had all been through so much together, the three of them, Elizabeth reflected, the long eight-month voyage back from Australia in a sub-standard ship, and Mary having to give birth to her first child on that ship, and then ... so soon after their arrival back in Scotland, that awful unexpected day ...

Elizabeth pulled herself out of her gloomy thoughts, remembering how fortunate she was, because as lonely as she sometimes felt at times, without the cheerful presence and support of George and Mary, she would feel totally lost, completely abandoned, and so would her son.

*

Later that night in the drawing-room, after Mary and the children had gone to bed, Elizabeth said, 'I will have to snap out of these doldrums of mine, George, they are wasting me physically, and I am wasting not only my time but also my life.'

George turned his face from the bookcase and looked over at Elizabeth, at her woebegone face which looked even paler above her black dress.

'You could start by disposing of your widow's

clothes,' he suggested, 'and start wearing some lively colours again.'

Elizabeth smiled faintly. 'What real difference would that make?'

'Well, people would treat you differently for a start. As soon as anyone sees you out dressed all in black, they remember you are bereaved and instantly lower their voices to a sympathetic hush.'

Elizabeth looked surprised. 'Do they?'

'They do. Have you not noticed?'

'No ... I suppose I just presumed everyone was as miserable as me.'

George put the book he had been considering back on the shelf and walked slowly across the room to sit opposite Elizabeth. Her need for a fire on a warm night like this perplexed him, but he was prepared to suffer it, suspecting her feeling of coldness was more in her mind than her body.

She was no longer the woman he knew in the past, the bright girl he had met when Lachlan had first brought him to Scotland, nor the energetic First Lady of Australia, the wife of the Viceroy Lachlan Macquarie who had helped her husband to make such needed improvements to the life and culture of that infant land.

Elizabeth had been thirty-one years old when they had arrived in Sydney, and forty-four years old when she returned, having helped to build a nation and turn a convict colony into a country. A woman who had been loved by all in New South Wales for her indomitable energy, friendliness, and most especially the fairness of her general attitude to others, especially the convicts whom she always treated with compassion, insisting they may be felons but they were still human beings and not just filth to be trampled on.

Oh yes, a great lady.

George had always liked Elizabeth, but his affection and admiration for her had never felt so strong as it did on that memorable night on the ship during the voyage back from Australia, near the port of St. Salvadore, when Elizabeth had worked so hard and stayed up for almost two nights without sleep to help Mary safely deliver their baby daughter.

No wonder Mary had chosen to name their child Elizabeth, without any protest from him.

Now Elizabeth Macquarie was forty-five years old, but she looked much older. In the past two years, since her beloved husband's death, she had aged ten years in appearance. She had always been slim, but now she was thin, very thin, and her lustrous copper-coloured hair was showing strands of grey.

Successive eruptions of crackling throbbed through the logs in the fire.

'Are you ready yet to resume contact with even your Scottish friends here on Mull?' George asked.

'No,' Elizabeth replied bleakly. 'During my years away in Australia both Murdoch and my sister Margaret over at Lochbuie have died, and as for my former friends, most of them seem to have emigrated to places like Canada or America.'

'Your sister Margaret has died? But she was younger than Murdoch, much younger, by at least twenty-five years.'

Elizabeth nodded sadly. 'What can you expect though. Poor Margaret gave birth to eleven children in less than twelve years. Enough to kill any woman.'

After a silence George said, 'Your friends in Australia have not died. Have you written to any of them yet?'

'No.' Elizabeth shook her head apologetically. 'I had nothing of cheer to write to them, so I wrote nothing at all.'

'Then they may think you are dead also.'

'What?' Elizabeth's blue eyes looked startled. 'Why would they think I am dead?'

George smiled. 'I said they may think it, not that they do.'

'Still ... you are right ... ' Elizabeth's expression flooded with thoughtfulness as she sat thinking back to those happy days in Sydney.

'So many letters keep coming from them all,' she said, 'and I have not answered even one.'

'Have you read them, the letters?'

'No, I have not even done that.' She looked at George, and for the first time in a long time her face did not look bleak as she smilingly said. 'I wonder how Mrs Ovens and Joseph Bigg are getting on? I always had a suspicion those two might end up married. Did you?'

George almost laughed. 'Not with Mrs Kelly around, no.'

'Mrs Kelly? Why, did *she* have her eyes on our carriage driver also?'

Now George *did* laugh, remembering Mrs Kelly, the widowed Irish cook in charge of the convict-servants in the staff-kitchen at Government House, and the best friend of Mrs Ovens; an Englishwoman who had travelled out to Australia with the Macquarie group solely to be a personal cook for the Governor's family.

But Mrs Kelly ... a woman who had served her time and then stayed in Australia after being transported from Ireland to Botany Bay for the crime of attempting to kill her lover because he had cruelly deceived her with another woman.

'Mrs Kelly hated men, all men,' George said to Elizabeth, 'but she loved gossiping and getting drunk on rum with Mrs Ovens in one of their kitchens every night, so I doubt she would allow Joseph Bigg to interfere with that friendship – not without attempting his murder first.'

Elizabeth actually laughed. ' I liked Mrs Kelly, she was so funny at times.'

She paused and looked at George curiously. 'Rum? Mrs Ovens too? Every night? Getting drunk on rum?'

'It was the worst kept secret in Government House. Everyone knew about the smuggled rum and the two drunken cooks night after night, everyone except you and Governor Macquarie.'

'So *you* knew, yet you did not tell us.'

George smiled. 'I think those nights made their days bearable. Their enjoyment was more to do with the shared companionship of two widows than the shared rum.'

'Still, I'm certain Mrs Ovens had a soft spot for Joseph, and I'm sure if he – '

'No, no, no!' George insisted. 'Mrs Kelly would

break his head if he tried to take away her gossip and drinking partner.'

Elizabeth's demeanour had completely changed, a new liveliness infused her voice as she stood up and walked over to the writing desk at the window. 'You are right, George, I really *should* read and answer some of these letters ...'

She opened a side-drawer of the desk and lifted out a thick pile of letters and began to quickly sift through them.'

'I think I'll start with the letters from Mrs Ovens. I know she has written a few because I recognised her very small handwriting ...'

'I'll say goodnight then,' George said, standing up and heading towards the door, but Elizabeth stopped him in his tracks.

'Don't you want to know what Mrs Ovens has to say?'

She turned the lamp up to full brightness and then began to quickly unfold a letter. 'You never know – she might have told me something about herself and Joseph Bigg, does that not interest you also?'

'Oh yes, it interests me avidly.'

Something in his tone made Elizabeth lift her eyes from the letter and look at him.

'You do understand that I am lying?' he said wryly.

'Now I do' she replied tersely. 'You have no interest whatsoever in any gossip from Mrs Ovens.'

'No interest at all,' George confirmed, lifting a candle from the sideboard to light his way upstairs.

Elizabeth could not help smiling at his typical

male behaviour, so reminiscent of her husband who detested any kind of female gossip.

As soon as he had left the room her eyes returned to the letter, her interest quickening as she read every detail written by Mrs Ovens, her eyes squinting over each word of the tiny writing, no doubt a habit developed by Mrs Ovens due to the cost of postage being charged by the page, smiling as she read one particular sentence that gratified her:

> *... Sir Thomas Brisbane is not the fine and lovely man that your husband Governor Macquarie was, we all still miss him so badly ... '*

*

George paused in the hallway, his thoughts also about Australia. He turned away from the stairs and moved towards the small study where Lachlan had spent so much time in the last few months of his life.

He sat down in the chair at the desk, the same chair Lachlan had sat in. George still missed him, and in his heart still privately mourned for him, the beloved man who had rescued him from a slave-trader in Cochin when he had been only seven years old and had brought him up like a son from then on.

George sat thoughtful, his face intent, the room flickering with light and shadow as his thoughts went back to that day in Cochin when Lachlan Macquarie had rescued him and changed his life. A young soldier in a red coat, only in his late twenties, and so enraged by the Dutch slave-trader whipping a small boy that he had taken out his pistol and pressed it to the trader's head, threatening to blow his bloody brains out if he did not release the child.

A young captain Lachlan had been then, but through the years no matter when his rank had changed, from Captain to Major to Colonel to General, George had always called him "Father", not in the paternal way of the West, but in the reverent tradition of the East.

George opened the bottom right drawer of the desk and lifted out two documents. The first, bearing the Governor's red seal, was a grant of two thousand acres of land in New South Wales belonging to Lachlan himself, which Elizabeth now owned.

The second document was a grant of one thousand acres of land in New South Wales, which Lachlan had given to George as a wedding present on the day he had married Mary in St Phillip's Church in Sydney.

George sat thinking about that sunny land, with its vast open acres and constant bright sky. Coming from the East the sun was like a magnet to him, he loved its warmth and cheerfulness, so good for the mind and so uplifting for the soul.

Only in summer could he bear the climate here in Scotland, although he should have been used to it, having been schooled for a time in London and then later in Edinburgh, but the dark skies and freezing cold of winter depressed him – and during the last winter, which had been full of sadness, he had often fought the impulse to leave Scotland and take Mary and his baby back to Australia, a country he had grown to love.

But always he had shunned the temptation away from him, because he had made a promise to Lachlan on the day before he had died, to take care of Elizabeth and young Lachlan, to remain a part of their family and never leave them alone without a man to care for them.

As well as that he possessed an indestructible bond of loyalty and love for Elizabeth and a deep affection for her son ... so no, despite how strong his desire could sometimes be, or how bright the sun and sky over Sydney harbour, he would continue to stay here in Scotland and devote himself to Lachlan's small family as well as his own.

Australia would just have to wait.

Leaving the study and walking back down the hall, Elizabeth heard his footsteps and called to him from the drawing-room, a smile on her face as he paused by the door.

'Mrs Ovens tells me that although Joseph Bigg is no longer the Governor's coachman. She read – *'he is still polishing the saddles and harnesses in the sunshine of the yard and he seems quite happy.'*

'That's good,' George smiled, thinking with affection of his old friend who had sailed out to New South Wales with them.

'Although,' Elizabeth added, reading the letter, 'Mrs Ovens says that he is beginning to look *"a bit bent in his frame these days, especially across his back, but I am sure, m'lady, that he will still be bent over polishing his harnesses until he's in his dotage, because of his love for all the horses.'"*

'But no mention of any love for her?' George asked.

'No, no mention of that at all,' Elizabeth chuckled, and picked up another letter. 'Oh, look, here's one from Sergeant Whalan. Do you remember that beautiful garden he had started to create around his home in Parramatta?'

George had seen Sergeant Whelan toiling in his beloved Parramatta garden many times, and as Elizabeth leaned forward and got stuck into his letter, George left her to it.

*

When he quietly entered the bedroom and placed the candle on the dresser, Mary pretended to be asleep but as he undressed she watched him with the drugged eyes of a besotted lover. Her attraction to George Jarvis had started on the first day she had laid eyes on him and every day the heat of her love for him grew stronger.

He slipped gently into the bed beside her and she lovingly extended her arms to embrace him, causing him to look at her with a surprised smile. 'I thought you would be asleep by now.'

'Hush now, hush,' Mary whispered and pulled him closer to her body, kissing his lips with an eager passion.

George succumbed to his beautiful wife without further speech until, in the darkness, her love set his blood on fire.

Chapter Five

The following morning, fully dressed, Mary woke him with a daylight smile and placed his whimpering daughter in the bed beside him.

'Last night Elizabeth M needed your company, and now it's Elizabeth J's turn. I'll be back for her in a few minutes, and Mrs Keillor says she'll be serving breakfast in half an hour.'

As soon as George took the child and sat her on his chest and held her there with his hands, all the whimpering stopped and she sat looking down at him, silent and smiling.

She was an exquisite child, his daughter. He could still remember those months at sea, after she had been born, when night after night as she lay curled up in warm sleep he had watched her for hours in a silent paean of ecstasy and gratitude. There was no way he could describe the depth of his love for her.

She was almost four now, and the time since her birth seemed to have gone by in a blink. Now she could walk and talk and ask him a lot of curious questions that he had no true answer for. Why were these flowers blue? Why were these ones red? Who coloured them?

'Papa,' she said, reaching to put her small hand on his face. 'Are we going to the loch today?'

'Do you *want* to go down to the loch today?'

She nodded her head up and down, slowly and definitely.

'We will go after breakfast.'

'Mama too?'

'Mama too, but only for a short time because I have my work to do.'

'Lachlan too?'

'Yes ... ah, no ...' George remembered that today was Friday, one of the days young Lachlan's teacher, Robert Meiklejohn, came to privately tutor the boy.

'No, Beth, Lachlan can't come to the loch today because he has to do his lessons in the study with Mr Meiklejohn.'

'Can I do lessons too?'

'Not yet,' George smiled, remembering the hated classrooms of his own education. 'Plenty of time yet before you start your schooling, Beth, and soon enough after that you will be crying and asking me *why* you have to do lessons.'

Mary returned to the bedroom and lifted Elizabeth down. 'Come on, my girl, let your papa get washed and dressed.'

George said, 'I've promised her we'll take her down to the loch – after breakfast – just for a short time.'

Mary, leading the child to the door, stopped and looked back at him. 'Just the three of us?'

'Yes.'

'Good,' Mary replied, then lowered her voice, 'because I want to have a talk with you, George, a *serious* talk with you.'

*

After breakfast, the sun outside was already

radiating a strong heat, making the morning perfect for a stroll down to the waters of Loch Ba, a freshwater lake at the back of the house.

Beth, whose cotton nightgown had now been replaced by a green dimity frock over white pantaloons frilling at the ankles, skipped and played and delayed the walk many times, stopping to crouch down and look at one flower after another with a litany of questions; and then stopping to examine a yellow weed which she decided was the nicest flower of them all, pulling it out of the earth to take home with her.

Mary chose that moment to start her serious talk with George.

'How long do we have to stay, George, here on Mull? It's too remote, too lonely. I love Elizabeth M, I truly do, but after General Macquarie's funeral she shut the doors of Gruline, shut them to the world.'

'That's because she did not want any visitors to see how devastated she was. Her Scottish pride would not allow any outsider to witness her grief.'

'I know, I know, but, George, that was almost two years ago, and we are all so isolated here on this island, so cut off from the rest of the world, even cut off from the rest of Scotland.'

George could not deny it as he looked at her silently.

'And as for the local Jarvisfield tenants,' Mary said despairingly, 'many of them have no English and speak only in Gaelic. They could be saying bad things about me and I wouldn't know it.'

George smiled. 'That's only the older ones, the

ones that look a hundred years old. Most of the younger tenants speak English.'

'Not to me they don't! Around me they speak only in Gaelic.' Mary shrugged. 'Probably because they know I'm English.'

'Why don't you go over to Tobermory once in a while,' George suggested. 'Meet some of the locals of the town. Most of them are fluent in English; they have to be, because of all the foreign boats that come in there. The people are friendly enough, and I've seen a few young women of around your age.'

At this Mary's face became sulky and she turned her head away as they strolled on.

Having been brought up in the city of Leicester, a place with many roads and streets and avenues, she found it hard to think of Tobermory as even a town, because it had only *one* main street – one single street along the sea front – all other paths led up to the various houses where the locals lived.

Even the town of Sydney, as young as it was, had many paved streets and beautiful buildings when she had lived there – a bank, a hospital, and many shops selling all kind of produce, including tasty spices and beautiful silks from India, colourful cotton and so many other things from Capetown, making Sydney a real town to visit, and all thanks to the hard work and planning of Governor Lachlan Macquarie.

She said all this to George as they strolled towards the loch, and George nodded. 'Yes, but what you must remember is that Lachlan Macquarie loved the town of Tobermory, as small as it is, probably even more than he loved Sydney.'

'How could he?' she challenged, 'A man with such vision? A man who – '

'A man who grew up here on the island of Mull, a man who posted all his letters in the town of Tobermory, so all his vision, his humanity and his compassion must have once started from here, from this Scottish island, from the place where his dreams and feelings began.'

When Mary made no answer, just continued walking in thoughtful silence, George looked at her sideways and asked somewhat cryptically, 'Tell me, Mary, what great man ever came out of Leicester?'

Mary looked at him, and smiled and then laughed as she slapped him reprovingly on the arm. 'George! Don't you dare start teasing me now!'

George was smiling. 'I'm just saying that although Mull has a sparse population, perhaps it makes up for in quality what it lacks in quantity.'

'Oh!' Mary said, exasperated, 'You are beginning to sound like a proud Scotsman who was born here.'

'Well, I *was* educated here.'

'Yes, in *Edinburgh*, a thriving city, full of people. And where is your loyalty to Australia now? How quickly it has faded.'

'My loyalty to Australia?' George stopped walking and looked at her, astounded. 'I have *no* loyalty to Australia.'

'But I thought ...'

'Then you thought wrongly,' he said seriously. 'To like a country, to love a country even, is one thing, but to feel *loyalty* to a country is something else. Australia is the place where I found my happiness, so how could I not love it?'

He turned to glance at his daughter, playing safely, running around a bush and chattering to herself.

'But as for loyalty, yes I *do* owe some loyalty to Scotland and this island of Mull, because the man who rescued me from the slave trade and brought me up from childhood like a son, was himself a son of Scotland, born here and now buried here. A great man.'

'And now known as the "*Father of Australia,*"

'No, the father of a boy – who died worrying about his son's care, worrying about who would look after him, look out for him, on a day to day basis, just as I would worry in the same way about the care of our daughter. Why are you so hard-hearted about this, Mary? It is not in your nature to be unfeeling or unkind, so why be so about this ... why?'

Mary bit her lip guiltily, knowing she was being very selfish, and was now showing no gratitude to Elizabeth Macquarie who had been so kind to her. She loved Elizabeth, she truly did, but she did not possess Elizabeth's gentry class to shield her against the cruelty of the world; nor did she possess George's dignity and intelligent manner that either charmed or saw off all would-be detractors because he was brown-skinned and of foreign birth.

No, she did not possess such armour against the cruel world. She was just an ordinary girl with many weaknesses and fears of her own, and only in Australia would she feel safe from castigation.

In Sydney she had lived in Government House and so was regarded as superior and a cut above all the rest. Not one of the population would dare say a word against her, especially not after she had become one of the Governor's household and then a member of his family by marrying George.

But here, in Scotland, they seemed to look down on anyone whose only offence was no more than being *English* – and she was English – worse even it seemed than being brown-skinned and a real foreigner like George.

'Mary?'

She looked at George, her wonderful husband who had changed her life, changed her heart and taught her that life can never be good if there is hatred in it, hatred for anyone – or fear, because fear was a poison that crippled the mind and eventually the body.

'I'm sorry, George,' she whispered, and then put her hands around his shoulders and hugged him close. 'I'm sorry for being selfish, I won't speak of this again.'

George drew back and looked at her with an uncertain smile. 'You promise?'

'I promise.'

'And will you go into Tobermory and get to know some of the people there?'

Mary nodded her agreement, but was unsure if it was a promise she would be able to keep.'

'Papa!'

Beth was walking towards them cradling

something in her small hands and, from the delighted expression on her face, it was something wonderful to behold.

'Look Papa, look Mama ...'

George and Mary looked down at the small slimy green frog captured within her hands. 'Can I bring it home with me?' she asked excitedly.

'No, no,' George said gently, 'because that would be unkind to the frog.'

'Why?'

'Because he must have water ...'

Mary stood watching as George led Beth back down to the stream, her mind returning to their conversation and the promise about Tobermory.

She had only once been over to the town and had quickly left it as soon as her purchases had been completed. And now, not even to please George would she ever consider attempting to make friends there, because she was too afraid that somehow they would discover that she had once been a convict.

Not that she had ever done anything wrong, well, not *very* wrong. She had been a maid in a house in Leicester, sharing an attic bedroom with three other maids, they had no mirror in the room, and Mary, seeing the mistress had so many mirrors in her bedroom, Mary often sneaked in there and borrowed a small mirror for the maids to use, especially when one of them had a night off, and the mirror was always quickly returned.

Until the night she was caught coming out of the mistress's bedroom with the small mirror in her hand, and the mistress – a woman of many natures and all of them mean – became so enraged at the maids using her mirror, she had Mary immediately arrested and charged with theft at Leicester Assizes, where she was sentenced, at the age of seventeen, to be transported as a felon to serve seven years in His Majesty's prison camp in Botany Bay.

The shame, the pain, the heartbreak of that time was all forgotten now, because she had been lucky. As soon as the ship had docked at Sydney, and John Campbell, the Governor's secretary, had come aboard to inspect the convicts, he had immediately decided that Mary looked refined enough and spoke well enough to be chosen to serve as a maid in Government House.

And it was there, in Government House, in the private apartments of Lachlan and Elizabeth Macquarie, that Mary met George Jarvis and instantly fell in love with him.

At times their romance seemed hopeless, because she was a convict and George was free, a member of the Governor's family, and in New South Wales no free person was allowed to marry a convict.

There were times, in those sunny days, when Mary thought she would die of longing, so consuming was her love for George Jarvis, and the worst heartache of all was Mrs Kelly and Mrs Ovens constantly warning her that Governor Macquarie would never allow George to have any personal relationship with a convict.

But they were proved wrong, because they did not understand the deep bond of affection that existed between Lachlan Macquarie and George Jarvis.

And later, solely due to the personal request of George – aided and supported by Elizabeth – Governor Macquarie granted Mary a pardon and her freedom, which allowed her and George to marry.

No, dear Elizabeth needed her and George now more than ever. The dream of starting a new life by returning to their own grant of land in Australia would have to wait until Elizabeth was more settled back here and young Lachlan had grown older.

Unless ... a new thought suddenly came into Mary's mind ... unless Elizabeth M also decided to return to Australia! She had many friends over there now, more than she had here in Scotland, and she owned a huge plantation of land just outside Parramatta which Major Antill was presently overseeing on her behalf.

A smile came on Mary's face as she looked over at George and Beth crouched down together by the bank of the loch, their fingers playing with the water.

No, Mary realised, it was not George she had to try and persuade to return to Australia, it was Elizabeth Macquarie ... all of them returning together.

Chapter Six

Although George Jarvis always seemed perfectly in control and unflappable, whenever life got too tough, or his problems with the women of the household seemed difficult to resolve, he sought solace by spending time with a special male friend who always listened calmly and silently, and never interrupted – his horse, which he had bought in Oban a year earlier, a handsome strapping horse which the owner had named Brodie.

In the stables, George smoothed his hand down the horse's sleek brown face and asked his friend, 'So what is the solution, Brodie? Where do my *true* loyalties lie? To the promise I made to my father to look after *his* wife and child, or to the desire of my own wife and the future of my own child?'

Brodie gave an upward shrug of his head, as if to say he didn't know the answer.

'No, how could you know?' George agreed. 'You're just a horse.'

George flopped down on the straw at the front of the box and continued the conversation.

'Your problem, Brodie, is because you are Scottish, born and reared here, so you don't know the difference between here and the rest of the world. Now, Elizabeth Macquarie, she is Scottish too, so her heart and soul have an affinity with this land, and especially with these intemperate Highlands.'

Brodie gave a small whinny of approval as if he

too had a love of these intemperate Highlands, the place of his birth.

George turned his head and looked languidly out across the stable yard, bright with sunshine.

'Of course, in summer it's different. In summer it's warm, bright and cheerful, but how long does summer last here?' He made a *'pfffff'* sound and snapped his fingers. 'Three or four months, then gone.'

George sat for a long moment thinking, and then he continued:

'In winter though, it is hard, Brodie. If Mull was a woman I would call her fickle ... fickle and capricious. Who knows what her weather is going to do next? Without any warning she drowns you in rain, then screams through the windows in many of her gales, bites you hard with her coldness, and then blows down the chimney trying to scatter the flames of the fire into the room. But then ... in summer, she changes her ways and becomes soft and beautiful again.'

After another long silence, George sighed resignedly and stood up, his hands brushing the straw from his jacket and breeches.

On impulse, he lifted down the saddle from the wall and then slowly led the horse out to the yard.

'A good energetic gallop will get rid of our frustrations. Are you game, Brodie?'

Brodie lifted his front hoof and scraped the ground eagerly, shaking his chestnut mane with excitement.

Minutes later the two of them were trotting easily down narrow winding roads while overhead golden eagles wheeled and flew and every field and hedge displayed an array of colourful wild flowers.

George took in every aspect of the various views, the hills, the lochs, and the volcanic cliffs in the distance, all presenting scenery that was breathtaking in its beauty.

'Yet only in her summer dress,' he murmured to Brodie, but the horse had seen enough; he had been promised a gallop and showed his irritation at being reined in.

George grinned and gave him a small kick with his boot, and Brodie joyously shot forward, racing at full speed for mile after mile over the land until they finally slowed to a careful trot on the steep downward slope that led into Tobermory.

When George entered the Inn for a cooling drink, Angus McLeod greeted him with a big smile of welcome.

'Och, Mr Jarvis! I've been wanting to see you and thank ye. My bad headaches ... I'm cured of them! Not a one have I had since you took away the wee skull and buried it in the sea.'

George couldn't help laughing, certain the removal of the skull had nothing to do with the cure of Angus's headaches. It was merely the suggestion of it. Such was the power of the mind in healing the body.

Chapter Seven

Despite being married to George, Mary had never relinquished her role as Elizabeth's personal maid. She tended to Elizabeth's needs, which were not many, just the usual duties of bringing her water to bathe in the morning and later buttoning the back of her dress. Even so, they spent a lot of time together, and so Mary was pleased to observe the change in Elizabeth as the summer months went by.

A change that had began with the opening of the letters from Australia. Strangely, Elizabeth seemed more willing to connect with the people of that far country more than she did with her friends or relatives here in Scotland, and that fact gave Mary renewed hope of their eventual return.

She sat knitting and smiling to herself as Elizabeth wrote page after page to Sergeant Whalan.

'Mary, do *you* remember Sergeant Whalan's lovely garden? You must have seen it during one of our stays at the summer house in Parrammata?'

Mary nodded. 'His garden was full of the most beautiful roses I have ever seen, especially the big yellow ones

'And all grown from seedlings sent to me at Government House from India,' Elizabeth replied.

'I would love to see how his garden looks now,' Mary said quietly.

'Oh, me too,' Elizabeth agreed in a yearning

tone. 'How I would *love* to see all the new shrubs and flowers he has imported from India and Capetown. He says his garden is now three times the size it was when we were there, so I'm sure it now looks absolutely wonderful.'

'Do you think you will ever go back?'

'To Australia?' Elizabeth pondered for a moment. 'Well, I do have land and stock there, and some wonderful friends – '

'Excuse me, Madam?' Cook was standing by the door, claiming Elizabeth's attention.

'Yes, Mrs Keillor?'

Mary was so delighted with Elizabeth's answer she had to leave the room and rush out to the back garden to sing out a note of delight.

It was coming – their return to Australia was on the horizon and coming closer – just a little more patience, a little more time.

*

Elizabeth's letter-writing to Australia absorbed her. Too much at times, George decided, because young Lachlan was turning to him more and more for answers to questions and general guidance as well as companionship in his daily life.

One evening in October, when the evenings were darkening early, George waited until Mary had taken Beth upstairs to bed before broaching the subject with Elizabeth.

He found her in the drawing-room, seated at her desk as usual and immersed in her writing.

'Elizabeth.'

She looked round. 'Oh. George, I'm just replying

to Reverend Cowper. Do you remember the day he married you and Mary in St Phillip's?'

'Have you given any more thought to Lachlan's education?'

Elizabeth's eyes widened. 'Well, isn't that strange – I was just writing on that very subject to Reverend Cowper.'

George sat down in one of the armchairs by the fire as Elizabeth continued:

'You see, I knew that Lachlan had planned for our son to go to Eton, but when he died in that sudden and untimely way, I couldn't bear to lose young Lachlan as well by sending him away to school in England, not so soon after his father's death, that's why I kept Mr Meiklejohn on.'

She glanced down at the letter she had been writing. 'I'm sure Reverend Cowper will tell me that my dear husband would have understood and forgiven me for not carrying out his wishes.'

'I'm sure he *will* tell you that, but at some point Lachlan should go out to school. Meiklejohn doesn't have the knowledge to teach him everything.'

'He doesn't need to know everything,' Elizabeth returned. 'He is the heir to this estate and when he's old enough he will become its laird and run it.'

'Yes, but right now Lachlan is innocent and unworldly and very shy in his manner. He needs the company of other boys.'

'Other boys? Well he has plenty of male cousins over at my sister's home at Lochbuie. Perhaps I should have taken him there sooner but I just didn't possess the fortitude to do it.'

She leaned her elbow on the desk and put a hand to her brow. 'I just couldn't face it, listening to people blabbing their sympathy and then neighbours coming in with their condolences and offers to come and visit and comfort me. And apart from that, Margaret's boys are such a *rowdy* lot.'

Which was just the kind of company young Lachlan needed now, George thought.

Elizabeth seemed uneasy about the subject and quickly ended it.

'Forgive me, George, but I really want to get on with this letter telling Reverend Cowper about Governor Macquarie's final days, which I know he will pass on to all our friends in his congregation. And I want them all to know that in his final weeks of life down there in London, all of Lachlan's final actions, all his meetings with politicians, and even his meeting with the King, were all done to help the people of Australia. I want them to *know* that his affection and thoughts to the last were of the them, the people in his favourite country, the one he ruled for so long and gave it the name of Australia.'

George nodded and stood up to leave, knowing Elizabeth's mind was too deep in memories of her husband now to be capable of giving any serious or sustained thought to the matter of her son.

Yet now that the subject had been mentioned, he knew that Elizabeth would give it thought, but not until after she had finished that letter of eulogy to Reverend Cowper about the husband she had idolised.

Ten weeks passed before the letter was

completed. It totalled forty-six pages in it final form, but tens and tens of pages had been torn up and started again until Elizabeth was finally satisfied with it.

Now it was December and a freezing winter had arrived. Young Lachlan and Beth were beginning to suffer cold after cold, both coughing continually and watery-eyed.

'I think she needs a doctor,' Mary said anxiously, her palm on Beth's forehead, 'she's burning up, I think she has a fever.'

George bent over his daughter, felt her forehead, felt the heat, saw how ill she was, and his heart began to thump. He would never forget that cold winter in Perthshire so many years ago when Lachlan and Elizabeth's baby daughter had died at three months from the bitter cold and pneumonia.

'I'd better check young Lachlan too,' he said quickly, and then headed across the landing to find Elizabeth in Lachlan's bedroom, bending over him and sponging his face.

'How is he?' George asked.

Elizabeth turned to him and George saw that her face was not anxious as Mary's face had been, it was white with terror.

'He's as hot as a furnace and yet he's shivering and saying he's cold.'

'Beth is the same. I'll go for the doctor and bring him back with me. Where does he live?'

'Dr McLean, he lives in Salen, the first house on the left as you enter the village.'

George moved to the window, looked out at the black night, then over at the clock on the dresser.

'It will be after eleven when I get there. Will he come out?'

'He'd better come out!' Elizabeth snapped. 'Salen is part of the Jarvisfield estate and he is living on Macquarie land! But George, *you* don't have to go – send one of the servants, one of stable boys.'

'No,' George said firmly. 'Beth is my daughter and too ill for me to rely on anyone else to bring a doctor as quickly as possible.'

Elizabeth sucked back a breath, relieved that George had taken charge of the matter, as he usually did these days. Always so calm, even in times of distress, George was the one person she felt she could always depend upon, no matter how bad the situation.

Young Lachlan opened his eyes, looked round the room and said croakily, 'Was that George?'

'Yes, my darling.' Elizabeth touched her son's forehead again. 'You are still so hot. Let me sponge you again.' She rinsed out the flannel in the basin of cold water and resumed sponging Lachlan's face.

'Where has George gone?'

'To fetch you a doctor, my angel.'

The boy smiled his angelic smile and closed his eyes tiredly again. 'I love George, Mama.'

'I know you do, my darling.'

Down in the stables George was speaking quickly and firmly to the stable boy he had ordered to bring him a lantern and fix it to Brodie's saddle.

'It's going to snow, Mr Jarvis,' the boy said uneasily. 'I can feel it in the air.'

'Then I'd better move swiftly,' George replied, mounting the saddle. 'Lead me out.'

Lifting his own candle-lantern and shivering in the cold, the boy walked ahead, lighting the way out of the stable and down the narrow path that led out to the road.

'Mr Jarvis, I could ride over for ye. I know the way to the doctor's house betterer than ye.'

George looked down at the boy, twelve years old and shivering like an old man suffering with the ague.

'You get back into the warmth now, Hector, and stay there. Did you put some extra candles in the saddlebag?'

'Aye, sir.'

'Then goodnight.'

And on that George rode into the darkness.

*

'His wee daughter must be bad,' Hector said to Mrs Keillor when he returned to the warm kitchen. 'He looked like nothing would stop him from venturing out.'

'Aye, and the young master too. Those children are not hardy like us, Hector, too much pampering.'

'Aye.' Hector squatted down by the fire and was inclined to agree. 'They're no' like us, are they? The other day Master Lachlan told me he was no' Scottish at all, he was Australian.'

Mrs Keillor sat back in her chair and thought about that. 'Well, he was born there, and he lived there until he was eight years old ... so, aye, that place must be his homeland, true enough.'

Hector looked into the flames. 'They're all foreign, except Mrs Macquarie. Even Mary is English.'

'Mary is a grand lass, English or no,' Mrs Keillor said fondly. 'The Mistress's personal companion she may be, but Mary has no uppity airs about her, nay, she's just a normal lass. So let me hear no bad opinion about her from ye now.'

'I wasna going to say anything bad about her, just that she's an English *sassenach*, that's all.'

Mrs Keillor yawned and looked at the clock 'Away to your bed now, Hector. I'm staying put here by my fire until Mr Jarvis gets back, just in case I'm needed to make hot drinks for the bairns or the mothers. I'll have meself a wee nap sitting here while I'm waiting, so go on now, away with ye.'

Hector got to his feet, but his mind was still curious. 'That place, Australia ... Da says it's the place where the English send all their criminals.'

'Aye, so I've heard, to a place called Bottomless Bay. But I'm sure that's thousands of miles away from where young master Lachlan was born and lived.'

'So which place was *he* born then?'

'A place called S*id*ney.'

'Sidney? That be a man's name.'

'Aye, so maybe that man S*id*ney was the first criminal the English sent out there,' Mrs Keillor wondered. 'But anyhows,' she yawned again, 'at least there's one thing we can be sure of – with a name like S*id*ney, he was no' Scottish!'

Chapter Eight

The air was bitterly cold. George wrapped his cloak tighter around him and pulled his three-cornered hat down low over his brow. The night was so black, with no moon at all, he could see no further than a few paces in front of him, lit only by the dim light of the lantern.

Heading for Salen, the narrow winding road had led him into a glen, long and dark.

He had never realised that riding through the glen at night could be so eerie, so black, so silent, no sound other than the clopping of Brodie's hooves.

Something flew past his face, an owl probably, or a bat. Looking around him, seeing nothing, but feeling the enclosure of the glen, he began to wonder if the Scottish were right about these glens being filled with spirits that only came out at night.

A shiver ran through his body, but then he checked himself, realising how foolish his thoughts were. If there were anything unnatural and unseen in the glen his horse would sense it, as all animals seemed to be able to sense the unseen. Brodie's ears would prick up, and he would react with a whinny of warning; but no, Brodie was plodding along calmly, as if knowing the way in the dark was one of his natural talents.

But still the eerie feel of the glen continued to unsettle George. Who knew what strange animals might lurk here?

Again he checked himself, deciding he would risk them all, spirits or night animals or anything else that came on his path: all that mattered was his sick daughter and getting a doctor to her. For his little Beth, his precious girl, he would risk the sight of the Devil himself and fight him if he had to.

The thought of fighting anyone took his mind back to that long ago time when Lachlan's regiment had crossed the Egyptian desert from Suez to the Nile, a march of over one hundred and fifty miles.

It all seemed such a long time ago now, those days when he was only sixteen, and how they had all hated the dry heat of that desert, marching under the sun for mile after mile with no shade from even an occasional cloud in the sky.

He felt the cold biting into his face and wished he could feel some of that Egyptian heat now.

At last he saw a light in the distance and knew they were approaching the end of the glen. Relief flooded through him and he leaned forward to pat the horse's long neck.

'You're a champion, Brodie. You would have made a great war horse if you had been bought by the British Army and not me.'

*

The light had come from the first house at the edge of the glen, Dr McLean's house.

The housekeeper answered George's knock in her nightcap, a thick shawl wrapped around her nightgown.

55

'Aye,' she said, 'the doctor must be still awake because I saw a light under the door of his bedroom.'

George realised that must have been the light he had seen when approaching the end of the glen, the light from the doctor's window.

'But bye! This is a very late hour of night to call, and Dr McLean is already in his bed.'

'Yet his light is still on,' George said, 'so he must be awake.'

'Aye, he must be,' she grunted, opening the door wider for George to enter, 'reading those books of his no doot!'

She led George into a parlour and bade him to sit down. 'And no doot ye'll be needing a hot drink yerself.'

George moved towards the heat of the banked-down fire. 'It's freezing out there,' he said. 'As cold as ice.'

'Aye, I'll stir up the fire for ye.' She moved in front of him and lifted the poker, stabbing into the base of the fire until the flames flared.

Who is it that's ailing?'

'My daughter.'

'Your dattur? A child then.'

'Yes, and a young boy, both are very sick and need the doctor.'

'Och,' the housekeeper shrugged, 'children are never as sick as they seem.'

'No, that's not always true,' George replied. 'Years ago in Perthshire when little Jane got sick, her cold turned into pneumonia and she died.'

'How old was she?'

'Three months.'

'Oh, a very *wee* bairn then.' The housekeeper pulled her shawl tightly around her. 'Aye, well that can happen when they're that young. But now, sit ye here and I'll go up to Dr McLean and then I'll heat ye up a dish of beef broth.'

'Thank you, but I don't need any refreshment.'

At the door she paused and looked back, as if suddenly remembering. 'What name will I tell him? What house is it?'

The Macquarie house at Gruline.'

'Macquarie? You mean ... the house of the young laird of Jarvisfield?'

'Yes, he is the boy that is sick, as well as my daughter.'

'And your dattur is?'

'Elizabeth Jarvis.'

'Macquarie, Jarvis ... Jarvisfield ... oh my!' She turned and quickly left the room, clumping up the wooden stairs as fast as her feet would take her.

George finally removed his cloak and sat down by the fire, holding his hands out to the flames and feeling the wonderful warmth, listening to the sound of voices in the room above and hoping the doctor was not going to be contrary about the late hour.

And as he sat there, looking into the flames, it suddenly struck him, as it must have struck the housekeeper, that there would be no doctor living here, no house standing here either, no human habitation at all – if Lachlan Macquarie had not bought the land and built the village of Salen.

This was the first village Lachlan had planned to

the last detail with his architect, and then arranged for the stonemasons to come in and build it – only six years before he had re-designed Sydney and turned it from a shabby collection of shacks into a respectable city with so many new and necessary buildings, including a hospital.

George smiled as he remembered those early days when Lachlan was planning the building of Salen.

A young officer in his late thirties, he had returned from India a wealthy man, and bought nothing of any extravagance except half of the island of Mull.

He had chosen the area of Gruline to build his Scottish home, but in Salen he wanted to build some comfortable houses where his new tenants could live in comfort. By the end though, Lachlan being Lachlan, he had insisted upon a grocery store, a blacksmith's, a doctor's house, and even a Post Office to make the village complete and independent of Tobermory.

George had not witnessed the building of the village, because as soon as they had arrived in London, Lachlan had forced him to attend a private boarding school for a full year, before moving him up to a college in Edinburgh. Yet here it was, the village of Salen, built and owned by Lachlan Macquarie, and now George was depending upon its doctor to come and attend upon Lachlan's son.

Footsteps on the stairs.

Moments later Dr McLean entered the parlour still wearing his nightshirt and nightcap and carrying a black bag. A man in his late forties, he pushed his spectacles further up his nose and peered at George, then held out his hand.

'Mr Jarvis.'

George stood and shook his hand. 'Dr McLean. My apologies for calling on you at such a late hour.'

'Och, tis something I expect in winter. In the summer I rarely have a caller at all, day or night, so I can't complain.'

He peered over his spectacles at George again. 'Mr Jarvis, yes, I have heard of you, but we have never met before this, have we?'

'No, sir.'

'Now tell me the symptoms of the two sick children, but first the boy, the young laird.'

George described the symptoms of the constant coughing, the watery eyes, the constant and miserable tiredness and now the high temperature.

'And my daughter's symptoms are exactly the same.'

'So, all in all, I would say they are symptoms that should not worry you overmuch, just one of the many maladies of winter.'

George instantly felt annoyed by the doctor's complacency. 'But the symptoms *do* worry me, sir. In particular, the constant coughing and the high temperature. Could they not be symptoms of developing pneumonia?'

'In some cases, yes, but let me tell you why children cough so much in winter. Firstly, they get a small cold in their head, and this is aggravated by the fires we burn in every room in winter, even our bedrooms, emitting smoke that aggravates the children's throats and makes them cough, as well as making their eyes more watery than usual.

'Secondly, the continual coughing puts a strain on their lungs and leads to increased tiredness. Also, as our bedrooms are kept much warmer in winter, when children are confined to bed they *do* get very hot.'

George looked at Dr Mclean, wondering if he was an absolute fool, or a very good and practical doctor?

Dr McLean opened his medical bag. 'Now I will give you a bottle of linctus to soothe their coughs, and some powders to reduce their temperatures, and then let the body do the rest of its natural work in the healing process. But you must – and I do stress this point – you must ensure that their bedrooms are not kept *too* warm, otherwise they could become dehydrated which then leads to strong headaches and very unhappy children.'

Well, he didn't sound like a quack, and George began to wonder if his visit here had been too hasty.

'Dr McLean,' he said hesitantly, 'forgive me for asking, but where ... did you ... do your medical training?'

'Oh, I practised on cows and sheep, the odd goose here and there, a few old cats, the odd young dog – but now I practise on humans.'

The alarmed expression on George's face made Dr McLean throw back his head in laughter.

'I'm jesting, Mr Jarvis, something I always do when someone dares to question my qualifications. I can assure you that I received my medical training in one of the best hospitals in Edinburgh.'

'My apologies, sir.'

'Accepted.'

'But Mrs Macquarie does insist that you come to Gruline House to examine her son, and I do request the same for my daughter.'

'Certainly, I will call on the young laird of our land if it is so demanded, but not until tomorrow morning, after I have had my night's sleep. To rush out now would be an unnecessary folly.'

George struggled with his thoughts, still worrying about Beth, yet reassured by Dr McLean's medical advice.

'I'll take the linctus and powders back with me now, but I can rely upon you to visit Gruline tomorrow?'

'Most certainly you can.' Dr McLean smiled. 'If only for the purpose of presenting my bill.'

*

As George rode away from Salen he saw that Hector had been right in his prediction: a powdering of snow lay on the ground and more snow was falling.

The blackness of the silent glen was beginning to feel eerie again, wild and desolate, not a place for humans at night.

George adjusted the pole carrying the lantern and bent it forward, giving Brodie more light on the ground underfoot.

A mile and a half or so inside the glen a wind began to whip up, rustling the trees and blowing the snow into George's face, as well as unsettling

Brodie.

Leaning forward and stroking the horse's neck, George started a conversation to distract him, to calm him, but Brodie was not listening, his concentration on the ground before him, snorting his irritation.

The air was so cold it was turning the falling snow into ice as soon it reached the ground and the horse began to slither slightly with every few steps he took.

Alarmed now, George wondered if they should turn back and seek refuge for the night in Salen, but he reckoned they were now deep in the middle of the glen, and it would be as long a journey to go back as it would to go forward.

The wind became even stronger. George bent forward against it, head low, continually patting the horse's neck to comfort him; but the wind, the snow, the ice, and the darkness of the glen despite the small light of the lantern, all wreaked their havoc on the man and his horse, causing Brodie to suddenly slither forward and go down on his front legs, sending George toppling over his head, one foot still caught in the stirrup.

Whinnying in pain, Brodie tried to stand, but the ice underfoot prevented him, the effort leading to both man and horse falling sideways off the road until they were crashing down over the rocks and boulders into the blackness of unconsciousness.

Chapter Nine

True to his word and his bank account, Dr McLean arrived at Gruline the following morning, just before noon.

He greeted Elizabeth with deference. 'My apologies for arriving so late in the morning, Mrs Macquarie, but the snow and ice on the road has made my journey here a slow one. How is the young laird?'

'Much the same.' Elizabeth looked past him to the closed front door. 'Is George not with you?'

'George? Oh, you mean Mr Jarvis? No, he left Salen last night. I believe he and his horse were heading for the much shorter route back through the glen.'

Elizabeth's breaths were becoming uneven. 'Did you journey here through the glen?'

'Good grief, no. I'm not up to riding a horse anymore, not with this touch of arthritis in my hip. No, these days I travel by trap, and so I took the main road from Salen to Tobermory, and then had to double halfway back again to reach you here at Gruline.'

Elizabeth's fists were irritably knocking against each other. 'But don't you understand my fear? If George left Salen last night and he has not yet arrived here, then something must have happened to him in the glen.'

'The glen?' Dr McLean finally understood and became equally as alarmed.

'Then something must be done! A search party perhaps? I am not exaggerating when I say that in this freezing weather, with all the snow and ice, it would not take very long for someone to die of exposure out in that glen.'

'You should have stopped him from returning then!' Elizabeth snapped. 'Seeing the snow falling, and knowing how cold it was, you should have offered him hospitality in your home until the light of morning. That's what we thought you had done.'

Dr McLean looked shocked. 'It never occurred to me ... He seemed determined to get back as swiftly as possible, and also ... well, he seemed so capable in every respect.'

Elizabeth had heard enough. She turned and left the doctor standing and headed for the kitchen where she alerted Mrs Keillor and then found Hector.

'Hector, I want you to wrap up as warmly as possible, and then you must ride to Robert Dewar and tell him a search party must be gathered amongst the tenants immediately. Every strong man and boy must stop what he is doing and start searching the route from here to Salen through the glen.'

Hector looked bewildered. 'For why?'

'Mr Jarvis left Salen last night and he has not yet returned. He must be injured, somewhere along the road through the glen. Tell Mr Dewar, tell any tenant you see, tell everyone – George must be found, and quickly!'

'What about his horse?' Hector asked. 'If Mr Jarvis was injured or hurt, Brodie would have come back here looking for help, aye, I know he would.'

'Or maybe Brodie is acting the dutiful sentinel and is standing guard over George until someone comes and finds him!' Elizabeth snapped. 'Now *go!*'

Hector fled, and Mrs Keillor made a small sound in her throat and gave Elizabeth a slight nod of her head to turn and look at the open door of the kitchen.

Elizabeth turned and saw Mary standing there, her hand to her throat and her face as white as a sheet.

'Mary ...' Elizabeth moved and bundled the girl inside her arms. 'Don't worry, Mary, we will find him, and all will be well. A few cuts and bruises, maybe even a broken leg, it happens all the time to riders, but George is strong and determined and he will recover quickly.'

'What if they can't find him?' Mary asked.

'Of course they will find him!' Elizabeth replied with certainty. 'Mary this is *Mull*, and these people are Scottish people, *Highland* people – they know every inch of the terrain and will not fear to battle it. And George is a soldier, you know that, all the time he spent with Lachlan and the soldiers of the British Army, marching across deserts, surviving without water. George will know what to do to keep himself safe until help arrives.'

Tears were slipping down Mary's face. She leaned closer into Elizabeth to draw in more of her comfort and reassurance, saying softly, 'Yes, George always knows what to do.'

Chapter Ten

When she was given the news, ten hours later, Elizabeth's reaction to George's death was that of a woman stunned.

It was not possible, George Jarvis dead? No, it couldn't be true!

Even when Mary screamed and screamed and then finally collapsed into a chair with heartbroken sobs, Elizabeth was unable to comfort her. She stood in the centre of the drawing-room, silent and staring wide-eyed at Mary, convinced this was all just a hideous dream.

Later, after Dr McLean had given Mary a few drops of laudanum to calm her and help her sleep, he came back into the room and said to Elizabeth in a matter-of-fact tone:

'She will sleep now, that will give her some respite. As for the two children, both are beginning to recover from their colds, just as I knew they would. They'll be up and about in no time.'

'So, there was no need for George ... '

'No need at all,' Dr McLean replied. 'And certainly not at night, in this weather.' He shrugged. 'But we must make allowances for all the parents of sick children, and Mr Jarvis did seem to be a very caring father.'

'George was very caring about everyone,' Elizabeth murmured, feeling sick with grief. 'Do you think Mary will be able to cope with this?'

'No, not for some time,' Dr McLean replied

quietly, his mind recalling the face of the beautiful young girl with tears still streaming down her face, even as her eyes closed under the drugging effects of the laudanum.

'She is heartbroken.'

Elizabeth nodded, and then her composure completely changed. She began walking slowly up and down the room, wringing her hands and speaking in tones of painful regret at having allowed George to venture out so late at night and in such bitter weather.

Dr McLean was hugely relieved to be able to escape when Mrs Keillor arrived to escort him up to his room.

'Now, I've put a hot-jar in your bed,' said Mrs Keillor, leading him up the stairs. 'And Maggie has got a good fire going in there now, so ye'll be nice and warm, Dr McLean, nice and warm."

'And I'll wake up with a blocked nose, a chesty cough and a bad headache,' the doctor retorted. 'Is there water in the room?'

'Aye, sir, a large jug of water for drinking or washing, whichever ye please.'

'Well, thank you for the hot-jar in my bed, that will do me fine.'

As soon as the door had closed behind Mrs Keillor, Dr McLean lifted the jug of water and poured some slowly over the fire, listening to it hiss and splutter and watching it darken.

'These women and their bedroom fires!' he muttered tiredly. 'What do they think blankets and bed-quilts are for?'

Mrs Keillor returned to the kitchen to find

Hector still squatting by the fire's hearth, and still crying profusely.

Maggie was bent over the boy, a hand on his shoulder, endeavouring to comfort him. She looked up at the cook, a hopeless expression on her face.

'Nothing I say to him does any good, Mrs Keillor. He canna be consoled!'

'Aye, well ...' Mrs Keillor nodded at the new scullery maid who was only a year older than Hector. 'He was very fond of Mr Jarvis was Hector, as we all were, Maggie.'

'I'm crying for *Brodie*,' Hector wailed. 'Three of his legs broken and a gash down his head! Do none of ye care that Brodie died too!'

'Ah, we do care, Hector, aye we do,' Mrs Keillor muttered sympathetically. She sat down in her chair, unable to restrain a tear falling onto her cheek. 'But Mr Jarvis suffered just as badly ...'

She lifted her apron and wiped at her eyes. 'And he was such a fine man, aye, such a *fine* man ... He'll be a sore loss to the family and this house, that's for sure.'

Chapter Eleven

On the day of the funeral, Mrs Keillor's kitchen was busy and unusually crowded due to the number of young girls – the daughters of nearby tenants – who had come in to 'lend a hand' with the serving of the food and drinks.

'By! It seems like only yesterday since these same bunch of grand people came to Mull for General Macquarie's funeral,' Mrs Keillor said anxiously, stirring a wooden spoon into a cauldron of simmering chicken soup. 'Do ye think they'll ken that my menu today is the same as the last time?'

'They'll no' notice,' said Lorna McLaughlin, a fifteen-year-old who had helped out at the previous funeral. 'They've come to pay their last respects to Mr Jarvis, and won't care about the food.'

Mrs Keillor turned and looked at the girl. 'How stupid are ye? Since when did ye turn into a blathering fool, Lorna McLaughlin?'

Lorna's eyes were wide. 'But Mrs Keillor – '

'But nowt!' Mrs Keillor snapped, her anxiety turning to impatience. 'Everyone knows that the *food* to be provided is the most important thing people think about after a funeral. Same as after a wedding. And it has to be *good* food, otherwise the occasion is a disgrace. Why d'ye think I stayed up all night baking and roasting?'

George was being laid to rest with Lachlan Macquarie Senior and his baby daughter in the small private cemetery on the estate, a short distance from the front of the house.

Maggie Kennedy – who had been standing at the front door of the house watching for the return of the mourners – came running back into the kitchen in shock.

'There's bad trouble at the grave. Mrs Keillor! Aye, there is! Master Lachlan is kicking and punching Minister Bannon and trying to push him away! He's no' letting him say the prayers for Mr Jarvis!'

'No!' Mrs Keillor would not believe it, ripping off her apron and running through the house to the front door where she saw the commotion in yon cemetery garden. Mr Bannon was down on his back now, with two of the male mourners bending to help the hefty cleric his feet, while Mrs Macquarie was trying to restrain her son.

Lord save us!' Mrs Keillor muttered in shock. Young Lachlan's face was contorted as he screamed out his rage:

'George wouldn't want a bigoted ignorant and unholy man like you saying his last prayers! You told everyone he was a heathen! Aye, some of the tenants' lads told me what you've been saying about George! Now get away from his grave and get off my land. Get off my land!'

Mrs Keillor had her hands over her mouth, her big eyes staring.

Of course it *was* his land now, she realised; he had inherited it from his father and now his mother was just holding it in trust for him.

'Get off my land!'

Mrs Keillor turned quickly and moved back

inside the house. 'I canna look nor listen any more, Maggie! It's too upsetting. Ye keep watching – and ye as well, Lorna – and then come back to the kitchen to keep me informed! By! Young master Lachlan! Always as sweet as an angel! Who would have thought it!'

Ten minutes later Maggie came running back in again to tell Mrs Keillor: 'Two of the gentlemen helped Minister Bannon into the trap. Hector is taking him away and back to his manse.'

'So what's happening now?'

Mary is going to say the last prayers. Tis a good thing they took the Minister away because Mary was looking like she wanted to hit him too, and she said something to him that I couldna hear. But now she's crying.'

'Go back out – keep me informed!'

Lorna crossed paths with Maggie as she too now ran into the kitchen.

'Mrs Macquarie called me over, and she whispered for me to tell ye that when they all get back to the house, everything is to be done as if nothing un... un – '

'Untoward?'

Lorna nodded. 'Aye, as if nothing un-to-ward has happened.'

'And young Lachlan? Now Minister Bannon has gone? Has he calmed down?'

'Och!' said Lorna. 'He's no' calm at all. He's weeping buckets! He looks even more heartbroken than Mary.'

'Oh no, that's no' possible,' Mrs Keillor said moodily. 'No one could be more heartbroken than

Mary is now.'

'Will I go back out?'

'Aye.'

*

'They're coming back,' said Maggie. 'The funeral is over.'

Mrs Keillor flew into a panic, barking out orders like a drill-sergeant.

'Ye, Lorna, take that tray of drinks to the hall and greet the mourners with it.'

Lorna quickly lifted the silver tray of crystal glasses filled with sherry and rushed out of the kitchen.

'And ye, Maggie Kennedy, 'ye do the same with the tray of whisky glasses, but only offer a glass to the gentlemen, no' the ladies.'

'Why no' the ladies, Mrs Keillor?'

'Because ladies usually prefer to drink nothing stronger than sherry – least, no' in public company anyways. Now *scoot!*'

Mrs Keillor turned and stood ranging her eyes over the food on the large table in the centre of the kitchen, judging its quality and quantity: three roasted geese and a shank of boiled ham, a joint of beef pickled with onion gravy; six large vegetable pies – the pastry on all of the pies as golden as they should be ... aye, the food was good enough and plenty enough ... and so *she* at least, had not let Mr Jarvis down. The feast she had prepared for his guests was as good as the one she had prepared for General Macquarie. Oh, and the chicken soup!

She rushed over to the cauldron and gave it

another stir. After their sherry and whisky the guests would sit down and need a warming dish of hot soup to banish the chill from their bodies after standing outdoors in such bitter weather.

Finally, she gave a short sit-down to herself in the chair by the fire, satisfied to know that all was as it should be in the house, having checked all the rooms earlier. Young Hector had got good fires burning in both the drawing-room and the dining room, a warm welcome for their guests, just as important as good food.

She sat back and sniffed with satisfaction. Mrs Macquarie would have no complaints, nor Mary, the widow – aye, both women should be very pleased with all the work she had done on their behalf.

*

In the drawing-room, her emotions still in turmoil, Mary Jarvis was finding it very difficult to converse with the other mourners, but as George's widow she knew it was her duty to do her best to be sociable, especially to those people who had taken the time and trouble to travel up to Mull, some from as far as London.

She accepted a glass of sherry and looked around at the guests ... most of them she did not know, and most of them seemed more eager to speak with Elizabeth rather than her.

There was only one gentleman she recognised, a man in his sixties, and he was standing with his back to the fireplace warming himself while drinking his whisky – a very stern-looking man,

Mary had always thought, although she personally had never spoken with him.

Lord Strathallan, the new executor of the Jarvisfield estate and young Lachlan's legal guardian, saw Mary's eyes on him and he smiled at her.

Hesitantly, she smiled back, and he immediately crossed the room to speak with her, very gently.

'Mrs Jarvis, my sincere condolences.'

'Thank you.'

'I remember George as a very beautiful young boy, only ten years old when I first met him, and well ... it is fitting that he should now be laid to rest in the same grave as Lachlan.'

Mary's interest instantly quickened. 'You knew George ... when he was a *boy*?'

Lord Strathallan nodded. 'The first time I met George was in China. Of course then and there I was not called Lord Strathallan, just plain James Drummond, a doctor attached to the East India Trading Company in Macao.'

Mary knew all about George's visit to China with Lachlan and Jane, Bappoo and Marianne, but he had never mentioned the fact that Lord Strathallan had been there too.

'Over the years, of course,' Strathallan continued, 'during my stop-off in India, and then my return to Britain, Lachlan and I became good friends, close friends, and during that time I came to know George very well too.' His face became stern and stiff again. 'It is very sad that he has died so young.'

Mary could not bear to think about that. She

looked across the room at a man who seemed to be hogging Elizabeth's attention.

'Who is that gentleman speaking with Mrs Macquarie?' she asked.

Lord Strathallan turned and looked. 'Oh, that is Charles Forbes, another old friend of Lachlan's from India. He returned to England some years ago and is now a member of our Parliament. He also knew George very well.'

Mary then spent a further hour in the company of Lord Strathallan while he pointed out various people to her and told her who they were, as well as numerous little stories about them, but the only stories she fully heard were the ones that contained scenes of George in them.

When the time came to go to the dining room to eat, Mary accepted Lord Strathallan's arm and was pleased to find she would be sitting next to him at table, simply because he was the only guest she knew, and she was also eager to hear more of his stories about George.

As she moved to sit down, one of the local girls serving as maids came and whispered to her. 'Mrs Jarvis, there's a man and a woman outside the front door, asking to speak to Mrs Jarvis.'

Mary looked at the girl perplexed. 'Who are they?'

'I don't know, I didna see them. Mrs Keillor just said to ask ye if you would mind going to speak to them. She said they've travelled down from Tobermory.'

Mary excused herself to Lord Strathallan and left the dining room, crossing the hall with trepidation.

She didn't know anyone in Tobermory.

At the open front door she saw a short wiry man with very bushy eyebrows and a short fat woman standing beside him, both muffled up to the nose with scarves and shivering with the cold.

'Yes?'

'Mrs Jarvis?'

'Yes.'

'Mr George Jarvis's widow?'

'Yes.'

'I'm Angus McLeod,' said the man, 'the proprietor of the Tobermory Inn. We came here on this sad day, if ye don't mind, to pay our last respects to Mr Jarvis, who we liked reet well, aye, very well indeed, and to give our sincere condolences to his widow.'

'Why ... thank you.'

'And I've brought you a gift,' said Mrs McLeod, opening up a parcel and taking out a small pillow covered in a white linen case on which the name *George* was embroidered in blue and surrounded by little blue embroidered flowers.

'It's just a little comforter,' Mrs McLeod said gently, 'something for you to hold on to in these first early nights of such sadness. I made one for myself when my wee boy was taken many years ago, and aye, it helped me through, having something with his name on to hold.'

Mary's heart was thumping and her eyes brimming with tears as she took the pillow into her hands, looked down at the name, and then held it close to her chest.

'You don't need to be told, I suppose,' Mrs

McLeod added, 'that those blue flowers are called "forget-me-nots". I would have covered the whole pillowcase in them but my time to finish the embroidery by today was so short.'

Mary was breathing slowly and painfully in an effort to calm her emotions. 'Please, come in,' she opened the door wider and beckoned them inside. 'Please, come in ... you must have some refreshment to warm you after your journey.'

She turned and saw Maggie Kennedy still hovering nearby and listening to every word.

'Maggie, will you take Mr and Mrs McLeod to the kitchen and tell Mrs Keillor to see that they are well looked after.'

'Aye, Mrs Jarvis.'

Mary turned back to the couple, too emotionally moved for any more words other than to say again, 'Thank you.'

And then turned and ran to her bedroom where she flung herself down on the bed, still hugging her new comforter and crying, 'Oh, George, George ... I miss you so much ... we *all* do!'

Chapter Twelve

Later, looking back, Elizabeth was able to pinpoint the time of George's death as the time of the sudden and disturbing change in the personality of her son.

Overnight, it seemed, Lachlan had changed from an angelic young boy into an absolute devil, vicious and violent in his tempers.

He had reacted to the death of his father with tears, but he had reacted to the loss of George with *rage* – fighting with everyone in the household and even managing to give Hector a bloody nose.

'You damn swine! Don't you *dare* say George was to blame for the horse's death!'

'He was! He shouldna have taken him out in the dark when I told him snow was acoming!'

At the sound of the raised voices Elizabeth had stepped into the yard only seconds after Lachlan had lunged at Hector, knocking the surprised stable boy to the ground and punching him hard in the face.

'Hoigh! Hoigh!' Mrs Keillor had cried in shock. 'That's no way for a young Scottish gentleman to behave!'

Lachlan had looked over his shoulder at the housekeeper with pure hate on his face.

'I'm not Scottish, I'm *Australian!* And I'm going back there! This country kills people when they come here – first my father and now George. I hate this place, I *hate* it!'

'He has always been such a *good* boy,' Elizabeth later insisted to Mrs Keillor, 'but he is still very distressed.'

'As we all are, Mrs Macquarie, as we all are, but that was a terrible lathering he gave poor Hector. And aye, it's left me dazed, because I wouldn't have thought young master Lachlan was capable of such violence in his temper.'

Two days later Elizabeth again found herself defending her son in response to complaints from his tutor, Mr Meiklejohn.

'He is distressed, as we all are, Mr Meiklejohn,' she insisted impatiently. 'You *know* Lachlan is a good boy. You have said so many times yourself?'

'He *was* a good boy,' Mr Meiklejohn replied crisply, 'but now he's behaving like a *crazy* person.'

'Crazy?' Elizabeth's expression became icy, her voice chilled. 'If that is your opinion, Mr Meiklejohn, then you may end your role as his tutor immediately.'

Meiklejohn paused for a moment, and then replied quietly, 'If that is your wish, Mrs Macquarie, but if you will pardon my temerity, may I also say, with all due respect, that Mr Jarvis was right ... it really is time that Lachlan was sent *out* to school. He's now at an age when he needs the company of other boys like himself.'

'Like himself? *Crazy* boys?'

'Bright boys, of his own age, and of his own class. Boys who will be his friends and help him to have some enjoyment in life, not cooped up in this house with bereaved adults. I'm quite sure if he *did* go out to school it would help him to recover from the loss of both his father and Mr Jarvis more easily.'

Elizabeth's expression was still cold. 'And what kind of school do you suggest for my son, Mr Meiklejohn?'

'The tutor hesitated for a moment. 'I would suggest a ... a *boarding* school, away from his home.'

'Away?' Elizabeth looked shocked at the suggestion. 'Away from his mother?'

'Away from his pain, his heartache, and his overwhelming feelings of loss.'

PART TWO

Chapter Thirteen

It was not until eight years later that Lachlan Macquarie Junior finally returned to his home on the island of Mull.

During those years he had been educated in England, at schools in Woodford and Finchley, and now, at nineteen, coming on twenty, he was a very different person in every way to the boy who had left the island all those years ago.

Disembarking from the ferry at Tobermory, he hired a horse from the local blacksmith and while it was being harnessed he decided to refresh himself with a drink and some food inside the Tobermory Inn.

Angus McLeod was at his counter, engrossed in conversation with another old local, and neither man seemed aware of Lachlan's entrance.

'And because there was such a sswell on the ssea we had trouble keeping the lobsster pots deep enough for a catch,' the local man was saying to Angus. 'Nay, tiss no' like the old days, twass much better then, there was more people on the island, more people to ssell to.'

Angus nodded. 'And these days – the high cost of everything! I dunno how I keep this place open, especially with the high price ye charge me for the lobsters.'

'Nay! I charge no more than any other fisherman, Anguss! *Everything* iss more costly these days. Now, how much were ye charged for the building of yer new boat? More than ye were charged for the building of the old boat I'll wager.'

'Aye, a lot more! And I'm thinking I was mebbe robbed on that, aye, robbed.'

'Good morning, gentlemen.'

The heads of the two men turned around to look at the tall golden-haired young man who appeared at first glance to have stepped in from a life of luxury, judging by the fine navy corduroy of the riding jacket and breeches he was wearing and the white silk at his neck.

'Good day to ye, sir,' Angus said, instantly recognising the young man to be of the Quality and jerking alert. 'Is it a room or a meal I can provide ye with?'

'Some breakfast please.'

'I have a nice quarter of grouse pie left,' Angus offered.

Lachlan raised a cynical eyebrow, a half smile on his face. 'That wouldn't be the same last quarter of grouse pie you offered to Minister Bannon eight years ago?'

'What? Eight years ago?' Angus looked utterly perplexed.

'When I was last here, in the company of Mr George Jarvis.'

'Mr Jarvis?' After a moment, Angus's eyes opened wide. '*Ye* were the young laddie with Mr Jarvis that day? The day he cured my headaches! Och, now I remember ye, aye, ye were with him when he took away my wee skull.'

The fisherman who clearly had a problem with his s's was now looking eagerly at Lachlan, eager to get a word in.

'If ye'll pardon me, ssir, but ye'll no' get a finer breakfasst than a good lobsster, sstraight from my own ssea potss and fressh ass the dawn.'

The thought of the ignorant and bigoted Minister Bannon chomping on that last quarter of grouse pie all those years ago made Lachlan smile at the fisherman. 'Lobster it is then. I'm sure it will taste delicious.'

The fisherman beamed. 'Thank ye, ssir, ye're a sshentleman.'

'As I recall, the dining room is that way?' Lachlan said to Angus, pointing down the small corridor.

'Aye, sir, aye,' Angus said, continually nodding his head towards the dining room door until Lachlan disappeared through it.

'Ye see, Anguss,' the fisherman gloated, 'sshentlemen will always prefer the lobsster to any old pie. Ye sshould take more of them off me.'

Angus's eyes were still staring at the dining room door, musing to himself. 'Well, now ... wait'll I tell Lizzie. And he's grown to be handsome looking too. When he was younger he was as bonnie as a lass, but all that's gone now. Aye, he's a man now, as true as men come and as fine as they go.'

Angus looked at the fisherman. 'D'ye know who that is, Donald? That's young Mr Macquarie. Home to the west after being schooled for years in the south.'

'I knew he wass a sshentleman.'

'Och, he's more than that,' Angus replied. 'He's

the new Laird of Jarvisfield. Least he soon will be, when he reaches the age of one and twenty.'

Angus jerked alert and waved a hand of dismissal. 'Now let me see to him and his breakfast, Donald, or he'll up and go. I'll need to heft in a bucket of water and get Lizzie to start boiling the lobster.'

Chapter Fourteen

The hired horse he was given was almost blind, plodding along dolefully no matter how many times Lachlan urged him on with his boot. The journey to Gruline seemed endless.

He took another deep breath of the air that was heavy with the fresh scents of summer and the clean smell of the sea. Only now, after such a long absence, and riding at such a slow pace, was he able to take in the true splendour and beauty of Mull's scenery, tranquil and sublime.

A world away from the noisy streets of London.

He thought back to those early days when his mother had decided he should be sent away to school; remembering how much he had wanted to go, and not wanted to go, finally deciding if he had to go anywhere his choice would be back to Australia, back to the sunshine and away from the deathly cold and ice of Mull's winters.

His mother had been horrified at the very suggestion of returning to Australia. 'There are no good schools there yet! And the schools your father opened are still in their infancy.'

He had then sought support for a return to Sydney from Mary, knowing how much she longed to go back, and wondering if she could take him there, telling her he didn't really need to be schooled anymore – he had learned enough from Mr Meiklejohn.

But Mary had changed since she had lost

George, looking almost as horrified at the suggestion as his mother had done, but for a different reason.

'George is here,' Mary had said, 'and I will never leave him. I'm content to stay here in Mull now, and no doubt I'll end my days here. Go to England, Lachlan. You may want to get away from your memories of your father and George, but I don't.'

He remembered being very surprised when Mary said 'England' because he had believed that if he was going to be sent out to school, it would be to Musselburgh in Edinburgh, the same school his father had attended.

But no, his mother had other ideas. England was her choice because only in England could she kill two birds with one stone – install him in school, and then rent a house in London from where she could carry on his father's fight for the people of Australia.

And fight she did, with the only weapons she possessed. She informed the parliamentary representatives of the Colonial Office that she would not accept a penny of her husband's pension until his reports on that country were published and presented to Parliament for debate.

The Colonial Office decided they might publish some of the papers, but thought it politic if other papers were suppressed.

It took three years for her to win the battle, helped and aided by friends of his father who now lived in London. And when the *Macquarie Papers* were at last printed as a parliamentary paper and submitted to the House of Commons, his mother finally agreed to accept the pension.

But it was not the end, just the beginning. By the time he had moved up to school in Finchley she had enrolled the help of Sir James Mackintosh in her determination to lobby Parliament for the right of the Australian people to trial by jury.

Meanwhile Lachlan just got on with his own life, enjoying the company of his own friends, although as his tutor once wrote to his mother – "*Lachlan is good-natured and good-humoured but shows no inclination to study.*"

Which was unfair, because he did study as much as any of the others, the only difference being that he did not seem to need to keep his head down for so long in order to show the tutors what a hard-working swot he was.

Lord Strathallan's son, William Drummond, also attended the same school in Finchley, and in him Lachlan had found his greatest friend and ally. By the time they were seventeen both were weary of being educated, truly bored with the whole tedious business of learning Greek and Latin and so many other useless subjects, preferring to sneak out at night to go into London and have as much fun as they could.

Of course they were found out in the end, much to the dismay of the other students who took great pleasure in hearing about their exploits, especially with the young girls from the music halls.

'Actresses, my darlings,' Drummond would tell them in his smooth intoxicated voice. 'All are actresses with no strait laces to untie.'

Neither had been successful enough to find out if

the actresses had any hidden laces to untie or not, but Drummond's bragging and lying tales were always amusing to Lachlan, and excitingly shocking to the others.

All in the past now, all learning and schoolboy misbehaving was over. The time to grow up and behave like a man had come.

*

After he had been riding for some time he recognised a few of the tenants' cottages spread here and there and realised he was on his own land and nearing home.

Wearily the horse began to slowly pick his way down the narrow track to the road that led to the house at Gruline.

Lachlan was now certain that the horse was not only half blind, but also half dead.

'I've been ordered to get a stable boy and send you back straight away,' he said despairingly to the horse, 'but after all this plodding I don't believe you will make it back before next week.'

The horse pricked his ears at the sound of his voice.

'Truth to tell, I don't believe you will make it back at all, not unless you are watered and fed and given a good rest in the stables overnight.'

The horse seemed to wake up, pricking his ears again and shaking his mane.

'Ah, you like the sound of that, do you? A good rest, eh?'

As the horse reached the steep bend onto the road a sudden fierce barking erupted into the air and a dog charged at the horse, making it stumble with fright and almost fall.

'Judas!'

Lachlan quickly dismounted and caught the horse's reins.

'Bugger off!' he ordered the dog, but the sharp-nosed collie began to move even closer to the terrified horse who was whinnying and trying to back away.

'Go on – *bugger off.*'

'Robbie! Robbie!' A girl came running around the bend. 'Here, boy, here!' she called, slapping her knees. '*Now!*'

The black-and-white collie immediately lost his ill temper and trotted over to the girl, allowing her to stroke his head and calm him into a gentle nuzzle, her long black hair falling over the dog's face.

She was about twelve or thirteen years old, and Lachlan was about to rebuke her angrily for the dog's wild behaviour; but then she lifted her head and looked at him with an apologetic smile ... and although his mouth opened, his breath stuck in his throat and no words came.

'I'm sorry,' she said. 'Robbie thinks he's a Celtic warrior protecting our animals and land.'

Lachlan stood looking at her, like someone hypnotised and speechless. She was tall for her age, and slender, wearing black boots and a pair of boy's breeches under a loose shirt, but of all the girls he had ever seen in his young life, he had never yet seen one with a face of such heart-stopping beauty.

'We've been waiting for you,' she said, and then tilted her head sideways and looked at him curiously.

'You *are* Lachlan Macquarie aren't you? I could barely remember you, and we both must look very different now, so you probably don't remember me at all. I'm –'

'I know who you are,' he said quickly, because he had known as soon as she had lifted her face and smiled at him. 'You're George's daughter.'

*

Mrs Keillor had prepared a feast fit for a king. 'If he caught the morning ferry he should have been here long before now,' she said to Mary. 'Is Mrs Macquarie getting impatient?'

Mary nodded. 'Beth has gone with Robbie to watch out for him on the road.'

'What I canna understand is why he didna come back with his mother a week ago?'

Mary sighed with impatience. 'Because he's no longer a child! He's a young *man* now and he probably wanted the freedom to come back in his own time and in his own way.'

'And how d'ye know what he wanted or didna want to do in his own way?' Mrs Keillor asked curtly.

Mary sighed again. 'All I know is what Mrs Macquarie told me. Lachlan chose not to return with her because he had been invited to spend a week at Strathallan Castle with his friend William Drummond. And as Lord Strathallan is still his legal guardian, Lachlan did not think he could refuse the invitation.'

'Didna *think* he could refuse ...' Mrs Keillor chuckled. 'Didna *want* to refuse I'm thinking. From what I've heard that Lord Strathallan is always having parties on that estate of his, *lavish* parties where there's always plenty of whisky and foreign wine.'

'That is not our concern nor our business, Mrs Keillor.'

'So what young man would not want to go there for a week, eh? I know I'd go meself in a flash if I was asked.'

'Exactly,' Mary said.

*

The old horse, still nervous of the energetic young dog, kept backing-stepping and rearing his head as if wanting to turn back. Lachlan held tightly onto his rein and walked beside him. He apologised to Beth for being so late and bringing her out to look for him.

'Oh,' she replied, carelessly dismissing his apology, 'what does time matter?'

And that was true, here on Mull, Lachlan remembered. Keeping in time with Time held less importance here than it did down in London.

'That dog of yours – '

'Is a *working* dog,' she said quickly, unwilling to hear any criticism. 'But he's still very young and he was probably trying to round up the horse in the same way he rounds up the sheep.'

Lachlan smiled. 'Young and stupid then.'

'Robbie's not stupid, no, not at all!' she insisted.

'He can round up sheep and cattle and even the hens better than any other dog on Mull. Robbie has "the eye".'

'The eye?'

'Aye,' she said, 'a dog with "the eye" seems able to mesmerise animals, especially the sheep.'

He was feeling a bit mesmerised himself, but not by the dog.

'And when you want the lambs up and out and dogged up to the hills,' she added, 'Robbie's the dog to do it.'

She was looking at him seriously with eyes of the lightest brown under black lashes, and the pale tan of her face made her look sun-kissed after a hot long summer. God, those eyes of hers reminded him so much of George, and she had also inherited much of Mary's pale loveliness.

He looked away, out over the fields, and couldn't stop himself thinking that – despite her boyish clothes – if she looked so beautiful now, at the age of twelve or so – how in God's name would she look at the age of sixteen?

Curiously he asked her, 'Why are you wearing boys clothes?'

'Why? Look at my boots!'

He looked at her boots; the soles and heels were very muddy.

'How so?'

'I took Robbie for a walk and a play in the stream. He doesn't like being washed so I have to pretend we are just going for a walk along the bank, but he always charges in, trying to round up the ducks, and by the time he comes back to the bank he's shaking himself so hard to get all the hated water off that he ends up nice and clean.'

Robbie raised a whiskered eye to Beth, knowing she was talking about him again.

'I often plough about in the mud of the vegetable garden too,' she said, 'and it would be silly to do that wearing petticoats and skirts.'

There was something about the breeches and loose shirt that clicked on a memory. 'Where did you get those clothes?'

She smiled guiltily. 'From the wardrobe in your room. I found them a few months ago. You left quite a few clothes behind when you went down to London. Do you mind?'

'Not at all,' he said smiling. 'Do they look like they would fit me now?'

Yet the fact that she was wearing his clothes caused Beth a sudden and strange feeling of embarrassment.

Robbie seemed to sense it, and rubbed his head against her leg. Beth bent to stroke his head and then returned to her former topic.

'Without the mesmerising eye, a sheepdog is fairly useless. Did you know that?'

'No.'

'And Robbie has the magic in *both* of his eyes.'

'Which is more than my horse has,' Lachlan said. 'Not even one good eye. The poor thing is almost blind. And Robbie there nearly frightened the life out of him.'

Hearing the tone of disapproval in the young man's voice, and sensing that the young man did not like him as much as his mistress did, Robbie sauntered over to Lachlan and began to sheepishly lick the back of his hand.

'He wants you to like him,' Beth said.

Lachlan laughed and bent to stroke the dog's head. 'I don't *dislike* him, I just feel very sorry for my horse. A number of times I had to dismount and walk part of the way just to give him a rest. He really should be put out to pasture and not hired out to anyone.'

Beth stopped the horse, turning to stand directly in front him, putting her hands on each side of his face and staring into his eyes.

'Aye, his sight is very bad. It's terrible that he should be still made to work in his old age. Why don't you buy him and put him out to pasture in one of the fields near the house?'

'Buy him?' It was an idea that would never have occurred to Lachlan, and it appealed to him.

'How much would you say he is worth?'

'Oh goodness, nothing at all,' Beth replied. 'But if you sent the blacksmith a few shillings more than he would expect for the horse, then I believe he will probably be over the moon and very relieved to get rid of him.'

Lachlan smiled, a perfect solution. 'The pasture field it is then,' he said.

She looked away from him, towards the entrance to the leafy lane that led up to the house, and from where Elizabeth had just emerged, a cloak slung loosely over her shoulders, her hands held out in greeting and her face smiling as she walked towards her son.

'My dear ...'

He bent and kissed his mother's cheek, and then suddenly remembered. 'I picked up a letter for you at Tobermory – it looks very serious, from a firm of solicitors.' He took the letter from his jacket pocket and handed it to her.

'They're not suing you for being a nuisance to the grand members of parliament are they?'

Elizabeth laughed. 'Let them dare!' She scrutinised the envelope and the name and address stamped on the back. 'Now this *does* look interesting.'

Mary!' Lachlan could hardly believe his eyes as Mary also strolled out of the lane. Mary had not changed one bit – still as lovely as ever. She walked towards him with the same expression of surprise, because *he* had changed so much.

'Oh my!' Mary laughed with pleasure. 'I was not expecting you to be so tall and ... and *grown-up!* I've been reminding myself that you're a man now, but I keep seeing you in my mind as the boy you used to be!'

'Oh, he's long gone,' Lachlan grinned, and seconds later he was pulled inside Mary's arms. 'Oh, my handsome! Come here and give me a hug like in the old days.'

Mrs Keillor then arrived on the scene, panting and puffing towards him as she hailed, 'Welcome the prodigal son! Home at last and I have a fine feast ready for ye!'

When Lachlan eventually looked around, Beth was walking away towards the lane in a long-legged young stride with Robbie following at her heels. Behind him the horse was hungrily tearing at the grass on the bank and munching ravenously.

'Let's all go inside now,' Elizabeth suggested, clearly eager to open her letter. 'Lachlan – were did you get such an old horse?'

Lachlan sighed. 'From a hard-hearted rogue in Tobermory.' He caught the reins and pulled the horse away from the grass, leading him forward. 'He badly needs to be watered and fed.'

In the stables, Hector – who was now also older and taller – had been feeling nervous and very uneasy about the young master's return, remembering how viciously Lachlan had once felled and punched him.

Yet when it came to discussing the state and pity of the horse, he and Lachlan were of one mind and in one accord.

'That blacksmith should be put in a box for working a horse this old and blind,' Hector said angrily. 'If twere up to me I'd guide him straight to the gallows for it.'

Lachlan nodded agreeably. 'He deserves no less.'

'He does, aye. Will ye be taking him back?'

'No. He's on Macquarie land now, and on Macquarie land he'll stay.'

'That blacksmith though,' Hector added, 'won't take it kindly. He's a tough old bastard and no' a man of peace.'

'And I'll no' be caring how tough he is,' Lachlan shrugged. 'The horse is here and here it stays and I'll send him due financial recompense, which is *more* than he deserves to get.'

'Aye, aye,' said Hector, nodding his head in concurrence. 'He deserves the gallows and no less.'

By the time the old horse was brushed down and blissfully lapping up water from a bucket, the two young men were almost friends.

*

Elizabeth waited until they were all seated at dinner before she revealed the details of her letter; although it was to Mary she gave the details and not Lachlan.

'Do you remember some months ago, Mary, I wrote and told you that my Aunt Henrietta had died in London?'

'Yes. She was very old though, wasn't she?'

'Oh, very old indeed.' Elizabeth placed her napkin on her lap as Mrs Keillor walked around the table serving ladles of hot chicken broth into the soup bowls.

'When I was at school in Hammersmith I used to stay with her at her house in Wigmore Street,' Elizabeth continued, 'but later, much later, when her son Lord Breadlebane married and started a family of his own, Henrietta removed herself to a smaller house in Upper Charlotte Street, just off Portland Place.'

Elizabeth then directed the rest of the information to her son, as it affected him the most.

'That letter, Lachlan, was from Henrietta's solicitors, informing me that in her will Henrietta has not only left to me her town house in Upper Charlotte Street, but also the sum of two thousand pounds.'

Mrs Keillor almost dropped the bowl of broth. '*Two thousand* pounds! Grief! – that's a fortune in money, ma'am!'

'A *small* fortune, yes,' Elizabeth replied, giving Mrs Keillor a look that said it was not her place to comment on it.

'So, now that we will have our very own London residence, Lachlan, I think I may return there shortly to carry on my work.'

'Your work?'

'Yes, for Australia – trial by jury.'

'Oh, Mother ...' Lachlan shook his head. 'Do you honesty think that one woman on her own –'

'But it won't be one woman on her own,' Elizabeth cut him short. 'In a few months time D'Arcy Wentworth will be arriving in London from Sydney, *also* to lobby parliament with me on behalf of the emancipists – and William Redfern should be arriving any day for the same purpose. Do you remember him, Lachlan, young Dr Redfern? He delivered you.'

Lachlan smiled. 'Yes, I do remember Dr Redfern, but not as far back to the day of my birth.'

'And also supporting us will be Sir Thomas and Lady Brisbane.'

'Brisbane? I thought you *hated* Brisbane?'

'I did.' Elizabeth shrugged. 'But that was before I had personally met him. However, one must be fair, and I must admit I was very surprised when he and Lady Brisbane called on me in London, and despite some initial tension between us, I found them to be nice people. Brisbane's whole attitude to Australia has changed. He had been Governor-General in Sydney for only a year before the Exclusives turned on him because he wouldn't do their bidding in their continued opposition to any rights for the emancipists. That's why he resigned and came back so swiftly. And Lachlan – these are the sort of people we need on our side – people who *know* New South Wales and *know* how unfair it all is there.'

Mary was nodding in agreement; but Beth, now wearing a blue dress, and knowing absolutely nothing about New South Wales – not even the fact that her mother had once been a convict there – was feeling utterly perplexed by it all.

'How is it unfair?' she asked Elizabeth. 'In what way?'

'Because of the *Exclusives*,' Elizabeth replied, and Lachlan turned up his eyes knowing Beth had opened the subject of his mother's deepest-held annoyance.

'"The "Exclusives" are a bunch of penny-farthing nobodys who emigrated as free-settlers to New South Wales,' Elizabeth informed Beth. 'And the word *free*-settlers suited them well, oh yes, because without a penny in their pockets they had arrived in Sydney seeking to build their fortune on the *free* government land grants and the *free* labour of the convicts. Ignorant upstarts who then set themselves up as the mock "gentry" of the country, or as they preferred to term themselves, the *Exclusives*.'

Lachlan could see that Mary's face was flushing a deep red, but his mother was so impassioned she didn't seem to notice.

'Mother ...' he said, attempting to change the subject

'My husband despised them,' Elizabeth continued, looking at Beth. 'He rejected outright their demand that all emancipated convicts should be forced to continue in a life of servitude to them – even though they had served their sentence - and he also rejected their demand that any man who had once worn leg-irons should *never* be accepted into any of the places frequented by free-settlers.'

Beth could not understand her indignation. 'If I was a free settler I would not wish to mix with murderers and villains.'

'Murderers and villains?' Elizabeth almost laughed. 'My dear, that is why the politicians here in England needs to *know* about New South Wales, the truth of it. The real villains are the magistrates and judges that send people out there for no good reason under law – other than to get rid of as many of England's poor as they can.'

'But murderers?' Beth protested, 'Someone who has actually *killed* another human being?'

'Murder,' replied Elizabeth patiently, 'is a capital offence, Beth, and it carries only one sentence – death. Anyone who commits murder is disposed of on the gallows. A very different type of felon to the ones unjustly transported to New South Wales. My husband was severely criticised by the Exclusives for what they called his "light-handed" treatment of felons, but that was because he knew that many of those felons were mere youngsters sentenced to seven years in Botany Bay for what he considered to be trifling misdemeanours ... such as a young servant couple getting married without their master's permission, or an eleven-year-old boy sentenced for stealing a pie, or a twelve-year-old girl sentenced for filching a strip of lace from her mistress's sewing basket.'

'A twelve-year-old girl – *my* age,' said Beth, blanching with horror at the very thought of it. 'And did *she* have to wear leg-irons?'

'No, never, at least not while my husband ruled. All young girls were usually employed as servants or sent to work in the government wool factory.'

Lachlan was watching Mary who had not touched a morsel of her food while his mother and Beth continued their conversation. As he remembered, this topic of the convicts was the only aspect of Australia that Mary had always preferred not to talk about – and especially with Mrs Keillor or any of the Scottish servants lurking nearby.

'Yes, the wool factory, I remember that,' Lachlan said quickly, looking at Beth, 'because Australia has such fine grazing land for sheep, but alas, no good sheep dogs – not like your Scottish collie with his magic eye.'

'No sheep dogs?' Beth looked disbelieving. 'So how do they round up the sheep?'

'The men do it. The only dogs in Australia are dingoes. Wild dogs who hide out in the bush and the forests, and the only thing a dingo would do for a sheep is eat it.'

'Tell Beth about my tame wallabies,' Elizabeth suggested. 'Oh, I was so fond of my wallabies, even if all they did throughout the day was sleep.'

And now the subject had been diverted to Australia's animals, Mary glanced at Lachlan and smiled, appreciatively.

Chapter Fifteen

The following morning, Hector brought out one of the Macquarie horses for Lachlan to ride.

'This is more like it,' Lachlan said admiringly, looking over the strong young horse.

'Aye, yon Mr Dewar got this one for Mrs Macquarie from a good trader over in Oban,' Hector said. 'And Mr Dewar was careful in his choice, seeing as the mistress is such a fine horsewoman. Three years old he is, and a nice nature, though sometimes he do get a bit frisky if he's made go too long without a gallop.'

Lachlan raised an amused eyebrow. 'I can't believe my mother does much galloping.'

'Nay, she takes it steady most of the time, that's why Wentworth will be happier with a young man on his back.'

'Wentworth?'

'That's what she named him. After some man who crossed a mountain.'

Hector glanced up at Beth who was already mounted on her grey mare, patiently waiting; dressed in a brown riding jacket and brown skirt and wearing a black three-cornered hat.

'Miss Jarvis likes to gallop though,' Hector grinned. 'You should see her go – fasterer than the wind sometimes.'

Beth pulled slightly on the reins and gave her horse's head a tug. 'And we are eager to be off.'

Lachlan mounted, back-stepping his horse to

allow Beth to lead the way down the lane. She knew all the tenants and had offered to take him round to meet some of them and introduce them to their future laird.

She set the pace of the horses to a trot, but once they were free on open land she sped up to a race until Wentworth was getting the fast gallop he so badly needed.

At times, to Lachlan, it felt as if he and Beth were moving together, racing pace for pace through the warm wind, and after his years in London the freedom and the speed felt exhilarating and joyful.

By the time they reached Robert Dewar's house they were both laughing at the fun of it.

Robert Dewar had come out to greet them. 'I saw ye both coming from yon distance. I thought the devil himself was chasing ye.'

Beth was still laughing as she jumped down. 'Mr Dewar, this is Mrs Macquarie's son, Lachlan. Home from England.'

When Lachlan dismounted she told him, 'This is Mr Dewar, our farm manager, he takes care of everything for us.'

As the two men shook hands, Dewar smiled amiably and said to Lachlan. 'I remember ye well. Ye came here once with your father, and a then a few more times with Mr Jarvis.'

'Did I?' Lachlan had no memory of it, but then he had blocked off a lot of memories when he had left Scotland all those thousands of moons ago.

After leaving Robert Dewar they rode over the land, stopping here and there to meet cottagers and their wives, declining all invitations to come inside for a drink or a bite to eat; pausing to talk with farm labourers while dogs barked and chased their horses as they rode off again.

One thing Lachlan noted remarkably was that every single cottager and farm labourer appeared to love the young girl on the horse. All appeared to know her very well, so she obviously did not spend much time cloistered up in the house.

'How do they all know you so well?' he asked her. 'Tenants are not usually so familiar with anyone from "the House".

Beth sat on her horse silently for a long moment, allowing the mare to chomp at the grass.

'I'm a working girl, just like Robbie is a working dog,' she said quietly. 'And all the people you have met today are my friends. It's not my choice to sit around a house all day, so I like to be out and about working with the people.'

'What about your education – schooling?'

'Oh,' she smiled, 'Mr Meiklejohn says I am a fine attentive pupil, and much easier to teach than you.'

'What?' Lachlan laughed. 'Meiklejohn is teaching *you* now?'

'Aye, he's been schooling me since I was five. He says I have my father's intelligence.'

'Oh, if you have *that*,' Lachlan told her, turning his horse around, 'then you already possess far more intelligence than I do.'

She laughed at his self-deprecation, and moments later they were racing again, towards Gruline and home.

*

And so it continued, all through the summer. To the cottagers and farm labourers the sight of young Mr Macquarie with Miss Jarvis at his side had become a regular occurrence. Like brother and sister they were in their manner, but not so in their looks. One older and one much younger, one handsome and one pretty, one with fair hair to his collar and the other with long flowing hair that was as black as coal.

Hector didn't like it, didn't think it was right.

'And why not?' asked Mrs Keillor.

'Well, he is what he is, a gentleman of land and property, and she is what she is, the daughter of his mother's maid.'

'Och, Mary is more than that to the mistress. She's one of the family, and well ye know it.'

'No matter how the mistress puts Mary in charge of the house an' all, and allows her to eat with them an' all,' Hector insisted, 'Mary's still one of us, one of the servants. But the way *he's* treating Beth now, like she's his own equal. He's spoiling her, and so now she's started showing me airs and graces that she never had before – airs and graces above her station.'

'Doona be daft.' Mrs Keillor chuckled. 'Beth has never shown any airs and graces, no to me and no to ye, so doona be making things up.'

In her chair by the fire, Mrs Keillor sat back and folded her arms, her eyes narrowing in thought.

'He's changed, he has.'

'Aye, ' Hector agreed. 'He's grown to be fair

enough in his ways.'

'Highly-strung he could be as a lad' Mrs Keillor continued, 'with a temper in him, but only for some of the time. Mostly he was full of fun and chatter and light-hearted. Now ... well now he just seems to be light-hearted all the time with no temper left in him at all.'

'She's too young to be alus going everywheres with him, and he's too old to be alus going everywheres with her.'

'Mebbe he's biding his time until she gets a wee bit older.' Mrs Keillor shot Hector a shrewd look. 'Same as ye are.'

'Me?' Hector's expression of annoyance gave way to one of surprise. 'I'm no biding for anyone.'

'Ye like her though, young as she is. Ye've seen the way the future beauty is beginning to show in her now.'

'I like her, aye, but I'm no biding for her!' Hector protested. 'Why would I do that? My family is pure Heiland and pure Scottish, and God' blood! – my father would no' allow our Scottish bloodline to be tainted by a foreigner.'

Mrs Keillor gawped at him in astonishment. 'Beth's no foreigner. She was reared in this house since she was a bairn in arms.'

'Aye, but she was still sired by an Arab from India or wherever it was Mr Jarvis came from. Her bloodline and stock is inferior. If she was a horse, a mare, she would no' fetch as high a price as a Scottish mare. A lot less would be her price, and that's only if anyone would be willing to take her at all.'

Mrs Keillor blinked, not sure if she fully comprehended what Hector had just said to her; but as unsure as she was, she shot him a look of fierce warning.

'Ye'd better be careful, me laddie, and make sure ye no' let the young master or Mary or Mrs Macquarie hear ye talking in that way about young Beth. Because if they *do* hear ye talking that way, ye'll be kicked out on your backside by the mistress, and likely Mr Lachlan will find his temper again and spill that pure Scottish blood of yours all over that lane outside.'

'But ye ken I'm right in what I said?'

Mrs Keillor shut her eyes tight and put a finger to her lips, shaking her head as she hissed, 'I don't want to hear it, and I don't want anyone to find me listening to ye. Go now, Hector, leave my kitchen, I'll no' be a conspirator with ye in this. I'll no' let ye talk about Beth like this. So go, *go* – before I stop being civil and take my big iron ladle to ye!'

Chapter Sixteen

At the end of autumn, worried about the chilling effect of Mull's cold winters on her health, Elizabeth decided to spend Christmas in London at her new home in Upper Charlotte Street.

Once again she failed in her attempts to persuade Mary to accompany her, but Mary would not leave Mull, and Beth would not leave Mary.

'You don't need me down there with you,' Mary said. 'You'll have plenty of company with all your visitors, and you said most of your aunt's servants are all still in residence.'

'Oh yes, the servants ... a fine enough bunch.' Elizabeth pouted. 'But I can't chat away with *them* the way I do with *you*. Mary. Oh, my dear, I *will* miss you.'

Mary smiled. 'I know, love, but you'll not miss me as much as you think you will. After a week or so you'll be so busy and the time will just fly past until it's time for you to come back again. Is Lachlan not going down with you?'

'I haven't asked him yet, but I see no reason why *he* would refuse.'

Elizabeth successfully persuaded Lachlan to accompany her, insisting she needed his help in entertaining the Australian emancipists who were now in London and who would be calling on her regularly.

'And Lachlan,' she reminded him, '*you* are an Australian by birth, so *you* should also be playing your part in all this.'

Lachlan was happy to agree, deciding he would also invite his friend William Drummond to spend some time with them down in London, and this time their visits to the music halls would be less of a rushed and hushed event.

On the day before their departure, Lachlan and Beth rode over to Robert Dewar's house and received the usual friendly greeting from the farm manager.

'I see the cold wind has stung some red colour into your faces,' he said, smiling.

'Yes, it was a cold run today,' Lachlan nodded. 'And the wind from the sea is fierce.'

'Well, seeing as it's the season, will you sit in and take some food and a wee dram with us, Mr Macquarie? We can leave business aside for an hour or so.'

'No food, thank you all the same, but a wee dram will warm the blood,' Lachlan replied, looking at Beth who nodded at him in agreement.

'A wee dram for myself also, Mr Dewar, she said, shivering.

Dewar looked surprised at her request. 'Are ye not too young for something so potent?'

'Not if it's just a wee one and you don't tell my mother.'

Inside the large parlour room of the Dewar's farmhouse, Lachlan was introduced to a few strangers – locals who appeared very pleased to meet the young laird – telling him they were just "looking in" on the Dewar family, seeing as it was near the time of Christmas and good will and cheer to all men.'

'And is it young Miss Jarvis ye have with ye?' one asked, and once again Lachlan found himself thinking that everybody on the island seemed to know Beth.

One of the locals tried to stand up to shake Lachlan's hand, but half way up he collapsed back down in his chair again.

'Are you all right, Mr MacLaren?' Beth asked anxiously. 'You don't look so well.'

'I'm fine, lass, fine, I've just got a load on.'

'A load of what, Mr MacLaren?'

'A load of wee drams.'

Robert Dewar laughed and made Lachlan and Beth sit in seats close to the huge fire where they both quickly drank their drams of the warming whisky.

Lachlan's glass was instantly refilled, but when Beth held up her glass again with hopeful eyes, Robert Dewar shook his head in silent refusal.

'Now your father, General Macquarie,' said Jamie MacLaren, leaning towards Lachlan, 'I knew your father verra well. I could aye tell ye many a story about him.'

'Ye couldna have known him verra well,' his wife intervened, 'because he was never here! He was alus away somewhere with the Army.'

'In his red tunic, and as fair as yourself,' MacLaren continued as if his wife had not spoken, 'but that was a long while ago, when he came back from India and before he bought the land of Jarvisfield.'

Lachlan was interested, asking questions, and

while his attention was diverted Beth slyly lifted his glass and quickly sipped from it.

More neighbours "looked in" as the afternoon went on and all hailed the young laird with great welcome. Mrs Dewar and her daughter handed round plates of thick slices of bread and cheese with slices of boiled ham on top, followed by plates of raisin and rum cake.

Some of MacLaren's stories were very funny to Lachlan, constantly making him laugh, because he knew they were all made up without a word of truth in them.

Beth leaned over and whispered to him curiously. '1817? Wasn't your father in Australia then?'

Lachlan nodded and spluttered more laughter while MacLaren continued in a proud tone, '"In my house" says he on that occasion, says General Macquarie – course he was only a captain then – "in my house, ye Jamie MacLaren, will alus be welcome!'

'But ye see, what I'm wondering now,' said MacLaren's wife, who had been watching Beth intently and not listening to a word her husband had said, 'what I'm wondering is ... where exactly were ye born, Miss Jarvis?'

'In the port of Saint Salvadore,' Beth answered happily, her cheeks flushed with too many wee drams.

'Saint who? So what place would that be?'

'Brazil.'

'Oh, Brazil ... so you're from a place called Brazil?'

'No, I was born on the ship coming from Australia to Britain, but at the actual time of my birth the ship had docked in the port of Saint Salvadore, which is at Brazil.'

Knowing that Mrs MacLaren had too much curiosity for her own or anyone else's good, Robert Dewar changed the subject to fishing. 'The next night we go out night fishing you should come with us, Mr Macquarie.'

'And the next time we go out,' Jamie MacLaren put in, 'we're going to try for a good catch in the waters off Calgary.'

Lachlan looked at MacLaren with some surprise. The man looked as if having "a load on" was a regular occurrence – surely not safe in a boat at night. 'Do *you* go night fishing too?'

'Aye, any fish on our table is alus a fish I've caught meself. Isn't that so, Peggy?'

He looked round for confirmation from his wife, but she had gone into the kitchen where she was whispering to Mrs Dewar and her daughter and two other women.

'She was born in a place called Brazil.'

'Oh, I ken where that is,' said Dewar's daughter haughtily. 'It's in Spain.'

'Is it?' Mrs MacLaren narrowed her eyes. 'Now that makes some sense of it all. I alus thought Mr Jarvis looked a bit Spainey ... those dark eyes and that black hair.'

'I alus thought Mr Jarvis was the handsomest man,' said Dewar's daughter, a plain girl of no remarkable looks. 'And such a *nice* man ... it was so sad what happened ... I cried when he died.'

In the parlour Robert Dewar interrupted another long story from Jamie MacLaren about General Macquarie, saying: 'It will soon be dark, Mr Macquarie, and the ride home will be even colder.'

'Yes,' Lachlan stood up, 'time to make a move.' Thank you for your hospitality Mr Dewar.'

His words were slightly slurred and his walk a bit unsteady.

Outside Robert Dewar was looking somewhat anxious. 'The local brew is very potent ... maybe ye've had a few too many drams, sir.'

'Don't be ridiculous,' Lachlan replied cheerfully. 'It would take a lot more than that to get *me* intoxicated.'

He quickly mounted his horse and almost fell off again down the other side, pulling himself back up in the nick of time. 'Boot missed the stirrup,' he said with a grin. 'Nothing to worry about, Mr Dewar. I'm as sober as Saint Salvadore.'

Beth laughed, not quite sober herself.

They rode off at a trot, and contrary to what Mr Dewar has said, the air was not colder but much milder, the sky blanketed by a warming layer of thick clouds and the wind from the sea had dropped.

Neither seemed willing to go any faster than a steady jog. 'Did you enjoy your afternoon at the Dewar's?' Beth asked.

'I did, yes,' Lachlan nodded, and his tricorn hat fell over his face.

He pushed it back on his head and laughed. 'With the exception of that damn MacLaren woman asking you impertinent questions. If she'd asked *me* where *I* was born I would not have said Australia, I'd ha' said I was born in Timbuktu – and then see what gossip she made of *that!*'

Beth chuckled. 'Isn't it always more simple to just tell the truth?'

'Stone me! Tell the *truth* to a nosy old gossip when it's none of her business to ask? I'd be poxed if I would!'

Beth felt a wet drop on her face and looked up at the black sky. 'It's starting to rain.'

Chapter Seventeen

'Twenty is too young to settle down to the running of your Scottish estate, my boy. Your *mother* may want you to do that, but your father would want you to get some more experience of the ups and downs of life first.'

Lord Strathallan had also decided to spend Christmas in London, and during an evening at the Macquarie house in Charlotte Street, decided it was time to give his young charge a few words of manly advice.

'Plenty of time for you to settle in the future, plenty of time. I was thirty-seven before I left the rest of the world to get along without me. And it was only a year or two before I left the wider world that I met your father in Macao. Now, how difficult would it have been for me to meet your father in Macao, in China, if I had stayed in Scotland, eh?'

'Very difficult,' Lachlan agreed. 'Even, dare I say it, physically impossible.'

'And remember, the Jarvisfield estate is not yours yet, not until you are twenty-one.'

William Drummond looked at his father with bleary eyes, having imbibed too much wine during dinner.

'And you are still his legal guardian for another year.' Drummond knocked back the last of his wine. 'So tell him, father, tell him what you want him to do.'

Lachlan laughed. 'I know what *you* want me to

do, Drummond. You want me to hold your hand while you march bravely into battle.'

'Your father spent his life soldiering in the Army,' said Lord Strathallan. 'Made a career of it.'

'And what was good enough for your father should be good enough for you,' William Drummond advised. 'At least for two or three years anyway. I've no intention of serving for longer than that – just enough time to get me the title of "captain". An officer and a gentleman and all that. Women love it!'

Lachlan sat musing: a few years in the Army may be interesting ... especially with a sociable crackpot like Drummond at his side. And it would also serve as a sort of tribute to his father; following in his footsteps, like a good son, if only for a few years.

'I think he's actually considering it, Father, I honestly do.'

And after a few years away in the Army, when he returned to Mull, Beth would be older, nearer to womanhood ... the time would go quicker, the years would move faster ...

'Well, Macquarie?' William Drummond asked. 'Are you seriously considering it, or are you just having a short nap?'

Lachlan looked up with an amiable shrug. 'The Army it is then, for two or three years, why not.'

*

When Lachlan returned to Mull in early February, Mary was shocked to learn that he and William Drummond had signed up as ensigns in the 42nd Regiment.

'Had you both been drinking too much when you signed up?' Mary asked

'Well, we didn't just *sign up*,' Lachlan replied. 'It was a process that required much thought – and much money!'

Mary frowned, perplexed. 'What does money have to do with it?'

'A man can't just walk into the Army, sign a paper, become an officer, and then climb up on horseback and get on with it. We had to *buy* our commissions.' Lachlan shrugged testily. 'Money opens every door.'

'What's wrong with you?' Mary asked.

Taken aback by the question, Lachlan stared at her. 'Nothing is wrong with me.'

'Why are you so irritable then?'

'I'm not irritable. You're imagining things.'

Mary made no answer, but she kept looking at him. Maybe she was imagining things, and maybe she wasn't.

Lachlan glanced at Beth, annoyed that she was showing no reaction whatsoever to the news of his imminent departure overseas, sitting by the fire doing her sewing silently as if the conversation was none of her concern.

Or was it that she was even more like her father than he had realised. George was always calm, even in distress, and never one for a rushed or a thoughtless response to anything.

'What say you, Beth?'

Beth paused in her sewing, but she did not speak, not until a few moments later when she asked, 'Where do you think they will send you?'

'I've no idea. I'm waiting for my orders to report. Probably first down to Portsmouth or Southampton to embark, then out to India or Egypt or somewhere in the East where the British have a presence. It definitely won't be anywhere as near to Britain as the European continent, Drummond assures me of that. No point, not since the defeat of Napoleon.'

Mary said, 'And your mother – '

'Will join me at whatever seaport it is and see me off. As will Lord Strathallan.'

'Did she approve of you joining the Army?'

'Well, she could hardly show any *disapproval*, could she? Not when she has spent all her married life as a soldier's wife.'

'Yes, but I know she was very anxious for you to settle down here on Jarvisfield and learn how to manage the estate. And there's also the – '

'We will miss you, Lachlan,' Beth said suddenly. 'India is so far away.'

'I will write, every week,' Lachlan assured her. 'Long letters filled with my news about every thing and every person I meet, be they sadhus, beggars, or bejewelled maharajas.'

Next morning, to everyone's surprise, the military dispatch containing his order to report was delivered by a horseman.

'Came in on the morning ferry,' he said. 'Military seals on it, so I rode out fast as I could.'

Lachlan rewarded him with some money, and then carried the dispatch into the drawing-room.

'Oh no, so soon,' Mary exclaimed in dismay. 'I was hoping it would not come for a few weeks at least.'

The sound of the horse had not escaped Hector's sharp ears, and when the horseman was brought around the back of the house and into the kitchen to have some refreshment before making his return journey, as was the Highland custom, Mrs Keillor was all ears.

'Military seals,' said the horseman, 'that's all I know.'

'His orders,' said Mrs Keillor to Hector. 'Must be.'

Panting and puffing with excitement, Mrs Keillor found Beth in the vegetable garden, kneeling and digging and wearing her male breeches again.

'Tis no' right for ye to be wearing breeches, m'lassie!' she said in disgust, then remembered why she had come out. 'He's got his marching orders – a horseman just brought them.'

Beth jumped to her feet and quickly brushed down her knees and then ran past Mrs Keillor who eventually caught up with her and followed her into the drawing-room.

'I'll kill Drummond!' Lachlan was saying angrily to Mary, his eyes aflame. 'He gave me no warning that *this* might happen!'

Mary held a hand over her mouth, and Beth wondered if she was trying to stop herself from crying.

'Well?' Beth asked. Where are they sending you? Is it to India?'

'No,' Lachlan replied through stiff lips.

'Egypt?'

'No.'

'Where then?' asked Mrs Keillor impatiently. 'Sakes alive – where's the Army sending ye then?'

'Timbuktu,' Lachlan replied.

No!' Beth gasped in astonishment. 'And only before Christmas you were saying – '

'He's not going to Timbuktu,' Mary said, still trying to stifle her laughter. 'Not as far as there.'

'No, but I wish I *was* going to Timbuktu!' Lachlan said angrily. 'Or even to Hell and back – anywhere but *this*!' He looked once more at the dispatch then walked over to the fire and dropped it onto the flames.

Mary took a deep breath and said steadily, 'They are sending him to Birmingham.'

'Birmingham ...' Mrs Keillor frowned. 'Where's that?'

'In the midlands,' Mary said. 'About halfway between here and London.'

Chapter Eighteen

Lachlan served only three months in training with the 42nd Regiment, before he transferred to the 2nd Dragoons.

'*If I am to spend my time in the Army based solely in Britain,*' he wrote home to Beth, '*then at least it will be more enjoyable if I do it on horseback.*'

William Drummond, of course, had transferred with him.

'They don't treat the horses right, them dragons,' Hector said to Mrs Keillor. 'They ride 'em too hard and too fast and they dig their spurs into 'em.'

'Nay.' Mrs Keillor shook her head, tired of Hector's sly digs and griping about the young master. 'Them horses are trained to be *war* horses, fit for battles, so the dragons canna be mooning and sopping over them all the while like ye do.'

'Aye,' said Beth, entering from the garden carrying a basket of herbs and coming in on the conversation. 'Those horses are soldiers too, serving their country along with the men.'

Beth hadn't looked at Hector as she spoke, and she heard him breathe heavily before he replied.

'Aye, but who *asked* the horses if they wanted to be soldiers, eh? Who lifted their hoof and got them to sign up? Nay, the horses wasna asked, the horses didna sign anything – they was just roped in whether they wanted to be war horses or no'. And then them dragons ride 'em like bulls.'

'Lachlan would never ride a horse too hard,' Beth insisted. 'He loves horses as much as you do, Hector.'

'Nay, nay *nay*! Don't say that to me!' Hector replied angrily. 'No one loves or cares for horses in the same way as me. But that's yer trouble, Miss Beth, ye is incapable of even *thinking* a bad thought about Master Lachlan, the golden boy of Jarvisfield. Not one bad word, not one bad thought, have ye ever had about *him*.'

Beth was looking at him now, her brown eyes gazing at him in a very direct way as she said quietly, very quietly, 'No, I have not ever had a bad thought about him, Hector, because he has never given me any reason to think anything but the best of him, the *best*.'

When Beth turned and walked out of the kitchen, Hector seemed to be having trouble forcing the saliva down his throat.

Mrs Keillor chuckled. 'There now, that's told ye.'

*

In the two years that followed, Lachlan came home to Scotland twice a year and, as always, spent most of his time riding out and about with Beth.

During the third year he came home in time to celebrate Beth's sixteenth birthday, and William Drummond came with him. Both were now lieutenants, and in Drummond's company Lachlan showed a difference in his behaviour and attitude that was not his normal way, Mary noticed.

Two weeks after their arrival, when Mary took the trap into Tobermory to collect some personal provisions, and then later dropped in to see the McLeods at the inn, she learned that the two young officers had already caused quite a stir amongst the young people of the town.

'Lord's my life!' said Lizzie McLeod. 'The two of them! And that young laird of Jarvisfield – well, whenever we see him he's as likely to be kissing as many girls passing his way as he can, or brawling with any lads who object.'

'But it usually ends in laughter amongst them all, lads and lasses alike,' Angus put in, having become quite fond of the two red-jacketed young officers who frequented his inn a few nights of the week.

'But that tall and broad one,' said Lizzie. 'The one called William. By! – He can knock back the whisky as easily as I can drink water. Isna that so, Angus?'

Angus nodded his head happily. 'Spend a fortune in here they do. I've had to up my stock of whisky just to keep up with the one called William. Mind, he wasna pleased when I said I had no wine.'

'William Drummond,' Mary said. 'He's Lord Strathallan's son.'

Angus banged his fist triumphantly on the counter and then looked at his wife. 'I told ye, Lizzie, I said that William had money to waste. And now we know where he got it – from his rich father.'

'Where does he abide?' Lizzie asked curiously. 'This Lord Strathallan?'

Mary shook her head. 'I don't rightly know, somewhere on the mainland, in Perthshire I think.

I heard William say one day that Strathallan Castle was about four hours ride to both Glasgow or Edinburgh, depending on which way you go.'

'And who made his father a lord?' Lizzie demanded to know.

Mary smiled. 'I don't know that either. All I know is that he is the 8th Viscount of Strathallan.'

'*Viscount?*' Angus was beside himself with excitement. 'And his son drinking in my inn, and even sleeping up in one of my rooms upstairs! Wait'll I tell the fishermen and my other neighbours.'

'Sleeping in one of your rooms?' Mary frowned. 'When was that?'

'Och, pay no heed to Angus,' Lizzie said quickly, catching Mary's arm and urging her down the passage towards the dining room. 'Come in to ma kitchen and have a drink and a bite before ye head back.'

Once inside, Lizzie McLeod rolled around her kitchen quickly making Mary some refreshment, but once she got her sat down and eating, Lizzie sat opposite her and began to tell Mary all the gossip she had collected since the last time she had seen her.

It was all tittle-tattle, mildly interesting, until Lizzie could not stop herself from telling Mary about William Drummond.

'I wouldna say anything,' Lizzie insisted, 'if Angus hadna let it slip out there. But the one called William, he's taken a room here on a few nights, and Angus is no' the only one who's been doing some slipping – because twice now, twice, I'm certain that one called William slipped a lass up there. I didna see her, mind, so I don't know which lass it was, but I know the giggling of a lass when I hear it.'

Mary's eyes were wide. 'And Lachlan? Did he take a room too?'

'Nay, he alus rode away on his horse, but I'd say he's as familiar with women as that William is. He's no angel, no saint, that I can tell ye, he knows what's what, that's for certain – but that William,' Lizzie rolled her eyes and then whispered, 'he's a *devil* for the lasses.'

An hour later, as Mary drove the trap back to Gruline, she thought over everything Lizzie had told her, every little bit of conversation between the two men that Lizzie had heard from deliberately eavesdropping or had accidentally overheard.

Finally, Mary thought she had the picture, and it dismayed her, concluding that Lachlan was no longer the refined and innocent young gentleman he had been when he had left Mull to go to the Army.

No, with no battles to fight and no war to fear, and under the influence of that rapscallion William Drummond, he had now learned to drink hard and had become one of the "fast set" of his regiment, and – from what Lizzie had overheard – many of their escapades had not only been dicey and disorderly, but had also been wickedly debauched.

At Gruline, as the trap rolled along the road towards the house, she saw the two figures on horseback coming along the road. They were not galloping or even jogging along, but keeping their horses walking at a slow but steady pace, their heads turned to each other as if in deep conversation.

At sixteen, Beth was no longer the girl she had been either; her body had curved out and she was showing all the signs of the beautiful woman she was going to be. She wore a long navy riding habit with cream lace at the neck and cuffs, and a black three-cornered hat which brimmed the fall of her lustrous long black hair.

A soft passion of love came into Mary's heart and eyes as she thought, 'Oh George, my darling, I wish you could see her as she looks now, your beautiful daughter.'

Normally Mary would have turned the trap into the lane and left Beth and Lachlan follow her in at their own pace, but today she sat waiting for them, and watching them.

Lachlan looked as happy in Beth's company as he always did, and Beth was laughing at him in the same happy way. They were close those two, very close, and always had been.

When the trap had been emptied and Lachlan and Beth had stabled their horses, they came into the drawing-room where Mary was sitting stiffly.

She glanced at Lachlan coldly but he didn't seem to notice, coming over to her and kissing her cheek in the same affectionate and respectful way as always.

'Where is your friend William?' Mary asked.

Lachlan shrugged carelessly. 'God knows. He declined to come riding with us, so he has probably taken himself off to Tobermory. He seems to prefer the business of that town much more than our country life here in Gruline.'

'He told me he likes going to Tobermory because he enjoys watching the fishermen,' Beth said.

Mary now understood the small smile of amusement that Lachlan gave to Beth when she said this.

Yet at dinner, Lachlan was so much his natural self, his old self, as refined and as good mannered as he had always been, declining to drink any wine and showing nothing more than fond companionship to Beth as he had always done; so much so that Mary found herself wondering if much of what Lizzie McLeod had told her about him had been mere gossipy exaggeration.

*

On the day they were due to leave and return to their regiment, William Drummond sat in the drawing-room still attempting to charm Mary; and even though she could not stop herself from laughing at his funny wit, Mary was still convinced that he was a rake of the first order.

Lachlan was busily walking from room to room, searching for Beth, eager to have a last half hour or so with her, when perhaps they could take a walk along the bank of Loch Ba and talk in private; and maybe he could even give her some hints about his hopes for their future.

Out in the stables, he asked Hector, 'Have you seen Beth?'

Hector was busily harnessing the two horses in

readiness for their departure. 'Aye, I know where she be.'

'Where?'

Hector pointed. 'Over in yon bluebell field talking and laughing with the two fat cows.'

Lachlan grimaced. Beth's love of animals had no limits ... but to go off like this on the morning he was leaving for perhaps another year was rather remiss of her ... or maybe she had a very good reason.

'Is there something wrong with the cows?' he asked.

'Oh, aye, there's a lot wrong with those two fat cows,' Hector nodded positively. 'They could thin down for a start. Ye never see a horse lolloping around with flesh bouncing in all directions like that. No' a *good* horse anyways – nay, no' *any* horse as I've seen.'

Lachlan was getting confused, and somewhat irritated by Hector's habit of seeing every aspect of life from an equestrian viewpoint.

'It's bad enough,' Hector continued, 'when Mrs Macquarie is residing here and those two cows come to help Mrs Keillor and do the cleaning work, but now they're over here all the time when none of the Macquaries are here, including ye – over here telling Miss Beth stories and leading her along by heir reins, leading her *astray* I say.'

'Hector, what the pox are you talking about?'

'She's over in yon first field,' Hector replied, tightening one of the girths. 'They alus sit propping up one of the trees down there.'

Lachlan walked towards the bluebell field. There

was a slight breeze stirring, but the morning sun had a soft warmth.

He walked down towards the loch until he finally saw the three of them ... lounging back against the thick trunk of the tree in the sunshine, and so wrapped up in their chattering that none were aware of his presence.

Beth was in the middle, between Maggie Kennedy and Lorna McLaughlin, lying back and smiling as she listened, while the two older females were sat upright, talking to each other over her head and laughing.

For one long moment he stood staring at Beth, at the seductive way she was lying back, without a care in the world. She looked like a beautiful dreaming princess in the company of her two older ugly sisters.

'Beth.'

Her brown eyes turned and looked at him; full of surprise, while the two others quickly pulled themselves to their feet and bobbed a slight curtsy.

'What are you doing?' he asked Beth curtly.

Beth moved to her feet and brushed bits of grass from the back of her dress. 'I'm enjoying the sun with my friends.'

'Your *friends*?'

'Aye, my friends, and you know them well, Maggie Kennedy and Lorna – '

'I know who they are,' Lachlan cut her off. 'I'm leaving shortly and I need to speak with you.'

Beth's brown eyes were wide again. 'Oh, is it *today* you are leaving? I thought it was tomorrow.'

Maggie and Lorna bobbed another curtsy and

bustled away as quickly as they could.

Lachlan watched them go, and then eyed Beth reproachfully. 'You shouldn't be so familiar with the servants, nor should you be lying back like that, like ... like a farm girl.'

Beth half laughed. 'But I *am* a farm girl, Lachlan, what else could I be, living on a farm as I do.'

'You do *not* live on a farm, you live in the laird's house.'

'But I do *work* on the farm.'

'Nobody makes you work on the farm. Nobody makes you go out helping Robbie to dog the sheep or work in the vegetable garden. Nobody makes you do *anything,* Beth. So why can't you do as other young ladies do and sew or paint or read books?'

'I *do* read books, and I also do plenty of sewing, but those are things I do in the evenings, when there is little else to do. Why are you suddenly taking on so?'

Indignation flashed darkly in her eyes. 'And to tell me not to become too familiar with servants when my own mother is a servant in your house!'

'Mary is *not* a servant – not on that level at all. She is much more than that to our family, much more.'

'She is now your mother's housekeeper, and before that she was *your* nursemaid in Australia. Was she not a servant then?'

'Oh, enough,' Lachlan shrugged. 'I just wanted a short walk and a talk with you.'

But it was too late for that now and both of them knew it. The mood was all wrong, and looking back he could see that Hector was already leading the horses out, saddled and bridled.

Lachlan's tone softened. 'I'm sorry, Beth, it's just that ... well, never mind that now, but next year I'll be back in time for your seventeenth birthday, even if I have to sell my commission in the Army I will, I promise.'

'Why?' She looked at him curiously. 'What's so special about my seventeenth birthday?'

'You are, Beth' he said softly. 'You are very special on any day or any birthday, but it's your seventeenth that I have long been waiting for.'

PART THREE

Chapter Nineteen

Elizabeth (Beth) Jarvis was a young girl of intelligence, but few complications. She had inherited not only her father's appealing good looks, but also his calm manner and dispassionate acceptance of life as it was, dealing with every day as it came, and rejecting most excuses to complain. Her nature was happy and gentle and considerate of others, and she considered herself very fortunate.

Her greatest love in life was the place in which she lived. Unlike others, she did not stand on the coastline of the island of Mull gazing out towards the wider world pining for more than she had, because she believed here on Mull she had it all.

Her home in the leafy countryside of Gruline was a secluded haven of peace, where the view of the green hills was stunning in the soft glow of a red sunset, and the silent serenity of Ben More and the smaller mountains calmed her spirit and then her eyes into a tranquil gaze, allowing her to dream.

And only here, in Mull, could she dream her favourite dreams.

As young as she had been when she had last seen him, she still had vivid memories of her father. Misty memories as if seen through a veil of thin white gauze; his wonderful smile when she looked up at him as he held her hand and walked her down to the stream, his calm voice as soothing as a summer breeze.

She had loved him then, and she loved him still, and the older she got the stronger she held onto her memories of him. As scant as they were, they were still enough to keep him alive in her heart and in her mind, and were added to over the years by the many little stories her mother told her about him.

And he was, very different, very special, and everybody had loved him.

And he was here, in the island of Mull, a fact that bound her mother to this island and one of the reasons Beth had such a great love for it.

But she also loved Mull for itself, a natural paradise where golden eagles cruised in the sky and red deer paraded harmlessly amongst the hills. And down on the shore she loved watching the otters languishing on the rocks, their nature as happy and as playful as her own, making her laugh when they used the wet sand on the beach in summer or the snow or mud on the rocks in winter to make a waterslide and then sliding on it into the water for no other purpose than fun.

And she also loved the *people* of Mull, oh, the people were the best of all; wary of strangers but possessing kind hearts and easy smiles, she had grown up in the bosom of their friendship and caring community and loved them all, even though some were quite loony in their ways, especially Kirsty Dewar who never got any of her facts right, yet could never be persuaded that she might be wrong.

'Halooo Miss Jarvis!'

Checking her horse, Beth looked round to see who the caller was – and waved to an old man who many years ago had emigrated to Mull from the nearby island of Ulva, accompanied only by his pet goose.

'Iolaire-suile-na-grein!' he shouted, pointing upwards at a huge White-tailed eagle flying above her, and Beth nodded, knowing that was Gaelic for *'the eagle with the sunlit eye.'*

She paused to watch the White-tailed eagle as it cruised towards the coastline and the sea to catch a fish to take back to the mountains for its dinner.

She rode on, thinking that although The White-tailed were the biggest of all the seabirds, they were also the *meanest* in her opinion, because they were always swooping down to steal the fish caught by the otters and swooping away again.

Reaching Gruline, she slowed and turned her horse into the lane leading to the house, her slim young body relaxing on the horse as it plodded unhurriedly towards the stables at the back.

Before she had even dismounted Mrs Keillor came running out of the kitchen into the yard to greet her, all abustle and apuff and excitedly holding up a letter.

'A letter – for ye – from Master Lachlan! It says he'll be home in a week or two, for your seventeenth birthday in May, and with him he'll be bringing ye a very special present.'

Beth curiously turned the letter over, front and back, and saw that it was still sealed with red wax.

'It's unopened, as it should be, a private letter to me – so how do *you* know what he says in it?'

'Oh I don't *know* what he says in it,' Mrs Keillor said with a grin, her eyes all-knowing, 'but I think ye will find, my Bethey, that my guessing is correct.'

*

Sitting in the drawing-room reading the letter, Beth learned that Lachlan would not now be able to return to Mull in time for her seventeenth birthday.

His letter explained why.

With very short notice, his regiment had been posted over to Ireland, to a place called Limerick, and the first remarkable sight he had seen there, remarkable enough to write home about, was some of the most stunning horses in the world. Magnificent thoroughbreds that raced so lightly over the grass with a natural grace and speed it took your breath away. He was determined to buy one, and bring it back with him.

Until then he wished her all the best, and reiterated his wish that in the meantime she would not, *please do not*, become too friendly and familiar with the common servants such as Maggie Kennedy and Lorna McLaughlin, and also *to please stop* wearing breeches.

'Well?' asked Mrs Keillor, hovering curiously by the open door. 'Well?'

'Well, men are so *unobservant*,' Beth said indignantly, folding the letter. 'I stopped wearing breeches almost a year ago.'

Chapter Twenty

Elizabeth returned to Mull, as she always did in the summer, but this year she looked worn out, complaining of a constant cough brought on by the infernal smog in London.

'Why they insist on having their fires burning night and day down there is beyond me,' she complained. 'Chimneys chuffing out smoke and polluting the air all the time, especially at night. I never allowed a fire to be lit in my bedroom. I remember only too well what Dr McLean said about that. Have you seen him of late?' she asked Mary.

'No, no need,' Mary replied. 'We have all been well.'

'He will have to come and see to my chest, but first I will wait and see if a few weeks of our clean Highland air will cure it. Where's Beth?'

'Oh, she's gone up to the hills with Maggie and Lorna and a few more of the locals. There's a bonfire up there today.'

'A bonfire! On a warm day like this?'

Mary smiled. 'Yes, but in a few hours time it will be Midsummer's Eve.'

'Is it? Oh yes, of course it is. And the young must be allowed to celebrate and have their fun.'

Elizabeth sat back in her chair and smiled fondly at Mary. 'Now, my dear, it's time for us to share all our news. You first.'

*

The young people of Mull always celebrated Midsummer's Eve, as did many of the older ones, gathering to welcome in the Summer Solstice.

Everyone brought delicacies of food and drink of some sort to share around, and huge baskets of trout brought by the young fishermen were grilled over the fire. Musical instruments were also brought to the gathering by those who had them, and the sound of tinkling fiddles echoed through the air.

Holding hands with Maggie Kennedy and Lorna McLaughlin, Beth was dancing in a circle around the bonfire and loving every minute of it. For years these two older girls had been her very best friends and she did not care if Lachlan approved of them or not.

Maggie Kennedy was singing happily and loudly as she danced, which sent Beth into fits of giggles, because the fisherman always complained that when Maggie Kennedy sang you could hear her far out at sea and it frightened the fish so much they dived straight down to the seabed and hid there until she stopped squawking.

Lorna McLaughlin had dressed herself up fine for the occasion, pinning a bunch of wildflowers into her hair and now they were falling one by one onto the ground as she danced.

Beth wore a simple green cotton dress with a wide black ribbon around the waist, as simple in style as her long black hair that had been tied back with a green ribbon.

'Ah, your fine Celtic headdress,' she said to Lorna when the dance was over, bending to pick up some of the fallen flowers.

'Aw!' said Lorna. 'Aw ... it took me hours to pick them flowers.' She looked at Beth's green ribbon. 'I tell ye what – you lend me your green ribbon, Beth, and ye can pin these nice flowers in *your* hair, the ones that are not crushed... look here's three that look as good as new, and a nice mixture of colours.'

'But with only one hairpin they'll fall out of *my* hair too when we dance again.'

'Aye,' Lorna whispered in a pleading voice, moving her face close to Beth's, 'but I need to look my best if I'm going to catch me a marrying man tonight, but ye've got one. You don't *need* the ribbon.'

'Me? What marrying man have I got?'

'Master Lachlan 'course. He's just been biding his time till yer old enough to be wedded and bedded. Ask Hector, that's what he do say. That's what *all* do say.'

Beth looked earnestly at Lorna and whispered back. 'And why do they *all* say that.'

''Cause of what they see – you and he alus everywhere together when he's here, and the way he *looks* at ye, Beth, even a fool like Hector kens what Master Lachlan has in his head. And lookit how he didna like seeing ye be so free with me and Maggie – that's 'cause he wants to make ye the *lady* of his house some day. But me, I'll be happy if I catch me a gleg fisherman, so give me the ribbon.'

Beth was a girl who rarely spent her time looking too seriously into the future, but now Lorna's words made her think about Lachlan's determination to come back in time for her seventeenth birthday ... and yes, the only reason for it's unusual importance was that he had probably intended to ask her to marry him.

The thought did not make her unhappy, it filled her with a pleasant warmth because she enjoyed being in Lachlan's company, and if their lives together were to continue more closely through a marriage then she would live on Mull forever and die happy.

She untied the green ribbon in her hair and gave it to Lorna. 'No, I don't want the flowers,' she said, shaking her hair loose, 'they will just fall off when I dance again.'

While Lorna fussed with her hair and the ribbon, Beth strolled over to where Maggie Kennedy was taking to a fisherman in a blue jersey, but to Beth's surprise Maggie's voice in response to the man's questions was no longer loud and normal, but doll-like and simpering.

Smiling, Beth strolled on. Thank goodness she did not have to spend *her* time looking for a suitable marrying man.

At the edge of the hill she stopped and looked up at the sky ... the golden globe of the sun appeared to be standing still, as it always did on Midsummer's eve. It was going to be a night that some of the fishermen would not bother to go out, because the sun stayed too high above the horizon and the time of darkness was short.

She stood looking out over Mull filled with contentment, loving its volcanic cliffs, it hills and forests and lochs. How, she wondered, could anyone wish to live anywhere else in the world?

As she strolled back to the bonfire she thought about Lachlan, and wondered if he was still enjoying his life in Ireland with all of its stunning horses.

*

In Limerick, Lachlan and William Drummond had just finished testing two of the finest horses in the county.

'Look at the legs, the sleek haunches,' Drummond said admiringly as his horse was led away across the stable yard. 'Thoroughbred, pure thoroughbreds, both of them.'

Lachlan grinned, filled with the same admiration and still exhilarated from the speed of the smooth ride. 'I think I might like to keep racehorses one day, breed them, train them, race them.'

Drummond cocked an eye. 'Not in Mull. The ground's not flat enough.'

'No, not in Mull, but maybe somewhere else in Scotland, somewhere flatter, on the mainland.'

'Not anywhere in Scotland, old chum, you would have to go further south, somewhere in England. Should be easy enough to get the land and some good stables down there. Get the staff to train them too.'

'Well, it's a long time off, something to think about in years to come. How long do you think we'll be based here?'

'Not long I'm told; no more than six months.' Drummond gazed around him. 'It's a peaceable enough place though. I've encountered no dangerous rebels, not one ... apart from you, that is.'

Lachlan's cheerful expression gave way to one of surprise. 'Me?'

'Yes, you.' Drummond bit his lip thoughtfully for a moment, and then explained. 'You see, those horses now, they're a very good example – would you be as full of admiration and want to possess one if they were not thoroughbreds? Can you not *rely* on thoroughbreds to be good value for money and give a better performance than any other breed?'

Lachlan frowned, confused. 'William, what the pox are you talking about?'

Drummond gazed around him again. 'Well, one has to use the same judgement with women as with horses. And well ... what you told me in confidence last night, about ... wanting to marry Beth Jarvis, well, it's just not on, old chum, in fact it's sheer madness.'

Lachlan's anger was rising. '*Why* is it madness?'

Drummond scoffed. 'Well if you have to ask *why* then you are obviously still more Australian than Scottish. The years in London and in the Army have not polished you well enough. And does Miss Jarvis want to marry you? Know you that?'

'No I don't know that,' Lachlan replied through gritted teeth. 'As yet I know only my own choice. But now I want to know *why* you think my choice is madness?'

Exasperated, Drummond looked at him as if thinking he must be the biggest fool ever born.

'Because she's a *half-caste* that's *why!* Mixed blood, and not even good blood at that. As fine a man as I'm told her father was, nevertheless my own father tells me that *her* father was an Arab of uncertain lineage, and her white mother is nothing better than a glorified Macquarie *servant*. Now look, do you honestly believe that any respectable doors of Scottish society would be open to you if you married someone like that? All doors would be shut to you. And as *for English* society – '

The smash of Lachlan's fist into his face sent Drummond toppling backwards. Shocked and dazed he half lay on the ground and then put a hand to his lips and felt the blood.

'Good God! It was only in your best interests – '

'You're lucky I don't kill you right here!' Lachlan said, enraged. 'I intend to marry her! And a pox on your Scottish and English society – and a worse pox on anyone else who disapproves or tries to stop me!'

*

Midsummer's Eve came in with mellow warmth, the glow of the sun still bright. A few new stragglers arrived on the scene laughing as they watched the dancers and then joined in the songs.

Across from the fire, Beth and Maggie and Lorna were propped up against a tree. Beth was chewing one of Mrs Keillor's pastries while Maggie and Lorna tucked in to grilled trout.

Maggie finished her trout and looked up and around the crowd of gatherers. 'Oh, there's Mr Dewar, he found time to come after all.

Beth looked over at Robert Dewar and saw a young man standing with him, his body half turned from the crowd and his conversation with Robert Dewar appeared serious.

She kept watching them, especially the young man whom she did not recognise at all, concluding he must be a stranger to these parts. He was tall and slender and wore a brown corduroy riding jacket and black knee breeches, grey wool stockings and black leather shoes. His jacket was of the finest cut, as finely cut as all of Lachlan's clothes. His hair was dark brown and the sun glinting on it showed it was washed clean as clean can be. He looked like a gentleman, but no gentlemen came to these Midsummer gatherings to welcome the Solstice which was usually only celebrated by the locals and farmers of the island.

Beth saw Robert Dewar starting to smile, and so did the young man, both of them smiling, followed by each shaking the other's hand as if coming to some form of agreement.

Finally the young man turned and looked towards the bonfire and Beth saw his face full on. The blue of his eyes showed up vividly against his sunburned face and oh ... oh ... so handsome.

Beth's attention was claimed back by Maggie who was chattering to her about something Beth could not now quite take in.

'Oh by!' Maggie said suddenly, 'I think ye have an admirer, Beth ... over there.'

Beth looked 'over there' and saw the young man looking at her in the same wondering way she had been looking at him earlier.

'Do ye know him?' Maggie asked.

Beth shook her head. She was certain she did not

know him. How could she know him when she had never known anyone so ... so *attractive*. For a long moment they looked at each other, and then, as if realising he had been staring – he turned away and slowly walked over to where Robert Dewar and his wife had settled themselves.

Minutes later Robert Dewar's daughter came running over to the three girls, breathless and excited.

'Miss Jarvis, my cousin John has just asked father who ye are. So *I* told him ye are from Brazil in Spain.'

'I am *not* from Brazil,' Beth objected. 'I was only born at a seaport there. And I do not believe that Brazil is in Spain either.'

'Since when did ye have a cousin hereabouts, Kirsty Dewar,' Lorna demanded to know. 'Since when?'

'And if he truly *is* yer cousin,' Maggie said dubiously, 'and ye're not making up more fancies in yer head, then why have we not seen him before now?'

'Oh! Maggie Kennedy! I *never* make up fancies, and he *is* my cousin, though only a third or fourth cousin, and no' one of us has seen him for years because he has been away in the Navy.'

All four looked over at the young man who was once again in conversation with Robert Dewar.

'Aye, a handsome lover he'd be,' Maggie said with narrowed, interested eyes. She cocked one eye at Kirsty. 'How old or young d'ye know him to be?'

'I think he's two and twenty, but he could be three and twenty.'

'The torch-fires! The torch-fires! Come aroon an' light yer torch-fires!' a voice cried.

Maggie and Lorna and even Kirsty jumped to their feet in excitement and rushed closer to the bonfire where Mrs MacLaren was handing out small wood and straw torches from a basket. One after the other each held their torch to the flames and then proceeded to form a ring around the bonfire, although it was only the females who participated in this ritual, believing as they did that any wish they made on this Midsummer's Eve would come true.

Beth stood watching as the ring of females began to sing an old Norse song as they danced in a circle around the bonfire, wishing she could join in, but both her mother and Elizabeth had always forbid her to do so because this was one part of the Solstice celebrations they did not approve of.

'It all looks a bit pagan to me,' said a quiet voice close to her ear.

Beth turned her head and looked up at the young man who had been with Robert Dewar.

'Like the ancient days of sun worship,' he said smiling at her.

She stood speechless, looking at him, at his brown hair, curling slightly at the edges above his collar, and those blue eyes, still so vividly blue even in this strange light of shadows and sun and fire.

'Yes ...' she finally answered, 'that's what my mother says ... this part of the ceremony is not Christian.'

'No, but then most of the people on Mull descend from either the Celts or the Vikings ...

mostly the Vikings. They may be Christian now, but the old ways still remain.'

'Are *you* from Mull?'

'No, I'm from Edinburgh, but my father descends from Mull, and now he is planning to return here.'

And then, as if suddenly recollecting himself, he said quickly, 'Your pardon, Miss Jarvis, allow me to introduce myself. I am John Dewar, a distant relative of Mr Robert Dewar and his family.'

'And Mr Robert Dewar told you my name?'

He smiled again. 'Only because I asked.'

Beth felt herself flushing, and wondered if he could hear her heart pounding? And *why* was it pounding? She didn't know what else to say, so she spoke the truth.

'This is the time I usually slip away, once the torch-fires have been lit. My mother is very strict about my leaving ... because of all the drinking and carousing afterwards.'

'Drinking and carousing ... even the young women?'

Beth nodded, flushing again at some of the tales she had heard from Maggie and Lorna who always insisted that *they* had never caroused ... well maybe a *wee* bit, a kiss here, a hug there, but nothing more than that, not until a proposal was on the table.

'If you are leaving, then may I escort you home, Miss Jarvis?'

A hint of an unsure smile passed her lips. 'I'm quite safe on my own. It's barely half a mile, less than that.'

'Then allow me to escort you for my own pleasure,' he said. 'My uncle is watching us, so he will know who is responsible if you come to any harm.'

Beth looked over and saw that Robert Dewar *was* watching them, and seeing her looking at him the farm manager smiled and nodded, giving his approval.

They walked for a time in silence. Beth looked up at the sky. 'It always confuses me ... if summer begins in June, then why is *mid*-summer also in June?'

'Because here in the northern hemisphere, this is the time when the sun is at its farthest point from the equator, and it's highest point in the sky, and when it appears to stand still.'

'And does it stand still?'

'According to the sundials it does, but only fractionally, for a very brief time. The description comes from two Latin words, *"sol"* which means sun, and *"sistere"* which means to cause to "stand still". Hence, the Summer *Solstice.*'

'Oh, I see ...' Beth smiled at him, admiring his knowledge. 'Kirsty says you are in the Navy.'

'Yes, a midshipman.'

'A midshipman? What is that?'

'A rank below a third lieutenant.'

'So, you are an officer?'

'A very *junior* officer.'

They had reached a stile between fields. He climbed over first, and when she then climbed onto the step he offered his hand to help her down.

Too shy to take his hand, she jumped down,

which made him laugh.

'Miss Jarvis, you look very feminine and very young but you jump like a boy.'

Beth nodded. 'I have always suffered the disadvantage of being young, from as far back as I can remember.'

He laughed again, and she quickly added. 'I mean, always being the *youngest* of the household, too young for this, too young for that. And I have *always* preferred breeches to skirts.'

His tone was surprised. 'But surely you don't go abroad *wearing* breeches, do you?'

'Yes, but only when I'm ploughing about in the vegetable garden, or helping Robbie to dog the sheep back down to their pens.'

'Do you not have a farm boy to do that, pen the sheep?'

'Oh yes, but Robbie prefers me at his side to anyone else.'

'Now that I can understand.'

She looked up at his smiling face, the orange rays of the night sun gleaming behind his hair, and for a moment she felt as if the world was spinning.

'If ...' she said on a breath, 'if you are in the Navy, why are you not at sea?'

'I'm on leave.'

*

At ten o'clock, although it was still light, Mary took a lantern, left the house and walked down the lane.

The older Beth grew the more she worried about her, especially on a night like this when the young ones got carried away with all their excited talk of this night being magical, as well as all the drams that would be secretly drank, even by the lasses.

She looked up at the sky, knowing the sun would set tonight around half past ten, so it would be darker on the return journey if she had to go all the way up to the bonfire to bring Beth home.

She paused, checked that the candle inside the lantern was still alight, and moved on.

She had only been walking for five minutes or so when Robbie came barking after her, galloping past her at speed, and Mary laughed. 'So she's near, Robbie, is she? Near to home?'

Moments later the barking became furious, echoing through the air, and Mary knew instantly that a stranger was also near, near to Beth, else why was Robbie so angry and making enough fuss to wake the dead?

Seconds later she heard Beth's voice issuing commands to the dog, and after a few short growling complaints Robbie calmed down ... All was well, nothing amiss.

She waited, and then saw two figures coming into view from around the trees and walking down.

Beth ... and a young man who appeared to be in his early twenties walking beside her ... He was not a local, and he was not dressed like a local either, so who was he?

Moments later Beth was upon her – her eyes sparkling radiance, her face illumined with smiles. 'Mama, this is John Dewar. He very kindly escorted me home.'

John bowed slightly. 'Ma'am.'

'Dewar?' Mary said. 'Are you related to – '

'Mr Robert Dewar? Yes. He is my father's cousin.'

'Oh well, then,' Mary smiled, feeling relief as well as surprise, 'you must come inside and have some refreshment, and also meet Mrs Macquarie, the owner of Jarvisfield.'

Beth was disappointed when John politely declined. 'Thank you, but the hour is late, and I have to be in Tobermory very early in the morning.'

He glanced quickly at Beth, and then back to Mary. 'But, perhaps I could meet Mrs Macquarie tomorrow ... in the late afternoon? Would she be in?'

'Oh yes, and she loves to meet new people, we see so few strangers here. You would be very welcome.'

Again he glanced at Beth. 'Until tomorrow then.'

He bent and patted Robbie's head, and then said his farewells and took his leave, pausing at the bank to look back and give a smile and a brief salute.

Beth returned his wave. Robbie began to bark again, but in a more friendly tone.

Chapter Twenty-One

The following afternoon, Elizabeth's welcome was warm and gracious. She instantly liked the young man on sight.

'A midshipman?' She seated herself back in her armchair and accepted a glass of port from the tray Mrs Keillor was offering around.

'Well, officially, I am now a mate.'

'A mate?'

'A midshipman who has taken his lieutenant's exams and passed. A sort of sub-lieutenant.'

'And how long in the Navy?'

'Five years, ma'am.'

'And have you seen much action?'

'Not as such. Since Napoleon's defeat at Waterloo and the peace with France, the Navy has been involved with other duties.' John smiled apologetically. 'And the war with France, of course, was before my time.'

'Yes, of course, so it was. Goodness, how time flies!' Elizabeth sipped her port. 'So what are these other duties our Navy is involved in? Your last voyage, where did it take you?'

Beth sat crumbling the cake on her plate with her fingers, anxiously fearing that John Dewar might perceive Elizabeth to be giving him the third degree, which she really had no *right* to do.

Mary felt no such apprehensions, knowing that Elizabeth was genuinely interested in all news from the wider world.

'Our last voyage took us down to the South Atlantic,' John replied, 'patrolling the waters off Africa.'

'*Africa!*' all three said together.

Elizabeth sat upright. 'What on earth is our Navy doing in Africa?'

'On earth, I couldn't say, ma'am, but on the sea our Navy is maintaining a blockade off Africa to counter the illegal slave trade.'

Now all three were *very* interested. 'But,' said Elizabeth, confused, 'there are *still* slaves right here in Britain! Why, down in London, in every gentleman's household there are black men and women who may be dressed very well in their master's livery, but they are most certainly *slaves*.'

'Not according to the law,' John said. 'Under the law they are now free men and women since the Slavery Abolition Act was passed in eighteen-thirty-three.'

'So why are they still there?' Mary asked with some perplexity. 'If they are free under the law why do they stay in those houses?'

John shrugged, he did not know. 'Probably because their conditions have changed. Under the law they must now be paid a wage for their employment and be free to leave at any time.'

'And our Navy?' Elizabeth asked. 'What is their role in all this, what exactly do they do?'

'Well, clandestine slavery still goes on,' John said. 'So our role is to stop and search all British trading ships to ensure they have no captured slaves hidden below in their holds.'

'And if they have?' Mary asked.

'We return the slaves to land and set them free, and the captain of the ship is fined one hundred pounds for each and every slave found on his ship, which can often rise to a colossal amount, dissolving any profit he hoped to make from his illegal trade.'

'And if he doesn't pay?'

'His ship is commandeered, but whether he pays or not, his licence to master a British trading ship is revoked permanently.'

'I see ...' Elizabeth nodded.

'Although ...' John added, 'I believe a new law will soon be coming into force, whereby the captain of any ship found to be carrying slaves will be regarded as a pirate and his punishment will be death.'

Elizabeth's face showed her disgust. 'In London, in the past, whenever I was invited by any lady or gentlemen to visit their home for a musical evening or supper or whatever the occasion may be, if I entered and saw they were using black slaves I immediately turned around and walked out.'

She looked intently at John. 'This new law ranking captains of slave ships down to criminals – when does it come into force, do you know?'

'No, all I have learned since coming ashore is that the Bill has been passed in Parliament, but still has to be passed by the House of Lords.'

'The House of Lords – that lot! A feasting pig will be eaten in Jerusalem before that lot pass anything sensible!'

'With all due respect, ma'am,' John said hesitantly, 'The House of Lords *did* pass the

Abolition Act.'

'And all thanks to the late Mr Wilberforce.' Elizabeth sat back. 'My husband was an ardent admirer of William Wilberforce. He was a *great* man indeed.' She looked at John. 'Do you agree?'

John set down his glass of port on the side-table, hesitant to answer, or perhaps hesitant to answer in a way that might displease his hostess.

'Yes ... I do agree that William Wilberforce was a great man ... but a major battle, such as the war on slavery, can never be won by just one man, and all credit should not unfairly be given to just *one* man. There was an army of campaigners throughout the Kingdom helping Wilberforce, all doing arduous and important work. And the hardest campaigner of all was Thomas Clarkson, have you heard of him?'

Elizabeth said 'No.' Mary said 'No.' While Beth sat silently leaning forward in her armchair, listening and gazing at John Dewar, as if entranced.

'No, few people outside of London and the Abolition Movement have heard of Thomas Clarkson,' John continued. 'But you know, although Wilberforce was the man who carried on the fight in Parliament, he could not have done it half so well without the constant gathering of information and public mobilisation against slavery organised by Clarkson.'

Elizabeth was gazing with soft eyes at the young man sitting in her drawing-room. He reminded her in ways of young D'Arcy Wentworth, one of the leading revolutionaries so passionate in his fight for the rights of emancipists in Australia.

'Your ship?' she asked. 'Which part of Africa?'

'Our watch is between West Africa and South Africa, but in the main we were stood off the port of Cape Town.'

'And your next voyage?'

'The West Indies, I believe. Jamaica.'

'Goodness,' Elizabeth said, her mood animated, 'my husband served in the West Indies – in *Jamaica*. He told me all about the awful slave markets there at that time, in quiet a lot of detail too. He found it all quite sickening. Perhaps I could pass some of those details on to you.'

'And we know Cape Town,' Mary added. 'Our ship docked there on our journey back from Australia.'

Elizabeth clasped her hands together in eager anticipation. 'Mr Dewar, it's been such a pleasure, but we have so much *more* to talk about – will you *please* stay for dinner?'

*

While Elizabeth went to refresh and change for dinner, and Mary went to the kitchen to give instructions to Mrs Keillor to set an extra place, Beth took the opportunity to ask their visitor:

'Do you know where the seaport of Saint Salvadore is? I mean – *exactly* where?'

'Yes, if you have an Atlas I can show you?'

Beth stood up and began to search along the bookshelves. 'I'm sure we do have an Atlas somewhere, but I believe all such books are kept in General Macquarie's study ... and no one is allowed to go in there, apart from my mother and Mrs Macquarie.'

She turned and met John's eyes.

He said, 'Why do you want to know where it is ... *exactly?*'

'Because ... ' she shrugged, 'well, I was born at sea, on the way back from Australia, but the next port of land the ship stopped at was Saint Salvadore, and so General Macquarie has my place of birth registered as Saint Salvadore. So I would like to know ... *exactly* where that is.'

'Oh, I see ... ' John glanced towards the desk near the window. 'If you have some paper I could sketch it for you in a line-map ... the *exact* location.'

'Oh yes, paper, we have plenty of *that!*' Beth said jubilantly. 'Elizabeth spends most of her time here writing letter after letter to people in London and Australia.'

She opened a drawer of the desk and took out a few sheets of vellum. 'Will a pencil do?'

'A pencil will do it better than a pen.' John joined her at the desk and the two stood together as he began to draw.

'The ship would have left New South Wales *here,*' he wrote the name, and then continued his pencil line, 'and then continued on through the Indian Ocean to *here* at Cape Town ...' He frowned. 'And then for some strange reason ... the ship must have veered way off its course to over *here* ... to put in at the port of Saint Salvadore in Brazil.'

'Why strange?' Beth asked.

'Well, unless it was in dire need of fresh water or

some other supplies, or somebody needed the care of a hospital or some other emergency, the ship should have gone straight up the Atlantic on course for Britain.'

They were standing close together, looking at the drawing as he marked out the correct line from Cape Town straight up the Atlantic Ocean towards ... 'North Africa and then Europe ...'

Beth's eyes were fixed on the clean lines of his fingers and his tanned hand as he drew ... aware again of that strange stirring in her body that she had felt for the first time last night ... It unsettled her, his *closeness* now unsettled her in a way she had never felt unsettled before. She had lived long enough on a farm to know the stirrings of the animals in their seasons, but her own sexual feelings had always been undeveloped or dormant, due to her age she had thought, so it had never concerned her. Until last night she had always thought that a woman's sexual feelings did not stir or come alive until she wed, part and parcel of the marriage contract, and certainly not until *after* she had been bedded.

'... past Portugal and Spain, and then France, across the Channel – '

'So Brazil is *not* in Spain then?'

'Not even near,' John said, smiling at her. 'Spain is *here* and Brazil is –' she watched his pencil skim back down and across the paper to '*here* – thousands of miles away.'

'I knew Kirsty was wrong,' Beth said, 'but she won't be told. So will *you* tell her how wrong she is about Brazil being in Spain. She's *your* cousin.'

'A third or fourth removed cousin,' he said, 'but I *will* tell her if you wish me to.'

'I do.'

Mary and Mrs Keillor passed the door of the drawing-room together heading for the dining room, with Mrs Keillor talking at the top of her voice about some complaint regarding the tablecloth.

John and Beth's heads were bent close together, still looking at the drawing on the desk when he murmured quickly, 'Miss Jarvis, would it be possible to see you tomorrow *alone*? If only to give me a chance to speak with you directly. Would that ... be at all possible?'

Beth glanced briefly into his candid blue eyes, and then returned her gaze to the drawing. 'I think,' she said on a quick breath, 'that might be possible, Mr Dewar.'

'You do?' he answered in surprised relief. 'Where?'

Beth stared fixedly at the drawing on the desk and then ran her finger along the line of the Atlantic Ocean. 'We could meet by the trees along the side of the stream.'

'What stream?'

She picked up the pencil, turned over the paper on which he drawn his line-map, and drew her directions in the same way.

'This is the front of the house *here,* and if you go across the field to *here,* you see a line of trees *here,* and just a few yards down you will see a stone boulder *here,* and if you go through the trees by the boulder there is a long bubbling stream behind it.'

'What time?' he asked.

'Sometime in the forenoon would be best ... say ten o'clock?'

'Ten o'clock,' John said.

'Can you ride?'

'Of course I can ride. How do you think I get between here and Tobermory?'

'Well, I thought that perhaps with you ...being a sailor ...'

'You thought that perhaps I went down to the sea each morning and *swam* to Tobermory?'

They were both laughing when Mrs Keillor came in and said dinner was ready to be served.

Chapter Twenty-Two

Upstairs, Elizabeth was far from ready. Not only was her chest still troubling her, but also the stabbing pain from her arthritic right knee was spoiling her enjoyment.

'Such a nice young man, and so interesting,' she said to Mary who was buttoning the back of her dress. 'And very different from the usual conversation we get up here. Am I done?'

'All done up,' Mary said, patting the last button into place. 'But really, Elizabeth, you can't expect the people up here to have the same conversations with you as those down in London. Down there it's all politics and parties and more politics. The people here are too hard working and too busy for all that talking. Farmers are more concerned with the animals and the weather and the fishermen are always having to watch the moods of the sea.'

'I know, my dear, I know, but the *mind* must also be kept working, kept engaged. I think I will take just a small spoon of laudanum to ease the pain in my knee.'

'Laudanum?' Mary stared at Elizabeth as she moved to her dresser and lifted a small bottle from the top drawer, followed by a slim wooden box that contained a small silver spoon. 'Where did you get that – in London?'

'Yes, from my doctor in Harley Street, Dr Chisholm. A good man, and very understanding of the ills that befall us as we get older. When the pain in my knee gets too strong, he says a small amount will help.'

'I don't think ...' Elizabeth had knocked back a spoonful of the laudanum before Mary could finish her sentence.

'I've read in the newspapers about laudanum,' Mary said, 'and I know all the ladies in London think it's a miracle remedy for all ailments, but I don't think ... I really don't think it should be mixed with wine or port, Elizabeth, and you've had quite a few glasses of port already today.'

'That's because my knee was hurting so badly, but don't worry, I shall be very circumspect about how much port I drink after dinner ... probably none at all.'

'Still,' Mary said, as they descended the stairs, 'I don't think Dr McLean would approve.'

'Dr McLean!' Elizabeth laughed. 'What does he know about anything outside Salen? I don't think that man has ever ventured further than Edinburgh.'

'And if he has not, what's wrong with that?'

Elizabeth paused and looked patiently at Mary. 'In medicine, as in all things, Mary, one must keep on learning about what cures, what does not cure, and any new advancements that may help a patient and ease their pain. And Dr McLean will never learn anything new if he never ventures away from Mull.'

*

Over dinner Elizabeth did much of the talking again, which pleased Beth, as it allowed her to listen while Elizabeth asked all the questions she would never have dared to ask, nor was it her place to ask.

Watching John Dewar's occasional, easy smile, and the way he pushed back a lock of brown hair that kept falling over his brow, she learned that he was in Mull for one reason only – to find and buy a house for his bereaved father to live in. Anywhere on the island would do, his father had told him, as long as it was in Tobermory.

'Why Tobermory?' Mary asked.

'Because he wants to be able to watch the sea from his front door, he says, so he can keep an eye on me.'

'All the way over in Jamaica?' Mary smiled. 'Well they do say that some of the Scots have second sight?'

'Ah yes, but it is my father's *first* sight that is beginning to weaken. His eyes are not as sharp as they once were, so now he is making plans for his eventual retirement. Not yet, not for a few years, but he wants to make some occasional visits to Mull beforehand so he is used to the quiet life when he does finally settle here.'

'Understandable,' Elizabeth agreed. 'Mull is like an entirely different world to the busy city of Edinburgh. What does your father do?'

'He is a tailor, at Mortimer's.'

Elizabeth almost spilled her wine. 'There you go again! My husband *always* used Mortimer's in Edinburgh. He insisted it was *the* finest gentleman's outfitters in the entire Kingdom, not just Edinburgh.'

'And they make all the uniforms for the Army,' John said, pushing back a lock of brown hair from his brow, 'I expect they made your husband's uniforms too?'

Elizabeth nodded. 'The last uniforms they made for him, before we left for Australia, four sets I think it was, or maybe five, but they looked just as good coming back as they did going out all those years before.'

'And are you residing on Mull with your relatives?' Mary asked. 'At the Dewars?'

'Yes, and if I fail to find a suitable house, Robert Dewar has agreed to keep on looking while I am away. He and my father were very close when they were lads. Both will enjoy being neighbours again.'

Elizabeth was looking perplexed. 'Forgive me for asking, Mr Dewar, but how on earth did the son of a tailor manage to enter the Navy as an officer? Did your father buy your commission?'

'No, ma'am, the Royal Navy has never allowed the sale of commissions. Advancement in officer ranks is solely by merit.'

'Why is that? Purchase of commissions are allowed in the Army.'

John answered with a faint cynical smile. 'I suppose the reason is that an officer in the Army can get away with incompetence on the field, but a captain of a ship on the seas must have the best crew possible if he wants his ship to stay afloat and prevent death by drowning of all his men.'

'Quite.' Elizabeth hesitated for a moment. 'But still, are there not certain requirements for entering at officer level?'

'The requirements are prohibitive, yes' John admitted. 'You must have a sound education and a fair knowledge of mathematics, which I do, having attended the Royal High School in Edinburgh. But I would have had no chance at all of getting a commission in the Navy without the patronage and letters of recommendation from Lord Donaldson.'

'The patronage of Lord Donaldson?' Elizabeth was impressed. 'And how did you manage that?'

'I managed nothing,' John confessed. 'My father has been Lord Donaldson's personal tailor for years at Mortimer's, and over time they have become very fond of each other. So when my father told Lord Donaldson of my desire to go into the Navy, he offered to provide all the documentation that was required.'

'But what of the cost?' Elizabeth frowned. 'It cost my son Lachlan a *fortune* to enter the Army. He had to buy everything – his commission, his sword, compass, spyglass – even his horse! But the most expensive of all was his uniforms – a fortune! Did you also have to buy everything you needed for the Navy?'

'I did, yes, compass, spyglass, everything – except of course the cost of my uniforms which were made for me by my father.'

'At Mortimer's?'

'No, in his time off at home. He is excellent at his craft, and whether it be in Mortimer's workroom or in his own home, his finished garments are always superb.'

Mary detected that John Dewar was not at all comfortable answering all these personal questions about himself and his father, but Elizabeth was so taken with him – *and* she was drinking far more than she should after that laudanum. Under normal circumstances Elizabeth was too much of a lady, had too much discretion, to question any newcomer in such a way, but today – and now tonight – she was acting like an impertinent old dowager.

On impulse, Mary felt the need to say something kindly to the tensed-up young man, something to make him relax again.

'I'm sure you look very handsome in your Naval uniform, Mr Dewar,' she said sincerely. 'I have always liked Navy blue on a man.'

'Mary!' Elizabeth turned to stare at her, slightly miffed and somewhat bleary-eyed. 'You said precisely the same to Lachlan when you first saw him in his red Army jacket. So which is it – your favourite colour on a man? Army red or Navy blue?'

'Both,' Mary replied. 'Army red *and* Navy blue.' She lowered her eyes and fingered the stem of her untouched wineglass. 'And, if you remember,' she said softly, 'George often wore navy blue.'

'George ... oh, yes ... dear George ...' Elizabeth's eyes became wide and watery as she stared off into the distance, lost in her own personal thoughts.

'George?' John said to Mary, but it was Beth who answered him with a small, proud smile. 'My father,' she said. 'Everyone loved him.'

'Loved? He is ...'

'Yes, in an accident, when I was small.'

'You see,' Elizabeth said sadly, looking at John,

'that is why your Mr Clarkson and the Abolition Movement *must* keep up the fight to abolish slavery in all its forms and in *every* country. I believe it's still rampant in India, especially Ceylon. And the terrible suffering caused by this human trafficking is nothing less than *evil*.'

She took another drink of port and then continued: 'Take George Jarvis for example – his mother was just a young girl of fourteen when she was snatched on a Tangier street in Morocco – a young Arab girl taken without warning from her family and shipped to India, sold to an Indian prince as a concubine, and then when her son was born he too was captured by more slave-traders and sold to someone in Cochin – a beautiful young boy of seven forced to walk naked around a slave-market with a rope tied around his waist and the slave-trader lashing a whip at him. How cruel! How inhuman! God knows what would have happened to that boy if my husband had not come upon the scene and rescued him.'

Mary was speechless for a moment, her blue eyes wide with horror as she moved to her feet and finally blurted out, '*Elizabeth* – how *could* you!'

In the silence that followed, it took Elizabeth a few seconds to come back to herself and look around her and realise what a monumental blunder she had made, what an *awful* mistake.

Her hands went to her mouth. 'Oh, Beth, my dear, I am so, so sorry ...'

Beth's face, in that moment, stayed with John Dewar for a long time afterwards – the pale skin of her face as if all the blood had drained away; the speechlessness of her shock; and then the pain that glistened in her dark eyes as she looked up at Mary. 'My father ... was a slave?'

'Your father ... ' Mary got out, her eyes brimming, 'was the most wonderful man in the world.'

'Naked ... and *whipped*?' Tears were now spilling down Beth's face.

'Oh, please, Beth, please don't cry,' Mary pleaded, 'I know how hurt you must feel but – '

Beth knocked her hand away and stood up. 'I'm not crying for *me* – I'm crying for *him!*'

And then in a fast dash Beth was gone, out of the room and out of the house into the night.

John Dewar was also on his feet, and also shocked by what had just happened. He looked questioningly at Mary. 'Until tonight – she didn't know?'

'No.' Mary shook her head and wiped at her eyes. 'It was something George never wanted anyone to know, especially Beth, and we ...' she glanced briefly at Elizabeth, 'we have always protected Beth from knowing anything she does not *need* to know.'

Elizabeth was sitting with her elbows on the table and her hands covering her face, deeply distressed 'I'm sorry, so very sorry, I don't know why or how –'

'*Laudanum!*' Mary cried. 'From your fancy doctor down in London! That's why! That's how! And I *did* warn you about taking that stuff and drinking wine as well.'

John Dewar made a move to leave. 'I think I

must go after her. She is still in deep shock, so she should not be out there alone.'

'Oh, thank you, thank you,' Mary nodded appreciatively. 'I was about to go myself but you will catch up with her more quickly than I. Please bring her back and tell her ... tell her it was all a drunken mistake! Tell her that Elizabeth was talking about some other man called George Jarvis and *not* her father!'

John hesitated only for a moment at the door, looking back disbelievingly at Mary. 'You know she will not believe that.'

Seconds later Mary heard the door of the house shutting behind him.

Chapter Twenty-Three

It was after ten and the sun was beginning its slow descent when John Dewar set out on his journey, convinced that Beth had run for the hills, running blindly, desperate to get away from the truth she had just learned.

He could still feel his own shock at the sudden and calamitous turn of events, but as he walked – his eyes searching around him every few steps – it now all began to make sense to him – the puzzle of why a blonde-haired and blue-eyed woman like Mary Jarvis had given birth to such a dark-haired, dark-eyed girl.

And Mary Jarvis – how old was she? No more than thirty-seven or thirty-eight. An attractive woman, still comely; but it must have been from her father that Beth had inherited her striking exotic beauty. No wonder so many of the islanders thought she came from a place called Brazil, which they thought was in Spain.

The only puzzlement was that none of the islanders appeared to treat Beth as *'an outsider'* which was a real puzzlement indeed, because in his own short time on Mull many of the locals had eyed him with narrow suspicion, some referring to him as 'a foreigner' because they knew him to have come from as far away as Edinburgh.

When he reached the hill where the bonfire had been lit on Midsummer Eve it was deserted. He cupped his hands to his mouth and called *'Beth!*

Beth...!' But only the seagulls answered him.

Some time later, having satisfied himself that she was not hiding behind any tree or bush or rock, he stood looking around him, wondering where to search next. He did not know Mull that well, but she did ... so where would she go?'

Darkness had fallen as he returned down the hillside, missing his footing occasionally, slipping and sliding in the dark.

Back at the lane leading down to the Macquarie house, he could see the glow of candlelight in one of the windows. Was there any point in going inside and saying he had not found her, when that would only cause greater distress for the women.

He turned in the opposite direction and began to walk again. Sleep would be impossible, knowing there was a heartbroken young girl out here in the dark somewhere on her own.

He walked for miles, constantly cupping his hands to his mouth and calling out *"Beth...! Beth...!'* but unlike on the sea, his voice brought back no echo, and no answer.

He walked on, down leafy lanes, over fields and up hills, not knowing where he was going in the darkness, but at least the orb of the moon was nearly full in its glow and the sky was bright with stars so he did less tripping and slipping.

His voice was hoarse from calling her name, and when he eventually arrived back at the house at Gruline the dawn-light was beginning to brighten the sky and it was after five in the morning.

It was not until he was walking down the lane to the house that it suddenly occurred to him that

Beth might have returned home from another direction after he had left, and was now sound asleep in bed.

But when Mary opened the door, and she saw him alone, her tears began to spill again. 'I'll make you some tea,' she said.

In the dining room Mrs Macquarie was also still up, still sitting at the dining table, her face weary and looking much older. And she, too, when she saw him alone, seemed to shrivel in her chair with dismay.

'No sign?'

He shook his head.

'Where did you look?'

'I don't rightly know. I just kept walking and calling her name, but I must have covered a fair few miles.'

'Poor Beth ... the young find it so hard to cope in matters like this, and Beth has always been so ... so *innocent* about the world beyond Mull.'

'Mrs Macquarie, I think you should go to bed now,' he said. 'You look in want of some rest.'

Elizabeth put her hands to her watering eyes and said quietly, 'All I want is to die.'

Exhausted himself, he sat down on a chair by the window and remained silent, knowing no words of his would console her.

Mary arrived carrying a tray of cups and saucers and a silver teapot.

'Not for me,' Elizabeth said, rising to stand and walking slowly and wearily towards the door.

Mary quickly set down the tray and moved to block her path, putting her hands on the older woman's shoulders and looking into her swollen eyes.

'Oh Elizabeth,' she said softly, 'you did not intend this, and we all make mistakes, and please believe me when I say I forgive you.'

'I don't deserve to be forgiven,' Elizabeth replied. 'And I know I will never forgive myself.'

For a moment the two women stood looking at each other, and John looked on as they both suddenly hugged each other, and remained hugging each other for a very long time.

'Let me help you up to bed,' Mary said. 'Nothing can be gained by you staying up any longer.' As they reached the door Mary glanced over her shoulder at John. 'Help yourself to some tea, I won't be long.'

John eventually moved over to the table and poured himself a cup of black tea, drinking only half of it, then turned and stood looking down the room, his hand to the top of his head in thought.

Where could she be? Out all night in the darkness?

Hell's flames! He wished Mrs Macquarie had not questioned him so much. If she had only stuck to polite niceties and not had such an enquiring mind the subject of the slave trade would not have arisen. And Beth would be out this morning, none the wiser, her usual innocent self, meeting him at the stream, and no doubt that dog of hers would be jealously circling them again.

His hand came down from his head, his eyes widening as a realisation came to him.

He turned as Mary came back into the room and

he said quickly, 'Can you give me something that Beth wears regularly? A glove, a hat, anything.'

'Why?

'Her dog – Robbie!'

Mary stared. 'Oh my goodness – yes! Robbie always knows when Beth is near or on her way home.'

She rushed into the hall and came back holding Beth's black tricorn hat. 'She often wears this, especially when she's out riding.'

John took the hat. 'Do you have a horse I can use?'

'No, we will take the trap, because I'm coming with you.'

John frowned. 'A horse would be much swifter.'

'It would,' Mary agreed, 'but if we saddle up a horse in the stables for you to ride without Hector's permission he will be wanting to know why – and *why* you are still here when you only came for dinner. And knowing Hector, he won't stop lurking and listening until he finds out *why*. And what happened here last night must never be learned outside the four of us – you, me, Elizabeth and Beth.'

'Yes, I understand.'

'I often set off in the trap for Tobermory this early, and I'm quite capable of harnessing the mare myself.'

'I'll help you.'

'No, we cannot risk Hector being up and about and seeing you, although he's never usually up and around as early as this, not until after seven when Mrs Keillor cooks the breakfast. Her room is above the kitchen but she never wakes before half past six.'

'So what shall I do now?'

'You go down the lane and wait for me by the trees. Have you had some tea?'

'Yes, thank you.'

'Have some more. I won't be too long.'

*

John was standing by the trees with Beth's hat in his hand when Mary turned the trap onto the road, Robbie wagging along beside it.

John bent and patted his head and then held the hat under his nose. 'Where is she, boy, where is she?'

As soon as he got the scent of the hat Robbie barked and started running around in circles of excitement.

John and Mary looked at each other.

'Don't be stupid, Robbie,' said Mary impatiently, 'we want you to – ' her sentence remained unfinished as Robbie darted forward in the direction of Salen and minutes later was gone from sight.

'At least we know which direction he is heading,' John said, jumping up on the trap as Mary chucked the reins and urged the mare to go faster than usual. 'Go girl, *go!*'

They had travelled two miles in the direction of Salen and still no sign of Robbie.

'What do we do now?' Mary asked miserably. 'There's two turnings ahead and I don't know which one to take. A fat lot of use that dog has turned out to be. He probably saw a rabbit and went chasing it. What do we do now?'

John was still holding the hat, still convinced that it was no rabbit that had sent Robbie off in a mad run.

'We do what we would do with humans,' he said, standing up in the cart and cupping his hands around his mouth and calling '*Robbie! Robbie!*'

Minutes later Robbie came tearing back towards them, barking and circling the trap and dashing off again.

'He's heading into the glen,' Mary said. 'Parts of the track there is so narrow I won't get the trap through.'

'Then I'll walk.' John jumped down and began running after the dog. Seconds later Mary threw down the reins, abandoned the trap, and ran after him.

Hurtling back again, and seeing John coming into sight, Robbie turned and led the way – running forward round a bend, and coming back – running forward out of sight, and coming back.

Half a mile on, Mary was losing her breath and her patience. 'How do we know he's not playing a game with us?'

'We don't know, so we'll just have to trust that he's not as crazy as he seems.'

They came to a part of the track that was narrow enough for only a single horse to pass through and shaded by thick overhanging trees.

John led the way and Mary followed close behind, both emerging to see Robbie standing at the side of the track in utter silence, gazing down into a gulley.

Mary felt her heart stop for a moment and put a hand to her chest. 'Oh, God, she whispered. 'Oh, God.'

Both moved to look down the side of the gulley and saw why Robbie was remaining so silent ... Beth was lying curled up in a ball, fast asleep.

'Oh God,' Mary said again, tears spilling down her face, 'I should have known this is where she would come ... but how could I have known ... it's years since I brought her here and showed her ... and she was only about ten years old then.'

'Showed her what?'

Mary gulped in her throat. 'She's lying in the same place where George was found ... when he died ... her father.'

John exhaled his breath. 'Then one can only deduce that she has probably come here many times since then. You stay here.'

He moved down the gulley, through stones and rocks, until he reached the sleeping girl and bent to touch her shoulder.

She did not respond.

He shook her shoulder more roughly this time, and she stirred, turning on her back and slowly opening her dark eyes, her face as waxen pale as someone who has been through a long illness.

'Come, Beth, come ... time to go home.'

She closed her eyes and turned away, back into the same position.

Mary could watch no longer, making her way down the gulley, snagging her skirt on rocks here and there, until she reached her daughter.

And then John stood watching as Mary did the strangest thing ... she stretched out the ground and lay at her daughter's back, putting her arms around her and cupping herself close into Beth's body, whispering tenderly into her ear, words about her father, loving, comforting words ...

'It wasn't as bad as it sounded, the whip never touched him, General Macquarie saw to that ... He was only seven, and from that day forward he knew only love, everyone loved him, and his life was wonderful, travelling all over the world, to the farthest parts of it, to China and Egypt and England and Sydney ... educated at the finest schools in London and Edinburgh ... One day he said to me, "Why does it hurt you so much, when it does not hurt me. I have no memory of that time, it was all so long ago and I was so young. It was like a dream that is forgotten as soon as the eyes open after sleep. You know the dream was a bad dream, but hard as you try you cannot remember any of it..."

After a short silence, Beth stirred and turned inside Mary's arms, her eyes confused, her voice weak. 'If he could not remember, then how did you know about it?'

'I never knew the details, not until Elizabeth told me. I made her tell me, I forced her.'

'How did she know?'

'General Macquarie told her. Don't forget, he was an adult at the time, capable of remembering everything, but George was just a child. And Elizabeth had to have an explanation as to why George had the name of Jarvis ... the same name as

General Macquarie's first wife.'

'And why did he?'

'Because Jane Jarvis *loved* him so much she legally gave him her own name of Jarvis. She was only twenty-three when she died.'

'And how old was General Macquarie then?'

'Thirty-one, I think. He was only a captain then, and years later, when he married Elizabeth, over time she and George became very close, very fond of each other. In fact, it was only because of Elizabeth's goodness and kindness that George and I were able to get married.'

'Why?'

'Well, because ...' Mary bit her lip as she thought of some lie to tell her daughter. One shock was enough.

'Well, because ...'

John heard no more, walking away up the gulley and away from a conversation that was none of his business, a conversation that under less traumatic circumstances would not have taken place in his hearing.

He looked around for Robbie who had disappeared again, and then later found him stretched out on the bench of the trap, asleep. What a dog – what a mad, crazy, harum-scarum loveable dog.

Without looking back, John continued walking in the direction he had come, out of the glen and onwards under the brightening sky, until at the end of two miles he had reached the Dewar's house.

'By!' said Robert Dewar when John entered.

'That was a long afternoon cup of tea over at Gruline.'

John blinked his eyes tiredly. 'We drank port.'

'It was a long drink of port then. Were ye asked to stay for supper?'

'I was.'

Robert's curiosity was burning. 'So what kept ye there all night? They musta liked ye to keep ye there so long. Did her ladyship ask ye to stay and play some cards? She likes a game of cards, Mrs Macquarie, just so long as there's no money gambling in it.'

'Yes,' John said tiredly, pushing his hair back from his brow. 'We played cards.'

'What game? Twenty-one or Twenty-five?'

John was tired of people questioning him. He sighed. 'No, we played whist.'

'Whist? Never heard of it. What kind of card game is that?'

'A game of intellectual exercise using both caution and mathematical calculations to work out the chances of winning the rubber.'

'Stone me, I think I'd prefer to spread manure over the crops than play a dreary game like that. And ye played this game all night, did ye?'

John nodded. 'It's a hard game to play. It can take all night.'

Robert Dewar could not believe it, would not believe it.

'In God's truth, are ye telling me that Mrs Macquarie and Mrs Jarvis stayed up all night and did not go to bed?'

'In God's truth, Mrs Macquarie and Mrs Jarvis

stayed up all night and did not go to bed.'

Looking at him, Robert knew that John had spoken the truth.

'And Miss Beth?'

'She did not go to her bed either.'

'The three of them – staying up all night – why?'

'You need four to play whist.'

Robert Dewar chuckled. '*Whist* – exercise and caution and all to win nothing more than a piece of rubber! God's breeches! That must be a card game for women then, because what kind of *men* would want to play a dull card game like that!'

'A lot of young men on Her Majesty's ships,' John said, turning to leave the kitchen and heading for the stairs and his bed – bumping into Kirsty at the open door.

'Oh, yes, Kirsty, good morning, and Brazil is *not* in Spain. Brazil is in Brazil.'

'No it's not.'

'Yes it is.'

'Who says?'

'I do.'

'Then ye are a liar, John Dewar,' she said haughtily and pushed past him into the kitchen.

*

John did not even attempt to keep his arranged appointment at ten o'clock with Beth later that morning. He saw no point in waiting down by the stream when he knew she would not appear.

Nor was he surprised that she did not appear later that afternoon when he called at Gruline. Only Mary appeared to be home, and she seemed happy to see him.

She led him into the drawing-room and then looked at him with some surprise. 'The sleepless night seems to have had no tiring effect on you.'

'I'm used to sleeping in four-hour shifts. And you? How are you?'

Mary shrugged. 'I had a few hours sleep this morning. Tonight I'll go to my bed early.'

'And Beth? How is she?'

Mary gestured for him to sit down, and then sat down herself, looking very tired.

'She is in her room, but whether she is now sleeping or not, I don't know. Whenever I go in she pretends to be asleep, keeping her eyes closed, but I always know when she is awake. So ...' Mary sighed, 'I've decided to leave her alone until she feels ready for some company.'

John sat thoughtful. 'And Mrs Macquarie?' he asked.

'Oh, the late night did not go well with Elizabeth. She's tired out. I made her go back to bed for a rest. Although she will not get *into* the bed, the most she will do is lie on top of it, insisting it's against the Scottish way of living to lie in bed in daylight.'

John stood to leave. The only reason for his visit today was to express his wish that all was well with the family, and after the cataclysmic night of events of which he had been a party, it was no less than Mrs Jarvis would expect him to do.

'Thank you for coming today, Mr Dewar,' Mary said sincerely. 'Thank you for ... everything.'

He smiled. 'You may call me John.'

'Oh no, too personal,' Mary said with a small smile in return. 'Elizabeth would be horrified.'

'Oh well, the choice is yours.'

Mary accompanied him to the door, and as he stepped out, he suddenly turned and looked at her, his eyes thoughtful.

'Mrs Jarvis ... back in the glen ... I'm sorry for what happened there, the accident, and the sad loss of your husband.'

'Oh,' Mary said quietly, a soft expression coming into her blue eyes, 'George has never been lost to me. He lives on in Beth, more and more he lives on in her. Every day, every year as she gets older, when she smiles, the occasional look in her eyes, I see George all over again, as clear as day, and that has always been a great comfort to me.'

'And now Beth will need a great deal of comfort from you.'

Mary nodded. 'We will comfort each other, we usually do.'

*

For a number of days Beth did not want to see anyone, talk to anyone, preferring instead to ride off alone and spend her time on the hills with only Robbie and the sheep for company.

Sitting alone she wondered and thought about the events of life, which seemed to come and go and change in tune and mood as swiftly as the seasons.

At least the only seasons she knew, the ones she saw on Mull. In spring the land came alive in colour, red and yellow and purple wild flowers growing along every roadside and hedge, followed by the long and warm days of summer when the sky was a light blue and you could clearly see all the neighbouring islands, and even the White-tailed eagles seemed less predatory in their mood.

And then autumn, a quietening down into subdued greens and browns, followed by the darkness of winter ... the season her heart was in now, winter.

Perhaps if she had been told ... bit by small bit, at an earlier time, the shock would have been less, the pain would have been less. It was not good enough for people to excuse it all by saying her father had been a child at the time, as if such brutality was felt less by a small child than a big adult.

Now she understood why the main thing she remembered about her father was his gentleness, in touch and tone, always gentle and always calm, and now she knew why. No problem, no turmoil, must have seemed beyond his coping, not when in his childhood he had suffered the worst – captured and forced into slavery – so everything else since then must have seemed easy and painless in comparison.

She dashed the tears from her eyes - *captured and forced into slavery* – what kind of a cruel world was out there? Well, she would not be a part of that world, no, never. She would stay here on Mull where life was safe and the people were decent and the animals were less cruel than humans.

In the days following at Gruline, Mary saw the

change in her daughter, the difference. Oh, she was not petulant or sulky and carried on her conversations with Elizabeth and Mrs Keillor and the cleaning girls in the same old friendly way, but Mary knew that her daughter *had* changed. She saw it clearly, even though the others didn't seem to have noticed or be aware of it.

All the happy innocence had gone from Beth's eyes. She had learned that the world could be a hateful place at times, as Mary herself had long ago learned also. But then George had come along and helped her to recover from the misery and depression of it all. But who, now – apart from herself – would or could help Beth to recover?

'Does Lachlan know?' Beth asked Mary one night as they sat sewing in the drawing-room. 'About Papa?'

'No,' Mary replied honestly. 'Lachlan knows no more than you did.'

'Do you think it would matter much to him, if he knew?'

'Lachlan doesn't need to know anything,' Mary replied tersely. 'Elizabeth will not make the same mistake again.'

'It mattered to John Dewar.'

'What?' Mary looked up from her sewing. 'Why do you say that?'

'Well, because ...' Beth kept on sewing, 'the last time I saw him he appeared like an apparition bending over me in the glen, and then he disappeared in a blink, obviously having decided not to travel part of the way back with us in the trap, choosing a long walk instead.'

'I believe he felt – '

'And it's been more than a week since then and he has not sought to visit us here again and enjoy our alarming company.'

'He did call here, Beth, that same afternoon, but both you and Elizabeth were in your bedrooms. He wished you both well.'

After a long silence, Mary said, 'John Dewar gave me the impression of liking you very much, Beth.'

'He gave me that impression too.'

'So don't you think that you are now being very unfair to him? He spent most of the night out searching for you, when most other men would have bid a polite goodnight and hastily returned their bed. And it was his idea to use Robbie to try and find you.'

Beth sat silent, no longer sewing.

'Perhaps,' said Mary, *you* should ride over and call on *him*, if only to thank him for being so kind and helpful to your mother.'

*

The following morning, Beth endeavoured to do just that. She rode over to the Dewars' house and was immediately forced by Kirsty to taste one of her freshly baked oatcakes.

'Oh, still hot!' Beth smiled, swallowed, and then asked, 'Is your cousin at home, or has he gone to Tobermory?'

'He's gone to Edinburgh first, and then to Portsmouth.'

'Portsmouth?' Beth frowned. 'Where is that?'

'In London. All the big ships dock in London's docks, especially the *Royal* Navy ships, because that's where the *Royal* Family and lives.'

With an air of preoccupation Beth looked around her, her eyes fixing on the open kitchen window through which she could see Mrs Dewar pegging a white sheet on the line to dry ... a white sheet that made her think despondently of the sails on a ship.

'So he's gone then, back to the Navy?'

'Aye, and he won't be back here awhile, no' for a long while, probably no' for five years, that's how long it was before we seen him again the last time.'

Beth looked at her. 'But was that not because he lived away in Edinburgh, and not because he was away at sea for all that time?'

'Och no!' Kirsty laughed. 'Ye're thinking of the trading vessels that come in and go out, Beth, like they do at Tobermory. But that's no' how the *Navy* ships do it – they go out and stay out for years.'

Riding back to Gruline, Beth was certain that Kirsty was *wrong*, as she was about most things. If Kirsty did not know the answer to something, she just made one up in her head, and then believed it to be so, no matter how many times she was corrected.

Elizabeth was in the drawing-room at her desk writing letters when Beth walked in.

'Elizabeth, is Portsmouth in London?'

'Goodness, no,' Elizabeth replied. 'Portsmouth is much farther south, in the county of Hampshire.'

'Are you sure?'

'Of course I'm sure. It was at Portsmouth that

my husband and I boarded our ship *The Dromedary* for our voyage to New South Wales.'

Beth flopped down into an armchair. 'I think the next time I go into Tobermory I should buy an Atlas and give it to Kirsty. She believes she knows where every place in the world is, but *all* her locations are wrong.'

'Kirsty Dewar?' Elizabeth laid down her pen. 'Surely, dear, that would be a waste of money? That poor girl can neither read nor write, so how could she read an Atlas?'

Beth had forgotten that.

'But *you* could read an Atlas, Beth, then you would not have to ask Kirsty the location of anywhere. There's one in the study, why don't you go and get it.'

Beth was surprised. 'But I thought no one but you or Mama was allowed to go in there?'

'Oh, that was when you and Lachlan were younger, but now you are old enough to know not to go anywhere near my husband's desk, or interfere with any of his papers on the shelves.'

'When is Lachlan next home?' Beth asked.

'Soon, he keeps telling me in his letters, very soon.'

As Beth walked out the room, tall and young and graceful in her navy riding habit, Elizabeth's eyes followed her and a sad ache thumped in her heart as she remembered her awful mistake ... Beth had suffered sore because of that, and yet the girl had tried hard not to cause anyone else to suffer afterwards ... such a forgiving girl, so genuinely kind-hearted, no malice in her at all, and *so* like

George.

Some words from her favourite playwright came into Elizabeth's mind, words from one of his sonnets,

*'Thou art thy father's glass, and he in thee
calls back the lovely April of his prime ...'*

Elizabeth lifted her pen and returned her gaze to her letter, quite sure that Mr Shakespeare would not have minded her mentally changing his word of 'mother' to 'father'. No, in this circumstance, Mr Shakespeare would not have minded at all.

*

Beth found the Atlas in the study, took it straight up to her bedroom, and the first place she tried to find in its pages was ... Jamaica. Wasn't that the place where John Dewar had said his next ship would be going?

A guilty flush rushed into Beth's face. Why was she looking for Jamaica, when she knew that in time she may be marrying Lachlan and *he* was in Ireland.

Chapter Twenty-Four

The long summer days of bright skies until midnight had passed into the shorter and cooler days of autumn, and now the murky cold weather of winter was making its way down the hillsides with black clouds settling into their hidden contours.

Elizabeth's health became a constant cause for concern as she suffered one cold after another and seemed unable to shake them off.

'You are getting old, m'dear,' Dr McLean told her, which led to a sharp indignant response from his patient, 'I'm younger than you!'

'Only by a year or so, and I have not polluted my lungs in the smog of London as you have done. Now keep taking your medicine, and again I prescribe rest, rest and even *more* rest, preferably in your bed.'

Elizabeth glared at him in disgust. 'You expect me to be a lazy lay-abed night *and* day!'

'Aye, if only to stop you hindering the natural work of your immune system.'

Later, as he took his leave, Dr McLean paused by the open front door and gave some final advice to Mary.

'At least *try* and make her stay abed for longer in the mornings, that would be some help.'

Elizabeth obdurately refused to stay in her bed, preferring to take her rest in the armchair by the fire, a warm shawl around her shoulders.

The arthritis in her right knee was a constant pain and, strangely, was only relieved by the soothing effect of Beth standing behind Elizabeth's armchair and gently brushing her hair.

'Oh, Beth, that's almost as good as laudanum,' Elizabeth sighed blissfully, 'and equally as relaxing.'

So whenever the pain in her knee was very bad, Beth reached for the hairbrush and began her ritual slow strokes that always sent Elizabeth into a mesmeric stare into her thoughts.

'You know, Mary used to brush my hair for me in Australia, but not as good as you, Beth, not as gentle.'

'Tell me about Australia,' Beth murmured, 'from the day you arrived there.'

'Oh, we were *all* so young then, back in those days in Sydney ... Lachlan, George, Mary ... and even *me,* all so young ...'

'I thought General Macquarie was older than you.'

'He was older than me ...' Elizabeth blinked. 'I suppose I must be remembering our earlier days, when I first met him, here in Scotland. He was thirty something ... and I was twenty-five. Goodness, it all seems such a long time ago.'

'Tell me about Australia,' Beth asked again. 'Tell me about the land and the people and the animals.'

So Elizabeth told Beth, day after day, so many things, but without any laudanum in the house there were no further slip-ups for Mary to worry about. Sick in body she may be, but Elizabeth's mind was as sharp as always.

'And now,' Elizabeth said, 'Reverend Cowper has told me in his last letter that John McArthur has been officially pronounced insane, which does *not* surprise me. All that scheming against my husband and the emancipists ... I knew no good would come of it.'

'But ...' Beth ventured, 'I read in the newspapers that John McArthur has done wonders with the growth of the wool trade in Australia.'

'Oh yes, that cannot be denied. He owned the best merino rams in New South Wales and he used them. But all that plotting and scheming ... no wonder his mind gave up under the strain.'

As always, Elizabeth's eyes finally closed, and Beth left her in silence to sleep.

'Even an hour or two asleep in the chair is good for her,' Mary said to Mrs Keillor.

Yet a short while later, as always, Elizabeth's coughing erupted and broke the sleepy silence of the drawing-room.

'Now ye *must* stay in bed!' Dr McLean warned Elizabeth on his next visit, and eventually she did so, getting weaker and weaker as the days passed, her face as white as the sheet under her hands, until Dr McLean sadly informed Mary, 'I think the time has come for ye to send for her son.'

Hector rode as fast as he could to Craignure to deliver Mary's letter in time for the packet boat over to the mainland.

Mrs Keillor made pot after pot of nutritious hot brose for Mary to feed to Elizabeth, in the hope that it would 'help to bring some of Mrs Macquarie's strength back.'

During the night, Mary and Beth took it in turns to sit in the chair by Elizabeth's bed and keep a watch on her, in case she awoke in need of anything to aid her comfort.

And then the night came when Elizabeth awoke, needing only the comfort of her Bible.

Mary remained sitting silently, watching her as she read, fearing to disturb her in such a religious moment.

Elizabeth finally let the book fall open onto the eiderdown, turned her head slowly and, looking at Mary in a very peaceful way, she held out her hand.

'Mary ...'

Mary leaned forward and clasped Elizabeth's hand in her own. 'What is it, love?'

'When my dear Lachlan died,' Elizabeth said croakily, 'it was my belief that his death was simply an interruption in our relationship, and that one day we would be reunited again. That's not a foolish belief, is it?'

'No, not foolish at all,' Mary answered, kissing Elizabeth's hand. 'Love is a strong chain. I feel the same about George, that his death is just a short suspension of space and time until he and I are together again forever.'

'Please God,' Elizabeth whispered, her free hand moving to rest on her Bible as she gazed so fondly at Mary, and then her eyes closed in sleep.

Mary sat back in her chair and kept up her vigil, unaware that Elizabeth's time in life had already passed.

*

Lachlan arrived on the morning of his mother's funeral in the company of Lord Strathallan. The weather had been bitterly cold for some weeks, and although Lord Strathallan was draped in a full-flowing elegant cloak, Lachlan wore a plain grey Army greatcoat over his uniform.

He appeared to be very shocked by the unexpected death of his mother, and deeply grieved.

Although afterwards, during refreshments at the house, Lachlan became resentful and defensive when Mary asked him why he had not been to visit his mother more often – especially as Lord Strathallan had just told her that Lachlan's regiment had been back in England for almost four months – and he had not even informed his mother of that.

'It's not as if I *knew* she was going to die, or even expected it,' he protested. 'I thought she would live to be at least eighty.'

The following morning, when Lachlan made the decision to accompany his former guardian in his return to Strathallan Castle, Mary knew there had to be a very good reason for his eager departure.

'Is your friend William Drummond at Strathallan now?'

'Yes.'

'And you prefer his company to ours?'

'At this time, yes, with everyone so sad and sorrowful here, what help can that be to me? It will serve me no good to stay up here in the back of beyond. I need cheering up. I need my friends in the regiment. And Mary – William Drummond has always been my very *best* friend!'

After he had left, Mary was fuming – not only because Lachlan had completely ignored all the tenants who had come out in the cold and rain to attend his mother's funeral – but also because he had not once looked in Beth's direction nor attempted to speak a word to her.

PART FOUR

Chapter Twenty-Five

For Beth, the rest of the winter seemed endless. There was no work to be done in the vegetable garden, and the land all around was bleak and dormant.

Not until late February was she able to make herself busy and feel useful again, staying up through the night helping the ewes to birth their lambs, and loving every moment of it.

'This one I'm going to keep,' she said to Robert Dewar, sitting on the straw in the barn with a small lamb in her lap.

The farm manager shook his head in refusal and laughed, 'Nay, I dinna think Robbie would like *that*. Now away home to your bed, lass, and get some sleep.'

By mid-March most of the lambs were up on the hills with their dams; and with the coming of spring the land became alive with colour again, pink and yellow wild flowers peeping out from under hedges; and then in April moving out in stronger and fuller groups along the verges and woodland banks.

The woodland around the Jarvisfield estate had its own population of fallow deer that were usually content to roam within their trees, but now a young stag was daring to venture down to the lane of the house and into the garden, chewing the heads off the daffodils.

Hector was getting annoyed. 'Another one!' he

said to Beth. 'Them deer have no right coming down here, an' if they come near my stables I'll get me knife and we'll be eating deer till summer.'

'Don't you dare!' Beth cried. 'The fallow deers have been here since Norman times, so they have more right to be here than *you,* Hector Allen from *Oban!'*

'Ah-haha,' Hector attempted a laugh. 'It's been many a long year since my ain people emigrated from the mainland over to Mull, as many as eighty years or more.'

Beth was not listening. She had walked in a creeping fashion around the back corner of the house to halfway down the lane, and now she was stroking the young stag's head in a gentle motion with her palm.

Mary opened the front door quietly and stood watching Beth, with Mrs Keillor creeping up behind her.

'By!' whispered Mrs Keillor. 'I've never seen a stag let a human get so close.'

'It's Beth's strange way with animals,' Mary whispered back. 'She seems to have a way of not frightening them away.'

Beth turned her head, saw them at the door and smiled. 'It's the same one,' she said quietly, 'the same one that's been coming down these past few days.'

'How do you know that?' Mary asked in a soft hush. 'How do you know it's the same one?'

'He's only got one antler growing ...' Beth moved her body back so they could see the one, small stump of an antler growing on the left side of the young stag's head.

The stag bent his head and continued chewing as Beth stroked his fawn-grey body. 'Oh, my beauty, your coat will be a lovely rich brown colour come the summer.' She turned her head to the women at the front door and smiled again. 'He's adorable, I want to keep him.'

Mary and Mrs Keillor exchanged a weary look. Of late they had heard this from Beth so many times about so many animals – always wanting to keep one as her own and take care of it.

'She's looking for something to love,' Mrs Keillor whispered.

Mary nodded. 'Or someone.'

'She's at that age now,' Mrs Keillor observed. 'Only a few weeks shy of eighteen.'

They watched as Beth slowly escorted the stag back up towards the woods.

'Reckon she'll be happier to see Master Lachlan when he gets home again,' said Mrs Keillor thoughtfully. 'Last time his visit was so short and they were both too upset about Mrs Macquarie going down the road of no return to have any idle talk to spare for each other. D'ye think aye, hen?'

'Aye,' agreed Mary, turning back into the house and cutting off any further talk on that particular matter.

*

The warm Atlantic currents brought a thick flowering to the island in May, primroses, harebells and bluebells abounded everywhere.

Beth took Robbie down to the flowing waters of

the stream to give him his usual wash. Robbie objected in his usual way, growling in complaint. Yet as soon as he saw two ducks cruising near the opposite bank he dashed carelessly into the water to round them up, sending an unseen baby duckling fleeing in fright.

'Robbie!'

The flapping of wings and din of quacks made Beth take off her shoes, pull up her skirt and run into the stream to get the dog away and save the duckling from harm.

Robbie was now barking fiercely in response to all the flapping and quackery.

'Robbie! Robbie! *Robbie!*'

Hearing the angry tone in her voice, Robbie swam to the bank, darted swiftly into the trees and disappeared from sight.

Beth looked closely and saw the baby duckling was now safely tucked under its mother's wings and both ducks skimmed swiftly past her, still loudly quacking their complaints.

Beth sighed. 'Oh, that mad bad dog!'

She stood in the stream, the water around her knees, and then began a slow wade back to the bank, stopping in shock when she saw a young man leaning against a tree on the bank, watching her tranquilly.

He smiled. 'Good afternoon, Miss Jarvis.'

She instantly dropped her skirt to cover her bare legs, her face flushing a deep pink as she stepped onto the bank.

'How l-long have you been standing there?' she stuttered.

'Not long.' He took a fob watch out of his white waistcoat pocket. 'By my calculation, I am only eleven months, three weeks, five days and fourteen hours late for our appointment.'

'What appointment?'

'To meet by the stream at ten o'clock.'

He was still smiling, and Beth's heart was pounding again. He was dressed in his Navy uniform and looked even more handsome than she remembered.

'I have no memory of any appointment.' She bent down to squeeze the water from her skirt, hiding her face as she waited for her heart to stop racing.

'May I help you?'

'No, no.' She slipped her feet into her shoes and then bent again to tie the laces. 'How did you know I was here?'

'I didn't know. I was on my way to your house and then I heard Robbie at war with some ducks followed by your voice in reprimand, so down I came, and what I saw ... was a sight worth waiting for.'

'Please stop smiling.'

'Why? It's a beautiful day and, unlike yours, *my* clothes are not wet.'

Beth was still flushing, gazing around her with an air of preoccupation and feeling that unsettled reaction again, *unsettled*.

He stopped smiling. 'Come on, I'll escort you back to the house and some dry clothes.'

'Why were you going to the house in the first place?' she asked as they walked.

'To pay my respects. I have just learned about the death of Mrs Macquarie.'

'Oh yes,' Beth said softly. 'We all still miss her.' And then she realised, a frown coming to her face. 'But ... for a man who was on his way to pay his respects to a bereaved household ... I hope you do not intend to give your condolences about Elizabeth's death to my mother with that happy smile on your face?'

John Dewar laughed. 'No, of course not. I'm just happy to see *you* again.'

'And yet, almost a year ago, you did not think to call on us at Jarvisfield and say your farewells.'

His laughter faded, and now it was he who gazed around him in hesitation before he answered.

'No, almost a year ago I felt no wish to go near the house at Jarvisfield again. Although, I should have done, I realise that now, if only to say farewell to your mother and Mrs Macquarie.'

Beth looked at him, perplexed. 'But not to me?'

'No, certainly not to you.' He hesitated again. 'At that time I had been told by Kirsty that everyone knew you would soon be marrying the young laird of Jarvisfield.'

'Oh, that's not true! There was a time ... but no, I believe Lachlan and I have both learned that our affection for each other was more like that of a brother and sister. A marriage is out of the question.'

'So I have been informed.'

She did not have a chance to ask who had informed him because they were now walking down the lane to the house and her mother was standing in the garden – staring at John Dewar as if seeing a ghost.

'Mr Dewar!' Mary called, coming out of the garden to meet them, a smile widening on her face. 'Oh, I *am* happy to see you again!'

Beth left them to go and get changed out of her wet clothes.

When she rejoined them, in the drawing-room, Mrs Keillor was placing a tray of tea and buttered scones on the small table in front of the fireplace, looking as delighted to have new company in the house as her mother did.

Beth moved to a chair nearer to the back window, but before she sat down she caught a glimpse of Hector lurking outside the window and listening. He quickly bent down, but too late, she had seen him.

'Where are you going, Beth?' Mary called after her as she swiftly walked out of the room again.

Outside in the yard she found Hector pretending to be bent over a wooden tub of washing that Mrs Keillor had left soaking.

'What are you looking for?' she asked him.

'Well,' said Hector, scratching his head with one hand while still searching with the other hand through the washing. 'There's a pair of me breeches I canna find, so I'm seeing if she's been washing 'em.'

'And is that why you were listening at the window?'

'What window?' Hector straightened and stared at her. 'I was by no window. I was here looking for my stolen breeches.'

'Stolen?'

'Aye, someone musta stole 'em if I canna find 'em.'

'Hector, it is very rude to stand and listen at windows when we have a guest.'

'A *guest?*' Hector replied indignantly. 'Well *he's* no guest that the laird would approve being in his house. No, I'm telling ye *no.*'

Beth was baffled. 'Why not?'

'He'll no' like *him*, the laird,' Hector insisted, 'He'll no' like *him* at all.'

Again Beth asked, 'Why not?'

'Because ye don't pit two bulls agin each other, do ye? And if one's red and the other's blue, then the red one won't like the blue one, no, I tell ye, *no.*'

Beth was wondering if Hector had been secretly drinking drams of the house whisky in order to spout such nonsense, but Hector was deadly serious.

'Tis like all that argumenting and quarrelling I hears in Tobermory. Who is the greater man – the Duke of Wellington or that Horatio Nelson? And I says it has to be Wellington, 'cos he's head of the *Army.*'

Beth was beginning to think she understood why Hector objected with such animosity to John Dewar in his Navy uniform.

'And you prefer the men of the Army?' she asked.

'Course I do!'

'Why though? They both serve the same country and are on the same side. So why do you prefer the men of the Army? Is it because your employer and laird is now in the Army?'

Hector stared at her incredulously as if thinking she must be a fool.

'Nay, tis 'cos the men in the Army serve alongside *horses*. Aye, tis the *horses* that pull their cannons and carry their officers into battle and lead the charge, and tis the *horses* that win their wars for them, aye! No' like those navy blues who just sail around in ships. Now Wellington – he alus rode a horse, didna he? But that Horatio Nelson – he couldna ride a horse could he? *He* could only ride in ships and that's why *he*'s dead and the duke isna.'

Beth turned up her eyes, turned around and walked back into the house, thinking she must truly be feeling *unsettled* to think she could even *attempt* to have a sensible conversation with Hector.

When she returned to the drawing-room, John Dewar was preparing to leave.

'So soon?' her mother said. 'Could you not stay for dinner?'

'Sadly, no. The new lady in my life is preparing a very special dinner for me tonight, and I promised her I would definitely *not* be late.'

'Your ... new lady?' Mary said, glancing quickly at Beth who looked equally as surprised.

'Yes, my new landlady. I am staying at the Tobermory Inn.'

'With Lizzie – Mrs McLoud!' Mary laughed in relief. 'Oh, if Lizzie made you promise that then she must be planning something very special for you.'

'Her cooking's not as good as mine though,' said Mrs Keillor with a sniff.

'So you are not staying at the Dewar's house?' Beth asked. 'Like last time?'

John met her eyes. 'No, last time I came to Mull to look for a house for my father and gave it very scant attention, spending too much time elsewhere. So this time I must stay in Tobermory until I find one, because he is getting impatient and also nearer to his planned retirement.'

'Do you think you will find one?' Mary asked dubiously. 'Tobermory is not a big place.'

'I think I might. The agent in Tobermory sent a letter to my father saying he might now have the type of house he is looking for. The front door and windows look directly onto the sea.'

He turned to Beth. 'Would you like to come and view it with me, Miss Jarvis. I share a berth with three other men when I'm aboard ship so my taste is not the best when looking for a land dwelling.'

'By! – You have to share a bed with three others?' Mrs Keillor was shocked. 'I'd've thought the Royal Navy treated its men betterer than that!'

'No, no,' John grinned. 'A berth aboard ship is a cabin – a room – containing sleeping berths. It is neither large nor small and is quite adequate for our needs.'

He again looked at Beth. 'So would you like to accompany me tomorrow, to view the house? If you're free to do so, that is?'

'I would love to,' Beth said eagerly. 'Yes, I would be truly happy to accompany you to view the house.'

When John smiled back at her, Beth realised she would probably be happy to accompany him to the ends of the earth if he wished it.

Chapter Twenty-Six

Beth left early the following morning, wearing her new brown riding habit and black tricorn hat. She had arranged to meet John inside the Tobermory Inn at nine, in time to meet the agent of the house at half past.

When she reached the inn's stables and handed over her horse to the stable boy, she wondered if she would need the horse again to reach the house. The town of Tobermory itself was small, but its population and houses were spread widely all over the hills.

John was standing in the morning sunshine outside the inn, waiting for her. He was no longer wearing his uniform, and nor was he wearing breeches, she immediately noticed. He was wearing straight-legged trousers down to the ankles.

'I saw you and your horse approaching through the window,' he said, taking her arm, 'I have already collected the keys from the agent. It's just a short walk up to the house.'

As they walked up the first hilly street she kept looking at his trousers. 'Are they a new fashion?'

'No, they have been the style for a number of years now, in the cities anyway.'

'In cities like Edinburgh?'

'Most cities, especially London, but yes, Edinburgh too. Although they have long been in fashion in the Navy.'

She smiled cheekily. 'Did your father make them for you?'

'He did indeed. He is after all my own personal tailor.' He looked over her brown riding outfit. 'Who cuts your clothes?'

'A tailor and his wife in Salen make all our clothes. Do you approve?'

'The cut is good, but the stitching is ...' he glanced at her apprehensive face, 'perfect!'

She smiled as they turned up another hill. 'There's the house,' John said, pointing. 'Just there on the left.'

Beth glanced up and saw a lovely white house basking in the sunshine on the side of a green hill. 'It looks bonnie and ... charming,' she admitted. 'And its windows are *gleaming!* Who owned it before? Do you know?'

'I've no idea of the name, other than that the gentleman who lived there liked to paint pictures of the sea and the harbour, hence the wide gleaming widows for light – which is exactly what my father is looking for, a house with a lot of light.'

When they reached the house it had a wooden gate and a short gravel path to the blue front door, and inside it was... 'Beautiful,' said Beth as they walked from room to room. 'And yes – so bright!'

The house had four rooms downstairs, one a kitchen, and four rooms upstairs; bright square rooms with a good fireplace in every one.

'And *here,*' John said, standing by the window of the downstairs front room, 'is where my father will spend a lot of his time, either hand-stitching a garment, or looking out to sea.'

Beth joined him at the window and both stood for a silent time gazing out to sea.

'Even the harbour looks enchanting from here,' Beth murmured.

'Yes.'

Her eyes fixed on the distant horizon of the sea. 'Why did you choose to go to sea with the Navy?'

John shrugged. 'Even as a lad, whenever I looked out to sea I always longed to be ... *out there* ... mastering the waves and the ocean, seeing what lay beyond.'

'I've never wanted to be anywhere but Mull. Does that make me dull?'

'Oh, sweet girl, no. It makes you ... stable.'

'So you think I'm horse-like then? I'm sure I'm not.'

They were still laughing and teasing each other as they left and locked the house.

'My father is coming to Mull on the evening ferry on Saturday, to see the house on Sunday,' John said as they walked back. 'Would you like to meet him?'

'Well, yes ... but why would he want to meet *me*? He sounds very possessive of his only son.'

'No, not possessive. My father is now very *dependent* upon his only son.'

'Dependent? In what way?'

'Emotionally. I'm all he has left now. I think that's why he wants to renew his relationship with the Dewar family here, and a few others he knows from Mull.'

'Yes, I would like to meet him.'

John smiled. 'And when you do, you can bring

him up to date on how Mull has changed since he last lived here as a boy.'

Beth laughed. 'Mull *never* changes. Not even Tobermory.'

*

They spent the day in the town, walking along the harbour watching the activity on the various trade vessels and fishermen's boats, taking a late breakfast, and then an early dinner at the inn, where Lizzie McLoud joined them and gave Beth all the latest gossip to take home to Mary.

For Beth it had been a wonderful day, so different to her usual day, and as she mounted her horse in the stables she felt sad at parting from John, until he mounted a horse also.

'What are you doing?'

'I'm escorting you home.'

Delighted, yet maintaining a straight face, 'There is no need. I would know my way home blindfolded.'

'I'm sure you do, but it will soon be dark and you are a young lady who should not be out alone at night. There are sailors in the town, Beth, sailors from the trading ships, and not all of them are gentlemen.'

Beth thought she detected a hint of Navy snobbery in his tone.

'So, in your view, a sailor from a trading ship is not so much a gentleman as sailor from a Navy ship?'

'No, that's not my view. When I say not *all* of them are gentlemen, I'm referring to men in general, no matter their status.'

He turned his horse around and led the way out of the stables and she followed until they were on the road out of town.

'In Edinburgh,' he continued as their horses ambled along, 'Mortimers is truly renowned as the finest outfitters for "Gentlemen" in the whole of Scotland. And indeed, so renowned is the quality of their designs and tailoring, the demand has now led to Mortimers opening a second establishment in London.'

'London?' Beth was impressed.

'Yes, but my point is ... in all the years that my father has spent measuring and dressing and speaking with all those "gentlemen" who frequent Mortimers, he says he has learned there are *two* types of men of the gentry: one type he would certainly regard as true gentlemen, but the other type he merely refers to as "gents".

He looked at her. 'And the same is true on ships, Navy or Merchant. Some officers have worse manners and baser instincts than the ordinary sailors who climb up the mizzen-mast.'

Beth nodded. 'I understand now.' She turned away to look towards the sea, a smile on her face as the gentle breeze lightly rippled against her hair.

'Apart from that,' John added, 'Angus told me there was a lot of trouble last night when a sailor tried to molest a Tobermory woman which led to some fighting between the local men and sailors down on the waterfront.'

Beth's dark eyes rounded as she stared at him. 'Here? In Tobermory? That's unusual.'

'Not when a foreign ship is in, apparently.'

After a silence as they rode along, Beth asked, 'Do you think your father will like the house?'

'I'm sure he will love it. Anyone would love that beautiful house.'

'But ... is it not on the big side for one man on his own?'

'Hardly, he will need a live-in housekeeper to do his cooking and cleaning for a start. Since my mother died he has been taking all his meals at a nearby hotel.'

'Tell me about your mother,' Beth asked gently. 'Not about when or how she died, but about her life.'

Darkness was looming by the time they reached Gruline. And by that time also, Beth had learned a lot more about John Dewar.

*

Mary was still up when Beth came in, sitting in the drawing-room waiting for her daughter's safe return from her day in town.

And so was Mrs Keillor, who seemed to be spending less time in her kitchen and spreading herself more widely around the house since Elizabeth's demise, Beth noticed; but her mother did not seem to mind.

'Did you have a good day?' Mary asked.

'Very good,' Beth answered, her face illumined again. 'It was the most perfect day.'

'And Mr Dewar?'

'Oh, Mama, he's *wonderful!*' Beth exclaimed with passion. 'He rode with me all the way home, and now he's on his way back to Tobermory in the dark.'

Mrs Keillor sat forward. 'Did he try to kiss ye when he said goodnight outside?'

'No!' Beth said hotly. 'He's a gentleman!'

'A gentleman, eh? An officer and a gentlemen, eh?' Mrs Keillor winked an eye. 'They can be the worst of all.'

'Oh, what do *you* know about men?' Beth challenged. 'And that mysterious husband of yours – I notice you have said very little over the years about *him*.'

'Oh, now, *my* husband,' said Mrs Keillor, sitting back and folding her arms, 'was the worst man of all. So the least said about *him*, the soonest forgotten.'

'So why did you marry him?' Beth queried.

Mary waved her hand impatiently. She knew all about Mrs Keillor's vanished husband, but tonight she wanted to know about Beth.

'When are you seeing him again, Mr Dewar?'

'Tomorrow. He's coming to Jarvisfield to see his Uncle Robert and the Dewar family, and then he and I are meeting to go for a walk together.'

Mary smiled her approval. 'Did you dine at the Tobermory Inn?'

'Yes, we did. And, oh ... Mrs McLeod asked me to tell you that those two gentlemen you and she were talking about some time ago – she said you would remember if I told you that one of them could down whisky easier than water.'

Mary searched her mind and then her eyes widened as she remembered the conversation –

about William Drummond and Lachlan.

'Oh, yes, two gentlemen from Perthshire, I think. Although I cannot remember their names or who they were.'

'Mrs McLeod said to tell you that a gentlemen over from the mainland and staying at the inn, said he knew that young man well – the one who drinks whisky like water – and it seems him and his friend are in bad trouble.'

Mary sat upright. 'What kind of bad trouble?'

'Too much drinking and gambling with cards in the gaming houses in England, and now both are in very bad debt.'

After a silence, Mary managed a careless shrug. 'What matter is that to us?'

'Debt is a terrible worrying thing though,' remarked Mrs Keillor. 'It's something I mercifully have no' had to fret about since the day I arrived at Jarvisfield.'

'Off to bed now, Beth,' Mary urged, and Beth was glad to say goodnight and run up the stairs to the privacy of her bedroom where, she was certain, she would *not* be able to sleep.

She was asleep as soon as her head hit the pillow.

Not so Mary, who paced up and down her bedroom endeavouring to make sense of the message that Lizzie McLeod had sent to her.

If William Drummond was in bad debt, then she could not see that problem being too difficult to resolve. His father, Lord Strathallan, was rich enough to buy his son out of any hole.

But if Lachlan was in bad debt ... she wanted to

know by how much?

Oh yes, Lachlan had changed drastically since he had entered the Army. From his letters to Elizabeth, Mary had deduced that he had become one of the 'fast set' in his regiment, but Elizabeth had not shown any real concern, seeming to be certain that *'time will give him wisdom.'*

Yet at the funeral, Mary had studied his face and known that Lachlan had been taught to drink hard and to play hard, and now this possibility of bad gambling debts.

She finally went to bed, but was unable to sleep, her mind churning over the amount that the bad debt might be?

She fervently hoped to God that it was not large enough a debt to put the Gruline house and the Jarvisfield estate at risk.

Chapter Twenty-Seven

There were no clouds in the sky, no wind, the afternoon sun streamed down the hills like a golden flood.

Standing near a tree by a small lochlin brook, shaded by overhanging branches, there was no talking between John and Beth. They were bending down, mutely watching a brown and yellow Willow Warbler sitting on a nest of eggs and calling to her mate.

'Hoo-eet! Hoo-eet!'

The nest was very close to the ground, set back in some scrub under the tree. The bird's calls to her mate continued repetitively until she suddenly gave a long *'Hweeeeeeeeeeeeeeeet!'*

'Oh, she's getting impatient,' John whispered, and Beth put a hand over her mouth to stop herself giggling.

'I think we should move away,' he whispered, taking a quiet step back. 'I don't want to be a witness to any domestic bird quarrel when her mate gets back.'

'Hoo-eet! Hoo-eet! *Hweeeeeeeeeeeeeeeet!*'

The last long impatient call sent Beth back-stepping down the bank in muffled laughter.

'I don't know why you're laughing, it's not funny,' John said seriously as they walked on. 'I know what it's like to feel so impatient. It's a half sister to agony.'

She stopped and looked at him. 'Do you mean,

when you are confined on your ship?'

'No, Beth, I mean *now*. Here under these shady trees with a bubbling brook and birdsong, it's the perfect place.'

'For what?'

'For finally relinquishing my impatience.' He pulled her into his arms and kissed her. Her soft lips were like half open petals.

When he drew his lips away, she looked at him in silence with her dark eyes, much darker than they had looked only moments ago, and then she put her hands to his face, her lips moving up to meet his, and she kissed him back.

*

Mary sat down at Elizabeth's desk and began writing a stern letter to Lachlan.

She had, she told him, got wind of a rumour that he had incurred some serious financial difficulties and so would be very relieved if he could inform her that this was not true.

She also sought to remind him that she had been his nursemaid in his infancy, and had continued to play a large role in his care and upbringing ever since then.

> *'And now that your mother has passed on,'* she wrote, *'and although you are now a grown man, I still consider it my duty to be concerned about your welfare, as your mother would expect me to be. The maintenance of the house has also been left to my care in your absence, so I*

*would be grateful if you could write
and assure me that this rumour of you
being in financial debt is wrong.*

    *Yours, as always, and with good
wishes.*

          Mary Jarvis

She sealed the letter, and then went outside to the stables to instruct Hector to get the trap ready.

'Is it to Tobermory ye be going?'

'No, Hector, to Craignure.'

'Craignure? Why so?'

'Is it your business to ask?' Mary relented and sighed, too fond of Hector to remain stern. 'I need to get an urgent letter onto the evening packet boat for delivery to the mainland.'

'I could ride it there for ye,' Hector offered. 'I'd be much faster riding a horse than ye would be in the trap.'

'No, Hector, thank you, but I'm in need some air and the journey will do me good.'

Mary's true need was seeing her letter delivered to the packet service with her own eyes, so that her mind could be certain that it was on its way to Lachlan.

'Reet then,' Hector said, turning away, 'I'll get the trap ready for ye.'

A short time later, as Mary turned the trap onto the road, she saw the two figures of Beth and John Dewar coming over the field, walking hand in hand under the slanting shadows of the late afternoon sun.

She looked away, her eyes on the road before

her, about to chuck the reins when she suddenly stopped and looked at the two figures again ... walking *hand in hand!*

'Oh my,' she breathed. 'Well thank goodness *some* things around here are going the right way.'

She chucked the reins. 'And let's hope they continue to do so.'

Chapter Twenty-Eight

On Sunday morning, Mr John Dewar Senior was not at all happy with the white house on the hill in Tobermory.

'What were you thinking, son, what were you *thinking* when ye chose this house? You could not have been thinking about *me.*'

He looked at Beth, as if deciding she must be the reason for his son's lack of due thought and consideration. Oh, not that he could blame him. She was a beauty that would turn any man's mind away from necessary concentration.

But this house now! It was a bad choice. He looked at his son. 'And you say you've already paid a deposit on it?'

'What is *wrong* with the house?' John asked in bafflement. 'It has everything you need – plenty of light, good-sized rooms – and the view of the harbour and the sea is perfect.'

'Perfect,' Beth supported. 'It's a lovely house, Mr Dewar. One of the finest in Tobermory.'

The older man looked at Beth, and then at his son, and then he shook his head wearily. 'You young people, you see the world with young eyes and expect everyone else to see it the same.'

'But you haven't even *seen* the other rooms with young eyes or not,' John said in frustration. 'Not the rooms at the back, nor the bedrooms upstairs, and not the garden either. Only *this* room have you seen, and yet you pass judgement. Is that fair?'

'I've seen enough,' his father responded wearily. 'I would have told you back down there on the path that this house was not suitable, not for me anyway, but I didn't have enough puff left in my chest to get a word out.'

'Oh,' Beth said, finally understanding the problem, but John was still baffled.

'It's too *high*, son,' his father explained. 'Up two steep hills. Sakes alive, for a while there I thought I was climbing Ben Nevis.'

'But ...' John looked at Beth and then at his father. 'Beth and I had no problem walking up here a few days ago, no problem at all.'

'That's because she's a Highland lassie, so she is used to it. And you're young and strong and active. But *me,* I've spent most of my life sitting on a chair in front of a sewing machine or standing at a table cutting cloth. So what makes you think my knees or my lungs would now become as strong as those belonging to a mountain climber? *Retirement,* did you say? *Rest,* did you say?'

John finally realised his mistake. 'I'll find you somewhere else.'

'Will you get the deposit back?'

'I don't know.'

'Why did you pay it in the first place?'

'Well, because...' John fluffed, 'I was, foolishly, certain that you would like it as much as I did, and because ...' he shrugged, 'my time here is short and I just wanted to get the whole business out of the way.'

'Out of the way?' His father gave him a slow smile of understanding. He turned to Beth. 'Come on, Miss, let's get back down to the Tobermory Inn for a seat and some refreshment. At least the descent will be a lot easier.'

*

'Oh, now, this is *my* kind of level,' said John's father, easing himself blissfully into a chair in the inn's dining room. 'And in fact, so is this entire street. So next time you go looking for a house for me, John, see if you can get one here on Main Street, or, preferably, one street above it. Just so long as I can sit in my own house viewing the sea without having a mountain to climb to do it.'

The descent down had been as easy as the walk up, to Beth's mind, and she could see John was thinking the same.

'But Edinburgh is a very hilly city,' John said to his father. 'That's why it never occurred to me – '

'Edinburgh is that all right, and its hilly streets were no problem for me in my young days. But now, with all my years of sitting and standing, even the hills in Edinburgh are a strain on my legs. At least the road between our house and Mortimers is a fairly flat walk.'

Angus McLeod arrived on the scene, followed by Lizzie, both eager to hear the result. 'Well, what did ye think of it?' Angus asked.

John's father smiled. 'It near killed me, Mr McLeod. The trek up there.'

Angus and Lizzie exchanged a satisfied glance. 'We thought that would be the case,' said Angus.

Lizzie agreed. 'I could no more climb those hills once in a day, never mind go up and down more than once for anything I might need. What if you wanted fresh fish in the morning, and then again fresh fish for your supper? What would ye do?'

'Starve,' said John's father.

'And what if ye wanted to pop down here for a glass or two of an evening,' Angus added. 'Or even a nice supper. How would ye get down?'

'Oh, getting down would be easy,' said John's father. 'It's getting back up that concerns me.'

'Now what will you have to eat?' Angus asked. 'But first of all, what will ye have to drink?'

'Oh, a brandy will heal all wounds,' John's father laughed. 'The smoothest and best you can provide.' He looked at Beth. 'And you Miss ...'

'Jarvis. Elizabeth Jarvis. But you may call me Beth.'

'As my son does.'

'Yes.'

So what will you have to drink, Mi – Beth?

Beth would have loved a tot of brandy to calm her nerves, but not wishing to make a bad first impression she requested only water.

John agreed to a brandy.

The conversation after that became natural and friendly and Beth decided she liked John's father, despite all the fuss he had made about a few small hills.

Lizzie had prepared them a light lunch of roast duck and vegetables, followed by apple tart and cream.

Beth found it difficult to eat the tart, because throughout the meal she had noticed John's father occasionally looking at her with a strange expression in his eyes. It discomfited her, made her nervous and killed her appetite as she kept wondering what he was thinking.

Maybe he was now noticing that her skin was not as pale as other Scottish girls, or maybe it was because he knew she could not be Scottish at all – not with an English name like Jarvis.

Lunch over, Angus brought him another glass of brandy and while the two older men exchanged more pleasantries, John touched her hand. He could see she was no longer relaxed, and lifted a questioning eyebrow.

'Jarvis?' said John's father when Angus had left the room. 'That is your surname, Beth?'

'Yes.'

'Well, I have been looking at you, and although it may seem strange after all this time ...' He paused for a moment, and then smiled. 'Y'know, my dear, I believe I have already met your father.'

'What?

John and Beth both stared at him. 'But how could you have met him?' John asked. 'He was in Australia for years, and then – '

'As I indicated, it was a long time ago.' Again Mr Dewar looked wonderingly at Beth. 'Is your father Mr *George* Jarvis?'

Beth nodded, speechless.

'And as a young man, was he a student at the college in Edinburgh?'

Beth nodded again.

'And was he ... a *brown* man, of foreign looks?'

Beth nodded yet again, too speechless with shock to say a word.

'I thought so.' John's father smiled in satisfaction and sat back.

'It's not often you meet a man like him in Scotland,' he went on. 'And I remember him well because on the day I met him, it was the blue jacket he wore that caught my attention. Oh, a handsome young man, we all noticed that. But while others were looking at his face, I was more interested in his coat.'

'But *where* did you meet him?' John asked curiously.

'Oh, didn't I say?' Mr Dewar sipped some brandy. 'We shared a coach from Edinburgh to Perthshire. The rest of the passengers were a rum looking lot. A woman eating a fried sausage, and a man in a red plaid cape who kept telling funny stories that were not funny at all. And then there was this striking young man who sat with his eyes turned to the window as if he wished to remain distant from it all.'

He took another sip of brandy.

'There was something about his bearing, a dignity and graciousness that was very lacking in the other passengers. But best of all – he was wearing one of *my* jackets from Mortimers. A mixture of wool and cashmere, a very fine yarn, in dark blue.'

He looked at Beth and explained. 'I knew it was one of mine because of the cut of the lapels, you see. Every artist knows his own work, and I was a master of my craft, even back then.'

Beth was looking at him as if mesmerised.

'So, as he was clearly a customer of Mortimers, I

asked for his surname. I was young and vain and thought it would be nice to know, seeing as he was wearing one of my own creations. And he told me his name was Jarvis – George Jarvis – just like Beth answered her name in the same way when I asked her – Jarvis. Elizabeth Jarvis. It's been digging away at my memory of all through the lunch. And the same dark looks as he ... and now John is saying he went off to Australia? Well that explains why I never saw his name on the fitting or order books after that.'

He smiled warmly at Beth, very warmly. 'Will you give my regards to your father, Beth, tell him I remember him well. Tell him I was the young man in the coach who vowed to him that one day I would become the head tailor in Mortimers, and I have been that for a long time.'

After a quick breath John quickly explained that Beth's father was no longer alive, due to a riding accident.

The response from his father was one of mortification. 'Oh, my dear, I *am* sorry ... but it's not every day or every year that you meet a man like your father, that is why I recall – '

Beth had risen to her feet and moved to his side of the table, tears glistening in her dark eyes.

She bent and kissed him on the cheek. 'Thank you,' she said softly, 'thank you. I will treasure that story of your encounter with my papa.'

'Beth?'

She glanced briefly at John as she pointed to the door. 'A little air. A few minutes. I won't be long.' And then she walked quickly out of the inn.

'Is she all right?'

'Your encounter with her father was ... very unexpected,' John said, 'even to me. Why have you not told me about this meeting with George Jarvis?'

'Why would I? It happened years ago. Before you were even born. And how was I to know that one day in the future you were going to start courting his daughter. And damn me, when I started telling her about it – I didn't know her dear father was dead.'

After a silence, John pushed back his chair and stood. 'I think we both need another brandy.'

'May I shrivel and waste if I have offended that lass. It was not my intention.'

'You have not offended her,' John said. 'She told you she'd treasure the story of your encounter with her father, didn't she?'

'She did.'

'So then?'

'So all is well and no harm done. That's a relief. But I still need that brandy. I'm aching sore after that hike up those hills today.'

'I'll fetch Angus.'

Later that night, in the privacy of her bedroom, Beth wrote in her diary:

The fact that our two father's met each other so very long ago, and now their two children have also met, although living in two different parts of Scotland and one often away at sea, surely that is a sign of Heaven at work and Fate at its best.

Chapter Twenty-Nine

Mary was surprised by how speedily Lachlan responded to her letter. Less than two weeks had passed and here was his reply.

> *My Dear Mary,*
>
> *I can assure you that you have been disgracefully misinformed. I know not where this rumour of my being in financial difficulties has come from, and can only conclude that it must have come from the dregs of some beggar's bottle.*
>
> *My situation has indeed changed, but only insofar as that I am now thoroughly fed up with the Army and seeking to sell my commission and return home.*
>
> *I believe I have spread my wings far and wide until they can reach no farther, and now I think it is time for me to marry and settle down as laird of my estate. Because of this I send you my deep appreciation for your care of the Macquarie house at Jarvisfield, and I look forward to seeing you all again soon.*
>
> *Yours fondly,*
> *Lachlan*

Mary did not know what to make of it. Return home? Marry? Settle down? She sincerely hoped that these three things did not also include Beth – not after the way he had ignored her at Elizabeth's funeral – and not after the way he had stopped writing to her after only six months or so in the Army.

And hadn't he also, after Elizabeth's funeral, referred to his home here as 'the back of beyond'. He seemed to have changed his mind and attitude about everything. So what had changed it?

And no financial difficulties'? The 'dregs of a beggar's bottle'? Well, there was only one way to find out about that.

Once again she instructed Hector to get ready the trap.

'Is it to Craignure ye be going again? To send another letter?'

'Yes, Hector, to Craignure.' She was too alarmed and too confused to bother with any conversation with Hector other than to agree with whatever he asked. 'Yes. Yes. Yes.'

Hector stood and watched her as she reached the end of the lane and turned the horse and trap to the north – not to the south as she should have done if she was going to Craignure.

He lolloped into a sprint down the lane after her, calling out, 'Ye be going the wrong way, Mrs Mary!'

She ignored him, and continued on in the direction of Tobermory.

Hector returned to the yard at the back of the house, and then sauntered into the kitchen to complain to Mrs Keillor.

'I'm the only one around here that's no' gone mad,' he said bleakly. 'There be Miss Beth, walking around all the time like she be in cuckoo land and still dreaming, and now Mrs Mary has gone round the bend in the wrong direction.'

Mrs Keillor made no answer as she placed a chicken pie in the black iron oven above the fire and then closed its two doors 'Mary never goes in the wrong direction to anywhere,' she said, reaching for a broom to sweep inside the fender.

'It could be the mare,' Hector said thoughtfully. 'Aye, it could be the mare. She's losing her nose.'

'Who's losing their nose?' Mrs Keillor said, sweeping.

'And ye must be losing your *ears!*' Hector replied huffily. 'I said the mare – *the mare*. She be getting old now and her nose scent is weakening so bad that she'd get lost if someone didna guide her all the way home.'

'So what's to worry? She's got Mary to guide her hasna she?'

'But I just *told* ye!' Hector exclaimed irritably. 'Mrs Mary has gone round the bend in the *wrong* direction. So *her* nose must be getting as poor as the mare's now.'

*

Mary knew exactly where she was going. As soon as she reached Tobermory and parked the trap, she headed straight for the Inn and sought out Lizzie McLeod.

'He says he's in no financial difficulties, Lizzie, so who was this man who told you he was in bad debt? Perhaps it's not true.'

'Aye, it's true enough,' Lizzie responded. She had taken Mary into her kitchen where they could sit down and talk in private.

'The man who told me is a footman over at Strathallan Castle. He was over here on a visit to some of his people who live down near Loch Frisna. I know him and his people well. He said young Mr Macquarie is there most times he is on leave – at Strathallan Castle – that's when he and the one called William are not frolicking in Glasgow or Edinburgh or card-gambling down in England.'

'But how did he know about any debts?' Mary asked. 'Surely a footman would not know anything as personal as that?'

'No, but one particular night he was on his way to Lord Strathallan's library-room with a tray of drinks, and when he approached the door, his lordship was roaring fury at his son – at both of them – saying they had seen their way through a fortune and *he* had no intention of bailing them out this time.'

'And when was that, Lizzie?'

'A day or two before I gave young Beth the message to give ye, so the night of his lordship's fury musta been just a few weeks before that.'

So Lachlan had *lied* in his letter, Mary realised. And the reason he was now trying to sell his commission in the Army was probably to try and raise some money.

'I'm worried about the house and estate, Lizzie. The main reason General Macquarie bought the estate and built Salen was so that his children would have a good living and a good future to inherit. And now his son has inherited and – '

'Och, his debts couldna be *that* much, Mary. The

Jarvisfield farm and lands must be worth a fortune.'

'And there's something else, Lizzie – Lachlan wrote in his letter about coming home and settling down to marry.'

Lizzie frowned. 'But that's a good thing, isna it?'

'Not if he's thinking of Beth.'

'Oh, nonsense!' Lizzie sat back and laughed at the very idea. 'Ye've no need to worry there, Mary, not now she's keeping company with young Mr Dewar. By! I could *eat* that young man I could. And a delicious bite he would make too!' She laughed saucily. 'But don't tell Angus, will ye?'

'I don't know though,' said Mary, her eyes thoughtful. 'There has always been a special bond between Beth and Lachlan, ever since they were children. How do we know she's keeping company with John Dewar only because Lachlan seems to have turned his back on her.'

'Nay, *nay!*' insisted Lizzie, her face straightening with seriousness. 'Ye only have to *see* those two together to know that whatever bond Beth had with Lachlan is gone.'

Mary hoped so; and driving the trap back to Jarvisfield she allowed her mind to dwell on Beth and John Dewar and how over the past few weeks they had spent so much time together. Every minute that could be spared was spent in each other's company.

She remembered Beth's sparkling eyes and radiant face on that first night John had escorted her home from the bonfire on Midsummer's Eve a year ago.

Oh yes, she realised, Lizzie was right. Any bond Beth had with Lachlan was gone now. Broken from the first day she had set eyes on John Dewar.

*

The following afternoon Mrs Keillor was grumpy with frustration.

'I don't know what I'm supposed to be doing, hen,' she complained to Mary. 'First ye tell me I have to be thrifty now with simple dishes and no waste of food, and now ye are telling me to make all the best delicacies I can for Beth to take on a picnic!'

'Yes, but tomorrow is their last full day together. He leaves the day after to return to his ship. But no, you are right, a fresh buttered loaf and some cold pork and cheese will be enough.'

Now that she had been let off the hook, Mrs Keillor relented.

'I suppose I *could* make a fruitcake, and mebbe some jam tarts – plenty enough for all of us. Hector loves his cakes and jam tarts. Although when I give him some extra tarts to take over yon to the farmboys, he never does – he feeds them to the *horses* instead. Now I willna give him any extra, no matter how much he pleads with me.'

Mary smiled.

'Aye,' Mrs Keillor decided, whipping on her apron. 'I'll get on with the food for Beth's picnic now, before I start preparing the dinner.'

Chapter Thirty

Beth thought it sad that John had never seen Calgary Bay.

'That's why I chose it,' she said smiling, 'as a special treat for you. Although maybe as you have seen a lot of the world and a lot of beaches, Calgary may not seem so special.'

'Well, it's been a hell of a journey, so I'll let you know when we get there,' John replied. 'If it is a disappointment I'm turning around and heading straight back.'

She checked her horse and looked back at him, and saw that he was not serious.

There was not much talk between them as they rode on, due to the single file tracks that made it necessary for one to ride behind the other.

He let her lead the way and let his mind wander as he looked around at the scenery and the sheep peacefully grazing on the green high hills, and then outwards to look at a rim of the blue sea in the distance. Just one more day here – and then back out there – sailing away from this peaceful paradise.

Well, maybe to others it would not seem like paradise, but for him, she made it so. What other time, and where else in the world had he ever stopped to watch a plump little Willow Warbler and listen to her calling to her mate?

Where else in the world had he taken the time to watch otters at play, and enjoyed it?

She had opened his eyes to a whole other world of the natural life all around them.

Heaven had blessed them. During his time here the weather had been sunny and warm, and at times very hot. Not even one day of cold winds or rain, just sun, sun, sun every day.

'Look!' she said as they came out from the trees into a clearing and sat looking down on the low rippling waves of the blue sea onto a long beach of pure white sand, surrounded by rugged green hills.

'This is Calgary Bay,' she said, 'and it's always empty, always deserted, apart from the wildlife of course.'

Later, when they had dismounted and led their horses down through the sloping dunes covered in green carpets of tender grass, and reached the white beach, he could not believe that such a stunning place could be found anywhere in Scotland.

The seawater was sky blue and so transparently clear and sparkling that he said with amazement, 'We could be on a beach by the Indian Ocean!'

And the sand, so white and as soft as powder. 'We could be in the Caribbean!'

'So you like it?'

'It's stunning! Beth, you could not have chosen a better place for ...'

'Your last day here,' she said quietly.

'Yes.' He met her eyes, and the mood changed.

She looked out to sea for a long silent moment, and when she turned back to him she was trying very hard to smile. 'Let's pretend it is your first day here, not your last.'

'No,' he said. 'Let's just make it the best day of all.'

*

Mrs Keillor would not have been pleased to know that the food she prepared was hardly touched, just a bite or two of cheese, a small cut of the bread.

Somehow, to John, the food in the bag seemed all wrong for a place of such natural beauty as this.

After a long afternoon walking hand in hand on the beach exploring the small inlets and pools, they eventually moved through the grassy dunes and collected enough pieces of light wood and twigs for him to make a fire and bring it to light with the help of his tinderbox.

Then John cut and cleaned and cooked the mackerel he had caught on the fire.

It was, Beth agreed, a more fitting meal for a place like Calgary Bay, and delicious.

'These fish must have been swept onto the shore on a wave this morning,' John said in wonderment. 'No wonder the fishermen of Mull do so well.'

'Fishing and farming are the only livelihoods on Mull,' said Beth, staring at the edge of the sea that was slowly retreating backwards. 'The sea is leaving us, the tide is going back out.'

Washing their hands in a small pool, they stood under the weakening rays of the sun watching the sea retreating farther and farther away, leaving only a few narrow slicks of water behind on the darkening sand.

'I wish this day could last forever,' Beth said.

John looked out to sea. 'I was thinking the same

thing.'

They walked towards the back of the bay and the base of the green dunes, reluctant to leave but knowing they must, until he looked back and saw a majestic purple and orange sunset colouring the sky above the sea.

It was so spectacular they stopped and sat on the soft grass of one the dunes to watch it, the colours magnificent in a sky of flame reds and pinks and purple and dark blues.

'Red sky at night, sailor's delight,' he murmured.

She reached for her bag and took out two glasses and a flask of wine.

'Do you like wine?'

John looked at the sky and said, 'The sun is well over the foreyardarm so, yes, it is late enough for me to drink wine.'

'Late enough?' Beth queried.

John smiled as he explained. 'A direction from the Admiralty – no officer to partake of any liquor until the sun is over the foreyardarm.'

'And what time is that?'

'Usually – just before noon,' he grinned.

She half filled the two glasses, gave him one, and then reached to clink her glass with his. 'To –'

'Ahhhh!' He swiftly moved his glass away from her glass. 'Naval officers and crew never clink glasses when drinking.'

'Why?'

'Because life at sea is full of superstitions,' he told her. 'And it's long been believed that the ring of a glass tolls the death of one of the sailors.'

She momentarily shivered at the thought.

'Raising the glass is enough.' He smiled and raised his glass. 'To you, Beth.'

She sipped her wine and sat looking at the far-off sea. 'Are you looking forward to being ... out there ... again?'

'No, and once I'm on ship and out there, I know I'll be wishing I was ... back there ... with Miss Elizabeth Jarvis.'

'How long will it take for you to reach Portsmouth?'

'From Oban by coach, seven days, or near enough.'

'That long – seven days!' She sighed dismally. 'So even Portsmouth is a long way from here.'

'Very long, especially when you're confined inside a coach with people who don't bathe.'

'How long will you be away?'

'About a year. Another eight months on watch at Kingston.'

'Is that in Jamaica?'

'Yes, we're stood off just outside Kingston's harbour, or patrolling between there and Hunt's Bay.'

'Last time ... did the Navy find any ships with captured slaves hidden in them?'

'Yes, but ... Beth, let's not talk about it. Let's just enjoy our time together today, and forget about tomorrow or any other time.'

'Just tell me – were the captured slaves freed?'

'Of course they were. They were brought up on deck and returned to shore in a cutter.'

'And the captain?'

'The captains were dealt with. No more

questions. Soon enough I'll be back there, but now I'm here with you and that's all I want to think about.'

They sat for a time in silent harmony in the full colour of a warm Hebridean evening.

John gazed around Calgary Bay, at the emptiness and the serene peacefulness of it all, and then lay back on the dune with a sigh and watched the magnificence of the sunset, his eyes moving up to the last seagulls flying overhead. It was an evening for fantasising, for dreaming ... even the hills seemed greener and higher with a kind of dusky magic in the air. He gazed at the sunset again, at all the amazing colours shading and shaping together like an artist's painting of an explosion in the sky.

'I've no wish to leave here.'

'Nor I,' she murmured.

'This is bliss, this Mull of yours.'

'So it's Mull you love, not me?'

'Yes, it's Mull.'

He glanced at her sideways and smiled, and then pulled her down beside him and kissed her.

'No, it's you, Beth, you ...'

He kissed her again, and even the kiss felt different to all the other times he had kissed her.

'Would you ...' she asked him softly, 'would you ever wish to *live* on Mull?'

'Yes,' he said honestly, 'if it meant I would be coming *home* to you.'

The lowering sun was now like a blazing fireball suspended over the darkening horizon surrounded by pink and purple rays of light, but they were no longer aware of the sky or the sea or the land; oblivious to all but each other as they kissed and let their hands move over each other, unmindful that the darkness was coming.

Time passed, a cool night breeze came in off the sea.

'We should have left here hours ago,' John said, sitting up and looking at the night sky.

Beth also looked at the sky, only now becoming aware of how late it was.

'It will be difficult and dangerous riding on the narrow tracks in this darkness,' she said.

She slowly sat up to join him and he looked at her. Her lustrous black hair had come loose from its ribbon and was now tumbled down over her shoulders.

'Even in the dark you look beautiful,' he murmured.

She smiled and touched her lips to his. 'So do you.'

'And in the dark you *feel* beautiful too.'

Her lips were moving on his. 'So do you.'

Seconds later he asked smiling. 'So are we forced to stay here all night? Just the two of us alone?'

'At least until first light. It would be cruel and dangerous to make the horses trek those tracks in the dark.'

'It would,' John agreed, and then moved down to where the two horses were tethered and removed the two blankets, as well as the two saddles to allow the horses more comfort also.

Then he led both horses down the beach to one of the many freshwater pools between the rocks and waited while the horses drank their fill before he led them back again to their tethering spot.

Returning to the dune, he found a secluded spot out of the breeze between two rocks and spread one blanket on the ground. When Beth lay on it, he sat down beside her and pulled the second blanket over her.

'John.'

'Are you warmer here?' he asked.

'I have not been cold.'

He had taken off his jacket earlier and now folded it to make a pillow for her head. Beth was gazing up at the half moon.

'John.'

He paused and looked down at her.

'Did you mean it when you said it was me you loved?'

Even in the darkness she could see his smile. 'I love everything about you ... most of all those beautiful dark eyes of yours.'

'It does not trouble you ... that my eyes are dark because I was made by two people who were not of the same race? When you first saw me, did you not see that?'

He looked at her silently for a long moment. 'Do you want to know the truth?'

'Yes.'

'When I first saw you, I did not see a girl made by two people of two races, all I saw was a girl that I thought must have been made in Heaven.'

He slid down beside her and she moved inside his arms, smiling, relieved of her anxiety, putting her hands around his neck and half strangling him with love.

He pulled one of her hands away and kissed her fingers. 'Or maybe ...' he said, 'I am still in some wonderful dream and you are not in fact truly *real*.'

She smiled. 'Then it must be my wonderful dream too, and maybe *you* are not real.'

He grinned, his eyes moving over her face. 'I think we should investigate further and try to find out for certain once and for all.'

His hands began to move down her body, lightly touching her breasts, her waist and her thighs like someone who needed to be reassured. 'Yes, you feel real ... you feel ...' He turned up his eyes and let out his breath.

She kissed his mouth and both lost their smiles as the grip of her hands on his shoulders became more urgent, their bodies quickening, moving closer.

In their hastening passion John suddenly became conscious of his obligations as a gentleman, but she was more in tune with the ways and freedoms of the natural world all around them and she hushed him, touching his face softly and whispering her love for him. She wanted him as much as he wanted her and she told him so.

'I *love* you.'

And then, to Beth, it all became so wonderful as he kissed her and turned her onto her back and her bodice became unbuttoned and the world began to spin again as she lost herself in the blissful spinning of it.

She had once thought that she would be happy to accompany him to the ends of the earth if he wished it, and now he was using his hands and his lips to take her there, to the ends of the earth ... until finally he took her there, on the blanket, on a dune in Calgary Bay.

An owl in a tree somewhere above began to complain about her soft cries into the night, which interfered with his own night calls.

And when, a short time later, they made love again, lost in their own tender love-dream, and her broken and heightening love cries again rose into the night, the owl complained louder and swooped down past them, returning to his tree ignored.

Beth knew she would never forget one single moment of this beautiful night of looking up at a navy sky and the crystal clear star fields sparkling across it, hearing only the occasional hoots of a passing owl and the waves breaking gently on the beach.

A magical and beautiful night of sweet worship and tender passion, and the night of her first sexual experience, the most blissful of all.

'*The night,*' she later wrote in her diary, '*when I knew that all I wanted was to be his wife, or die unwed.*'

PART FIVE

Chapter Thirty-One

At the end of October, Mary received another letter from Lachlan.

> *My Dear Mary,*
>
> *This is the briefest of notes to inform you that I am betrothed to marry Isabella Hamilton Dundas Campbell, a daughter of the Laird of Jura and Craignish. The marriage is to take place after Christmas, following which Isabella and I will be returning to my Jarvisfield Estate.*
>
> *I am sure you will be happy to have a full house again, and I am also sure that Isabella and Beth will become good friends.*
>
> *Yours fondly,*
>
> *Lachlan*
>
> *PS: I am also happy to tell you that I now own a number of fine racehorses that I keep at a very good stable in Bunbury in Lancashire.*

Mary was so delighted she showed the letter to Beth, who was equally as delighted. 'Oh, that's *wonderful* news. And yes, I am sure Isabella and I *will* become good friends.'

Mrs Keillor was not so pleased. She sat back with a sigh. 'A new mistress, eh? Y'know what this means, Mary? It means I'm going to be kept cooking night and day with all the fancy dishes they'll be wanting every night.'

'Oh, I don't think Lachlan ever had much of a taste for fancy dishes,' Mary replied.

'No, but what about his future lady wife, eh? He says she's a daughter of the Laird of Jura and Craignish, so she must be used to good food and fancy living. And they'll be entertaining their friends, 'course they will – inviting them over to Mull to stay. By! For this to come at my time of life, just when I was getting comfortable with having little to do.'

She unfolded her arms, frowned, sat back and folded them again. 'There's only one thing forrit – ye'll have to get Maggie and Lorna in here working full-time once the laird is back with a wife. Will ye do that?'

Mary nodded, not really listening – too happy in the knowledge that Lachlan was now truly preparing to settle down, and with a wife that was not her precious Beth, especially in view of the difficulties that would now present due to Beth's relationship with John Dewar.

Oh yes, she had known, as soon as Beth had come back that day in July after staying out all night with John Dewar, she knew their relationship had become more intimate, but Beth had refused to answer all questions, so Mary had eventually stopped asking them.

She had tried very hard to be angry with John Dewar, but somehow she could not blame him. If she was to blame anyone it would be Beth, but knowing how much Beth loved that young man, it was hard to blame her either. Two young people in love, just like she and George were in Sydney. And they had also been unable to wait.

Oh, George, my dearest wonderful darling George...

'Racehorses, eh?' said Mrs Keillor curiously. 'If he's bought racehorses, why is he keeping them down in England if he's going to be living here?'

Hector, who had been lurking and listening by the kitchen door, stepped in quickly and answered her. 'If they be racehorses, *real* racehorses, then he'll need somewhere to train 'em, won't he?'

'So why canna he train them here in Mull?'

'Too rugged, not flat enough. Only place flat enough here for him to give racehorses a good run, is on one of the long beaches.'

'So why canna he do that then?'

Hector shook his head as if thinking Mrs Keillor was now as mad as the rest of them. 'If the horses are going to *race* on grass, then they must be *trained* on grass. He won't get much good out of 'em on race courses if they've been trained on *sand*. Any fool would know that.'

'Aye, and that explains why *ye* know it,' Mrs Keillor answered with a decorous sniff. 'Mary, he's been lurking and listening again.'

Mary was lost in thought, their voices merely mundane sounds in the background.

And obviously, she was thinking, any financial difficulties Lachlan may have had in the past were now behind him, otherwise he would not have been able to afford to buy a number of racehorses to stable in Lancashire.

She couldn't help wondering what this Isabella Hamilton Dundas Campbell would be like?

Well, she finally decided, it didn't really matter *what* she was like, because as Lachlan's wife, and a young lady new to Mull, she was determined to make her feel very welcome.

*

A late winter afternoon in February brought the latest Mrs Macquarie to the Isle of Mull, and her new home in Jarvisfield.

Wrapped in a heavy seal-skin cloak against the bitter cold, she looked small in height, but when the cloak was removed, Mary could see she was indeed a petite girl, with light brown hair and large blue eyes, and a face and manner that seemed nervous, but very sweet.

By the glowing light of the candles Mary could clearly see Lachlan's face ... and the change the years had brought to his looks. His face was leaner, harder, and looking slightly older than his twenty-seven years. Still handsome though, yes, but the years of fast living had taken their toll.

But his manner was light and happy and young and in this respect he was Lachlan again, back to his old self.

'Mary, this is Isabella, my wife of almost two weeks.'

'Welcome,' Mary said, taking the girl's hands in her own. 'I hope you will be happy here in Jarvisfield.'

The girl still looked nervous. 'I'm sure I will,' she answered. 'My husband has promised to take very good care of me.'

'That I have. And Isabella ... there is Beth ...'

Both seemed to pause and hesitate as Beth came out of the shadows into full light with a warm and welcoming smile on her face.

'Hello, Isabella, I'm sure you are going to *love* Mull when you get to know it, but you will not see it at it's best until spring arrives.' She gave the girl a light kiss on the cheek, and then turned to Lachlan, unable to hide her delight at seeing him again. 'Welcome home, stranger. We have missed you.'

'Beth …' It was he who moved to give her a light kiss on the cheek but his manner was stiffer, and he quickly drew away.

'So,' he said cheerfully to Mary. 'A good fire and a light meal is what we need now. Are our rooms ready?'

'Everything is ready,' Mary agreed. 'And it is more than a light meal that Mrs Keillor has prepared for you.' Mary looked over her shoulder. 'Where is she?'

Mrs Keillor came rushing into the hall wiping her hands on her apron. As soon as she saw Lachlan she was startled – he looked taller and older and more authoritative in his bearing – He looked like what he was – a young Army officer.

She immediately dipped a slight curtsy. 'Welcome home, sir.' And then, finally noticing the girl. 'Welcome, ma'am.'

Isabella gave a small laugh. 'It's so strange to be called "ma'am", but now I am married I will have to get used to it.' She looked up at her new husband adoringly. 'Won't I, dear?'

'How old are you?' Mrs Keillor asked

audaciously, certain the girl was no more than seventeen.

'Isabella is the same age as Beth,' Lachlan said, glancing briefly at Beth. 'Almost nineteen.'

Beth laughed. 'Lachlan – how easily you remember! You always had a strange way of remembering my age, even when I myself forgot it.'

'Come into the fire now,' Mary urged, leading them into the drawing-room. 'Isabella, would you like some tea to warm you up?'

Isabella nodded with her sweet smile. 'Yes, please.

'No tea for me, Mary,' Lachlan said quickly. 'Just wine.'

When Mary entered the kitchen, Mrs Keillor had a grim look on her face.

'She seems nice enough,' Mary said. 'So why the face?'

'I don't like the look of him,' Mrs Keillor brought a knife down hard to split a turnip in half. 'I think he's pretending to be very happy when he's not. And that wife of his is too thin. I hope she's not been starving him as well.'

'Don't be ridiculous,' Mary laughed. 'She is not responsible for what he eats. And I would not say she is thin. Her figure is very neat and slim.'

'Leastaways, officers always get good food in the Army, so I reckon he'll be glad to get back there.'

Mrs Keillor could not have been more wrong, because when Mary returned with the tea and a decanter of wine, she learned that Lachlan had resigned from the Army four months previously.

'There's no fun or excitement in peacetime

soldiering,' he told her. 'I was hoping for battles and charges and the camaraderie of men spilling blood on the battlefield together, like the Army was in my father's time. Now that was a *great* time to be a soldier, defending one's king and country. But now...' he shrugged dismissively. 'Now we have a girl on the throne, supported by her German consort who always appears wearing a magnificent uniform, but I don't believe he has ever seen any *real* service either.'

'I think it's wonderful to have a *queen* on the throne now,' Isabella said excitedly. 'And they say Queen Victoria is very fond of Scotland.'

'She can stay fond of it, as long as she stays away from it!' Lachlan said. 'As I remember the last female on the English throne spitefully ordered the death of our Mary Queen of Scots.'

'Husband!' Isabella said, offended. 'Mary Stuart was a *Catholic!*'

Mary Jarvis quickly excused herself from the conversation, after an apology about needing to instruct Mrs Keillor about dinner. She did not care for discussions about any kind of politics, nor indeed did she care who was on the throne in London, because it mattered little to life here on Mull.

Beth remained, interested. She asked Lachlan. 'What do you think of our Navy?'

'Our Navy?' Lachlan drank some wine. 'The Royal Navy is the greatest navy in the World. Britain's naval power dominates the seas. But what are our great ships doing now – in peacetime? They are chasing after trading vessels that might have a few slaves in their holds.'

Beth also excused herself, leaving the room and standing in the hall for a moment, bitterly disappointed and hurt that Lachlan had obviously forgotten that her father had once been a captured slave.

But then ... she remembered, Lachlan did not know that, just as she herself had not known. And knowing how much Lachlan had always loved her father, and over the years hearing from Mrs Keillor and Hector how crazy with grief he had become after her father's death, she could not blame him, only forgive him.

She returned to the drawing-room and sat down with a smile on her face. 'Only another couple of months and then the bluebells will be out,' she said cheerfully to Isabella. 'They grow everywhere around here. But I can also take you to some other lovely parts of Mull. Do you ride?'

Isabella grimaced. 'Only when I have to.'

Lachlan smiled. 'No, Beth, unlike you, Isabella is not a good horsewoman. She much prefers lying in bed all day, and loves it even moreso since her wedding, don't you my darling?'

The blush that coloured Isabella's face sent Beth out of the room with another excuse.

Something was wrong with those two, Beth decided. Something was *very* wrong. She could only judge from her own experience, but she was certain that John would be incapable of embarrassing her like that in the company of others, or even in private.

Yes, newly-weds those two may be, but

something was just *not right*.

Mary realised the same when she approached the dining room later that evening.

As she approached the door carrying a tray, she heard Lachlan and Isabella, who were already seated, arguing in hushed tones.

'But it's just not *normal*, having housekeepers and servants dining at the same table,' Isabella was saying. 'Father and Mother would never allow it at home.'

'And this is *my* home, not your father or mother's home,' Lachlan replied in low anger. 'And Mary and Beth are part of *my* family, always have been, because they are *George's* family, his wife and daughter. Even my father would be shocked at your suggestion, not to mention my dear mother. Listen, Isabella, you *must* understand – Jarvisfield is *their* home too, and legally so. My father's trust decrees that all and every one of the family of George Jarvis and his descendants shall have a home on Jarvisfield *for ever.*'

'Yes, I understand that, a home on the estate, and I don't at all mind them living here in this house with us as staff, but not to dine at the *same* table.'

Mary quickly turned about and headed back to the kitchen where she lay down the tray and stood with head bent, one hand on her hip and the other on her brow, taking a number of deep breaths.

'What's up?' Mrs Keillor asked, frowning at the tray and tureen of hot vegetable broth. 'Don't they want the broth?'

After a long silence, Mary pulled herself

together, and said firmly, 'Mrs Keillor, I want you to go into the dining room and remove two of the four place settings. Apologise and pretend you have set them their by mistake.'

'I did no such thing!'

'I said *pretend* that you did.'

'Why?'

'Just do it. I'll explain later.'

Mrs Keillor looked keenly at Mary with her sharp eyes, and then nodded and left the kitchen.

Mary followed her out, and quickly went upstairs to pop her head inside the door of Beth's bedroom.

Beth looked up from her diary.

'We are eating in the kitchen tonight. Don't go near the dining room.'

'What?' Beth laid down her pen. 'Why?'

'I'll explain later.'

*

Later, as they ate their dinner at the kitchen table, and after Mary had revealed the conversation she had overhead, their was utter silence for some minutes.

'Oh well, ho-hum,' Beth said with a shrug. 'Food is food and one table is not much different to any other table, so why fret about it. Allowances must be made for newly-weds I suppose.'

'It's not that they are newly-weds,' Mary explained, attempting to be fair in her thinking. 'It's just that ... well, life in the Macquarie household has always been different to others, more relaxed in the way it has been run, with little regard to convention and customs.'

'That's true,' Mrs Keillor agreed.

'I mean, it was the same back in Sydney. Governor Macquarie brought the wrath of the Exclusives to his door because he occasionally had emancipists dining with him at his table in Government House.

'That doesn't surprise me,' said Mrs Keillor, chomping on a mouthful of beef. 'A prince of a man he was, but no pomp in him, none at all. And a *fair* man in all his ways.'

'But for Isabella,' Mary continued, 'that's not the way things have been done in *her* home, which obviously adheres to all the conventions, and that's what she is used to. And Lachlan ... well, his duty and loyalties now belong to his wife, and not to his former nursemaid or her daughter.'

'Aye, and so ye are both banished to the kitchen now,' Mrs Keillor said. 'By! Who would ever have thought it? Not Mrs Macquarie, that's for sure. The *old* Mrs Mrs Macquarie I mean.'

'She wasn't that old,' Mary responded. 'She was only in her late fifties.'

'And sorely missed,' said Mrs Keillor, looking at the glowing fire and its red flames.

'Still,' she added cheerfully, 'ye are both better off eating in here with me in my kitchen and kept warm by my big fire. Aye, it's much warmer in here than sitting in that draughty old dining room, isna it now?'

Mary made no answer, still despondent about it all, but Beth smiled in response, 'It is, Mrs Keillor, much, *much* warmer than the draughty dining room.'

'That's my lass!' Mrs Keillor said with satisfaction. 'And yer mother will get used to eating in the kitchen soon enough.'

Mary half laughed to herself, thinking back to all those nights she had sat eating in the kitchen at Government House in Sydney with the two cooks Mrs Ovens and Mrs Kelly. But then ... that was before George, and before she became Mrs Jarvis and part of the Macquarie family.

Chapter Thirty-Two

Apart from the dining arrangements, life at Gruline carried on as it had always done, and Mary could find no big fault with the new Mrs Macquarie, just minor things that often irritated her and sent her into a mood of frustration.

Isabella's manner was always mild and polite, as a young lady usually is with her servants, yet at other times she could be very friendly and was always seeking out Beth's company.

Beth was happy to oblige, occasionally going on long walks with Isabella, showing her the Mull countryside, and then both girls would return talking cheerfully together, and always holding bunches of the earliest spring wildflowers.

Yes, apart from the changed dining arrangements, Mary decided that Lachlan's wife was nice enough – until the night Isabella stepped into the kitchen after dinner and looked around in a searching way. 'Where is Beth?'

'We've just carried the tub up to her room,' Mary said, drying her hands with a towel. 'She's about to have her bath.'

Isabella bit her lip for a moment, disappointed. She turned to walk away, then quickly turned back.

'Mrs Jarvis, do you think Beth would agree to be my maid? My *personal* maid? To help *me* at my bath time? I nearly slipped and fell the last time.'

Mary stared at her, her blue eyes flaming. 'Now let's get one thing clear. *I* may be a servant here, but Beth is not! She is here, legally, under the Macquarie Trust, because she is the daughter of George Jarvis, and she is *not* here as a servant!'

Isabella looked shocked and flummoxed. 'But I ... I need help with my dress and ... and my hair.'

'If you cannot manage without a personal maid, then you must send for the one you had at Craignish,' Mary replied. 'I trust you *did* have a personal maid at Craignish if you're looking for one now? So I suggest you send for her as soon as possible, but in the meantime, *I* will assist you with your dress and hair.'

'What's wrong?' Lachlan appeared behind Isabella, his face concerned. 'What's all the fuss? You sound angry, Mary.'

Isabella said quickly, "No, no, it's nothing, we were just talking about matters to do with the household.' She forced a fake smile onto her face. 'Thank you, Mrs Jarvis, goodnight.'

Lachlan did not look entirely convinced, and his concern seemed to be all for Mary. 'Is all well, Mary?'

'All is well,' Mary nodded. 'I'm off to bed shortly.

Goodnight, Lachlan.'

'Goodnight, Mary.' He nodded and walked away, following his wife.

'By!' said Mrs Keillor, when they had gone, 'I thought ye were going to punch m'lady then, I did!'

'I don't do such things,' Mary said dismissively. 'But I did *feel* like taking her by her bustle and throwing her out the kitchen door there. *Where* does she think she is – in a hotel in London? This is the back and beyond of Scotland, for heaven's sake! And she must have *known* that before she came, because he has said it often enough.'

'He has, true.'

'Why, even Mrs Macquarie, older as she was, and even when she was a younger woman in Sydney, never expected nor asked me to attend on her when she was naked in her bath!'

Mary was still so angry she had to sit down. 'She's entitled to a personal maid, if she needs one – but not my Beth!'

'And y'know,' Mrs Keillor put in, 'I don't think Master Lachlan would be happy to see Beth reduced to being his wife's personal maid either.'

*

Lachlan was not happy about many things these days. He had accepted his limits, and had returned to Mull to settle down, but at a price – a high price!

So a few days later, after seeing his accountant in Tobermory, he rode back in a fury to the Macquarie house in Jarvisfield, dismounting and throwing the reins to Hector in the yard before marching into the house through the kitchen door, and then looking searchingly into the drawing-room and then the dining room.

'What is wrong?' Mary asked him, coming down the stairs.

'Where is she?' he demanded through gritted teeth. 'That wife of mine, *where is she?*'

Mary did not know. 'If she's not down here, then she must be up in her room, I presume.'

'Still in her bed again – and it now almost noon!'

Mary watched him charge up the stairs and then all she could do was remain at the bottom of the stairs and listen, and what she heard was not pleasant.

'*Ten thousand!*' she heard him rage. 'That's the dowry your father promised me for marrying you, *ten* thousand – not *two* thousand. How in hell can I pay off all my debts with a shortfall of eight thousand? I was promised *ten* thousand!'

After a silence – no doubt a *shocked* silence – Isabella sounded just as outraged.

'*Ten thousand pounds?* My father does not have that kind of money. He has other daughters who will need dowries, and he has always said the dowry for each would be *two* thousand.'

'Drummond assured me that your father had agreed *ten* thousand!'

'Who? William Drummond? That man is a liar and a braggart and you should not believe a word he says.'

'*You* told me ten thousand! *You* boasted it to me! You said whichever man was lucky enough to get you would receive your dowry of *ten* thousand pounds. So it's *you* that is the liar – not William

Drummond!'

'And is that the only reason you married me – for money?'

'*Yes!*'

The desperation in his voice was clear, but what came next was vicious.

'Isabella, forgive me, I *did* intend that one day I would settle down here peacefully on my family estate with the woman I love – but sadly that woman is not *you!* And although I agreed to the ten thousand pounds, I would certainly not have married you for *two!* My racehorses cost almost that!'

Mary had to move quickly down the hall as he came running furiously down the stairs and out through the kitchen to the yard. Minutes later he was back up on his horse again – leaving Hector staring after him.

'I havna tightened the girths!' Hector shouted, but Lachlan recklessly rode on, eager to get away from the house as fast as he could.

Mrs Keillor had also been listening and had ducked into the dining room when she heard Lachlan coming down the stairs.

Now she returned to the kitchen and she and Mary stared at each other in consternation.

'So now we know,' Mary said sadly. 'The marriage was nothing to do with love, just a bargain to clear off his debts.'

'A bad bargain then, if he was promised a dowry of ten and only got two.'

'But even *two* thousand pounds is an almighty sum of money,' Mary said. 'When you think that our farm manager Robert Dewar earns only eighty pounds a year, and that's *good* pay.'

'Does he? I only get thirty.'

'Yes, you get twelve shilling a week – and that also is *good* pay!'

'Along with my bed and room and all the food I can eat, so I'm not complaining. How much do ye get, Mary?

'I get nothing from this estate,' Mary answered honestly. 'My money comes from a trust that General Macquarie left to George. And Beth's money comes from a separate trust that George left to her.'

They moved to sit down at the table where Mary slumped for a moment, her hands to her head as she said sympathetically. 'That poor girl.'

'Why? She hoodwinked him. Boasting about her big dowry.'

Mary suddenly jolted upright. 'Now don't you *dare* say a word about what we heard from upstairs today to Hector or anyone else on Jarvisfield.'

'Me?' Mrs Keillor looked at her wryly. 'I heard nothing at all. I was in the dining room tending to my own business.'

'And in particular – not a word about this to Beth. I don't want her to get dragged into it or become involved in any way. And what she doesn't know, can't trouble her.'

*

Throughout the rest of the day Mary kept venturing upstairs to knock on Isabella's door and see if she needed anything. She felt sorry for the poor girl, to be so disillusioned so early in her marriage, and in such a cruel way.

Unsure whether Mary and the staff had heard the quarrel, Isabella said she was feeling unwell, and so would stay in bed. And no, no, she did not want anything to drink. And when Mary knocked again later, no, no, she did not want anything to eat.

'Just to sleep,' she said tiredly, stretching out on her side and pumping the pillow under her head and then moving one leg over the other into what Mary concluded must be her favourite sleeping position. 'I have a weak constitution.'

'She eats like a bird at the best of times,' Mrs Keillor observed when Mary returned with the dinner tray. 'A pick here, a pick there, no wonder she's so thin and tired all the time.'

'God help her though, she's away from her home, in a strange place, so it must be difficult for her.'

'Difficult for who – Isabella?' asked Beth, walking into the kitchen, her hair soaking wet.

'Yes, she is feeling ill,' Mary said. 'And so will you be if you don't get that wet cloak off you.'

Beth removed her cloak and draped it over a wooden chair near the fire to dry.

'Oh, the rain! Only a short way riding back from the Dewars' place when I looked up and saw the low black clouds and knew I was in for a heavy soaking.'

She bent over the fire, squeezing the rain out of her long black hair. 'Poor Isabella. As soon as I change I'll go in to see her.'

'No don't – leave her be,' Mary said quickly. 'She's asleep and ... Lachlan is out.'

'Out? So where has he gone, do you know?'

Mary didn't know, but she could make a very good guess, and if she was right then Lachlan would not be back for days.

'Strathallan Castle, I think.'

Chapter Thirty-Three

When Lachlan rode up to the front door of Strathallan Castle, William Drummond came down the steps to greet him with an eyebrow raised in surprise.

'On your own? Is the honeymoon over? So soon? When I married I did not see the light of day for over a month!'

'Damn you, Drummond!'

Drummond caught the reins of the horse. 'Hang on and I'll call you a groom, but oh, I forgot –' he said with a laugh, '*you* are a groom!'

'I'm a fool,' Lachlan snapped, dismounting. 'And why did you *lie* to me?'

'I have never *lied* to you.' Drummond's laughter faded. 'Who says I did?'

'Isabella.'

'Oh good grief, I knew it! That's what women always do y'know. As soon as they get a husband they immediately try to turn him against all his friends.'

'Yes and *she* lied to me also! Am I now a laughing stock?'

'Not in this house you're not,' Drummond said, leading the way up the steps. 'This is beginning to sound serious, let's talk in the library.'

*

'Taste this,' Drummond suggested, pouring out two glasses of dark amber wine. 'It's a new Madeira I had shipped in a few days ago, and in my view, it's quite fair.'

Lachlan tasted the wine and then looked darkly at his friend, envying the difference between them. Upon his father's death William would become the 9th Viscount of Strathallan, and would receive all the property and money that went with that title. And even now he had plenty of money of his own – a yearly allowance that most men could only dream of.

'Why did you tell me that Isabella's father had agreed a dowry for her of ten thousand pounds?'

'Yes,' Drummond nodded. 'That was the amount, I'm sure of it.'

'How sure? Did he actually *say* that amount? Did he actually *say* ten thousand pounds?'

'Well ...' William thought back. 'I approached him on the matter, on your behalf, telling him that Isabella had made it very clear to me that she wished to marry you, and he was not only agreeable but keen, oh yes, very keen.'

'I know that. But what did he say then?'

'Thank you, Lord Strathallan.'

'William!'

'Ah.' Drummond knocked back his wine. 'Well, after I had told him that I was not Lord Strathallan *yet*, and that my father still appeared quite hale and hearty, he said he was very agreeable to an engagement between you and Isabella, even a short one, very agreeable indeed.'

'And the dowry?'

'Yes, I told him that as my father had been your former guardian since boyhood, I asked if Isabella was correct in saying her dowry would be ten thousand pounds? And he ...' William frowned as he thought back, 'he ...'

'Dammit!' Lachlan was losing his patience. 'Did he *agree* to that amount of ten thousand pounds? Did he verbally *agree* that amount with you?'

'Well, now that I think about it, he did not exactly agree it, in words – but then he did not *deny* it either. He just raised his glass and suggested we toast the happiness of the young couple's future.'

'So he did not agree ten thousand, but he did not deny ten thousand either – so you were taken by Craignish but it is *me* who now looks the fool!'

'Why, what happened? Did he pay you only five?'

'Two. And it was not paid into my bank until *after* the marriage.'

'Lord save us; I don't believe it. *Two* thousand. The canny rogue.'

Lachlan refilled their glasses. 'We've both known for some time now, William, that marriage for me could not be a matter of preference.'

William nodded.

'And that if I wanted to get free of my debts then I would have to marry for land or money. So I married for money – a girl that is likeable enough, but only in small doses. Now I find that the money I married is only a pittance of the amount I need.'

'So what are you going to do?'

Lachlan looked at him, a forlorn expression in his eyes. 'I don't know. Your circumstances are so superior to mine, so as a last resort, I was hoping you could help.'

Drummond did not answer, his eyes on his finger as he ran it around the rim of his wineglass on the desk.

'I could end up in a debtor's prison,' Lachlan said bleakly. 'Would you enjoy seeing me in there – in a debtor's prison?'

'It would be an entertaining sight, I must admit,' Drummond said smiling, 'but only for a few minutes, then it would pall.' His face straightened. 'No, we can't allow that to happen.'

'So you will help?'

Drummond nodded. 'I'm sure we can come to some sort of business arrangement.'

Lachlan's brow puckered. 'What sort of business arrangement?'

'Jarvisfield. If I was to lend you all the money you needed –'

'Ten thousand pounds.'

Drummond nodded. 'Say ten thousand pounds. Then I would need you to put up a section of the Jarvisfield land as security.'

'Agreed.'

'Also, no more gambling, that is the cause of your damnation.'

'You started me, you led me into it – *you* were the one who insisted on us going to the card games every night.'

'Ah yes, but I could afford to play, and so could you, until you started trying to recoup your losses. First rule of gambling – wager only as much as you can afford to lose.'

'And I lost everything.'

'You lost more than that, old chum. You lost

your senses when you recklessly bought four racehorses before you had even received the dowry, whatever the amount. That was a big mistake.'

Lachlan closed his eyes and put his head back on the cool green leather of the armchair. . 'I know, I know, I know ...'

'And there is just one other thing,' Drummond said thoughtfully. 'If I send a messenger with a note for my solicitor to call tomorrow, to draw up our business agreement, I will expect you to return to your wife and make the best of it. If you throw her aside I will not be able to support you. In a few years or so I will be the next Viscount Strathallan, eligible to take my father's seat in the House of Lords. I now have a reputation to protect.'

Lachlan sat with his head back, gazing at the ceiling ... wishing he was dead, a sweet release from it all ... If only, if only, if only he had stayed on Mull and never joined the Army, his life might have turned out so different ...

He sat up and looked at William Drummond. 'Agreed,' he said wearily. 'I'll go back and try and make the best of it.'

'It's the only way,' Drummond said, refilling the glasses and regaining his humour.

'Now Lachlan, I implore you, no more of this tedious talk about money and debtor's prisons. It's as foul as being forced to eat pig's kidneys. Stay a few days and regain your spirits, and by the time you return to Mull your financial difficulties will all have been sorted.'

'Yes,' Lachlan said, realising that he was

indebted to William Drummond in more ways than just financially. William had come to his aide, as he had always done. He had always been a friend when a friend was needed, and always a very good friend indeed.

He said, 'Thank you, William. You have my sincere gratitude and appreciation.'

'Oh *uffff,*' Drummond laughed. 'We have been friends for too long to need that kind of talk. I propose a toast. He raised his glass. 'To hell with the creditors!'

'I'll drink to that,' Lachlan laughed, his spirits brightening. 'But *you* are my main creditor now.'

'Then to hell with me!' Drummond knocked his wine and looked for a refill.

'And now, my favourite toast of all, which is quite fitting in the circumstances.'

'Which is?'

'To our wives and sweethearts – may they never meet!'

Lachlan laughed. 'Oh yes, I will *definitely* drink to that!'

Chapter Thirty-Four

Upon his return, life at Gruline House went on as much as usual with Lachlan doing his utmost to make the best of his marriage, and Isabella regaining her health and spending less time in bed.

With the onset of spring, Beth was back in her breeches, ploughing about in the vegetable garden, while Hector looked on disapprovingly.

'He willna like it,' Hector warned her. 'The master. He willna like ye wearing those breeches again.'

'These breeches,' Beth replied, 'are *his* riding breeches; old ones he had no further use of.'

'So ye stole 'em?'

'No, I asked if I could use them and he didn't seem to care.'

'Then *he's* changed hasna he? He used to hate ye dressing up in breeches and ...' Hector scratched the back of his head in an angry motion, 'and tis *no'* right and *no'* fair I tell ye!'

Beth straightened up and turned to look at him, her dark eyes puzzled. 'What's not fair, Hector?'

'Those *breeches,'* Hector exclaimed pointing. 'He alus gave his old breeches to *me* – so what am I going to do if ye keep stealing 'em from me?'

'Hector, I'm sorry, I didn't realise – '

'And them's *good* breeches,' Hector pointed out. 'Made in Edinburgh to last for years. Made o' the best codroy!'

Beth looked down at her corduroy breeches,

tucked at the knee into black boots. 'So I'll clean them and give them to you,' Beth said. 'It was simply because of the heavy rain –'

'Ye got mud on 'em – look, wet mud. My horses don't like wet mud.'

'And are the horses going to be *wearing* the breeches?' Beth asked dryly.

'Don't be doltish! Tis *me* who'll be wearing 'em!'

'Then when I'm finished I will clean the breeches and give them to you,' Beth said wearily.

'And no mud on 'em?'

'And no mud on 'em,' Beth repeated, walking back to the house.

'And ye willna steal any more of my breeches, will ye, Miss Bethy?' Hector called after her.

Beth refused to answer, feeling in a rare gloomy mood. Summer seemed to be taking so long to come, and all the excessive politeness in the household was making her anxious. Lachlan's constant politeness to his wife seemed forced and shallow. Isabella's meek politeness in response to him was stiff and tense. Her mother and Mrs Keillor were always whispering. Even Maggie and Lorna were always whispering about something or other. But nobody was whispering to *her* about anything.

Up in her bedroom she peeled down the breeches and stepped out of them.

She was being kept in the dark about something, as if she was some delicate child that needed protecting.

She slipped on her petticoat and then a warm grey tweed dress and fastened the buttons down the front, buckled the belt around her waist.

In the mirror she looked at herself and saw a healthy young woman of almost nineteen, an age to be respected.

Discontented, she stood thinking for a few minutes, looking out across the water of Loch Ba, and then she quickly turned and left the room to run down the stairs, lifting her cloak from the hallstand, throwing it around her shoulders and tying the cords.

Minutes later she was back in the yard, saddling her horse without needing any help from Hector, mutely refusing to be hindered by his protestations or babble.

And then she was riding away from the house, doing what she always did these days when she felt discontented, riding towards the sea.

Finally she drew rein on the cliff; sitting very still on her horse, staring out over the ocean while her dark hair blew about her face in the wind.

She sat there for a long time, staring out far and wondering, as she always wondered, in which direction lay Jamaica.

*

She was about to turn her horse around and ride back when she heard another horse behind her. She looked over her shoulder and saw the rider was Lachlan.

He hailed her with a smile and she turned her horse about and took a few paces down to meet him.

'Lachlan?'

'Beth.'

'What are you doing here?' she asked with some surprise.

'Like you – out riding to nowhere.'

She smiled. 'I rarely go riding to nowhere. I fancied a closer look at the sea.'

'Why?'

'It's calming. Don't you find it so?'

He gazed out to sea. 'There are not many things I find calming these days. Anyway, the sea looks quite rough, as if there's a storm brewing.'

'Rough or smooth, the sea always has a comforting effect on me,' Beth said as she rode on.

'You never seemed to care so much about the sea before. It was always the land you loved.'

'I love both,' Beth said. 'I love everything in and around my island. I love life.'

He looked at her strangely. 'Yes, and you always have done, haven't you?'

She drew rein and looked at him with concern. 'Lachlan, is anything wrong?'

He seemed about to answer, then paused. 'No, nothing.'

They continued at a walking pace. 'I miss the old days, you know, when I was young.'

'You are still young, Lachlan, still in your twenties.'

'Yes, but sometimes I feel as if I've seen it all and done it all and none of it was worth a spit. And while I was doing all that, I missed out on all the best parts, all the *good* things of life.'

She felt a pang in her heart. He was unhappy, very unhappy, and it hurt her to know that.

He smiled at her as the horses walked on. 'It was good in the old days, wasn't it? When we were both so young and would ride everywhere together; over to the farm manager's house all the time, sitting with the locals and listening to all their talk of the day. And Mr MacLaren, do you remember him?'

'I still see him regularly.'

'And is he still telling all those proud and fabricated stories about himself and my father?'

'No, not as I have heard. He still loves his fishing though. And still often has "a load on" but usually only at the end of his day's work.'

Lachlan nodded. 'It was all so simple then, simple but *good*. Every morning was a new day to get out of bed and enjoy.'

'Lachlan ...'

'And then I joined the Army and a whole new world and it all seemed so exciting then.'

He looked heartbrokenly at the girl he still loved, the *only* girl he had ever loved, the girl whom Drummond had referred to as a *half-caste* and the daughter of a servant of low blood – '*Yes, beautiful and perfect for a regular and delightful tumble in the hay, but never to be thought of seriously as a wife.*'

And then, when he had made so many friends amongst the other young officers, he knew they would be of the same opinion.

Weak-minded and easily led, not much of a man really, and certainly not a good and strong-minded man like his father.

His disgust with himself became so potent he angrily kicked the sides of the horse and abruptly rode off at a gallop, leaving Beth far behind him.

He did not return to the house at Gruline for two weeks.

Upon his return, after only three days and another enraged quarrel with Isabella, he left again. And this time Isabella left also, in tears, to return home and spend some time with her family at Craignish.

Chapter Thirty-Five

Beth was tired out waiting for the summer. Every day of May had seemed so long, and June was almost through to its end and still no sign of John returning.

Every moment of every day she expected to look up, or turn around, and see him standing there, smiling at her; but at the end of every day she went to bed disappointed. To wait for a year had been hard enough, but to wait even longer was almost impossible to endure.

Her waiting finally came to an end in the second week of July when a letter arrived, addressed to:

Miss Elizabeth Jarvis
Macquarie House
Jarvisfield
Isle of Mull

The postmark was Portsmouth, which made her give a little cry of delight.

'He's back in England!'

The sender's name was written on the back of the cream square of vellum sealed with red wax.

Lt. John Dewar RN,
The Fountains Inn,
Portsmouth.

Mary was relieved to hear that John Dewar would soon be on his way back to Scotland. Another day of watching Beth looking so discontented and impatient she simply could not tolerate.

'And he's written to tell you he is on his way?' she asked.

'But, Mama, it takes seven days to get here by coach! *Seven* more long days to wait!'

'No,' Mary said, thinking about it. 'The mail coach is faster than the stagecoach because it doesn't stop to pick up passengers and it travels through the night – what's the date?' Mary looked at the date of the postmark. 'There you go – five days ago, so he must be following close behind. Well, are you going to open it?'

'What?'

'The letter.'

'Oh *yes!*' Beth was so excited her fingers had trouble unsealing the letter carefully so as not to tear any of the paper, unfolding it carefully, surprised to find it contained *two* sheets of paper.

She sat down on the edge of an armchair and read:

> *My Dearest Beth,*
>
> *Arriving back in Portsmouth I find that my leave ashore is for only two weeks, which does not provide me with enough time to get up to Scotland to see you and back again to Portsmouth in time for our next voyage.*
>
> *This has vexed me greatly as I have spent so many months looking forward to seeing you again.*
>
> *The reason for such a short leave ashore*

is due to all officers and crew of our ship being immediately commissioned to join the Royal Navy's "West Africa Squadron." The British Government has now established a settlement in a place called Sierra Leone, and the duty of the West Africa Squadron is not only to run down and capture slave ships but also to transport in our ships as many former slaves who are too frightened of recapture or reluctant to return to their own country, and so they are being brought to settle in this new land of Sierra Leone – or which those former slaves who have already arrived there have named it – "Freetown."

I have not yet learned how long our time out there will be, but I'm told it could be for almost two years from sailing out to return. So once again that half sister of agony will accompany me daily in my impatience to return home and see you again.

But, Beth, although I hate to say it, in all decency I must say it. I cannot allow MY duty to the service to put any kind of hold on your life, especially as you are yet only nineteen.

So despite the "understanding" we made with each other in Calgary Bay, I feel bound to release you from it, as you must be free to keep company with any man who may come along and capture your interest during the coming two years while I am

away at sea. (If that should be the outcome,
then the sorrow will be mine)
   So all I can do now is send to you my
apologies, my regrets, and my love.
                              John

Beth must have read the letter four or five times before she finally looked up, and then silently handed it over to her mother. Although by then, judging from the fleeting expressions moving on Beth's face while she had read each page, Mary knew it was bad news.

Reading the letter, Mary did not understand the second last paragraph. 'What "understanding" is he releasing you from?'

Beth did not answer, because she had already left the room, throwing on her cloak to go walking towards the hills.

Robbie saw her go and leaped into a mad dash after her, barking with excitement.

In the weeks that followed Beth spent most of her time up in the hills with only Robbie and the sheep for company.

Mary grieved for her, knowing it was the release from the 'understanding', which was hurting Beth so much, even more than the wait of another two years.

He should not have written that, Mary decided. She understood *why* he had felt duty-bound to write it, but still, he should *not* have written it, a big mistake.

In so many ways Beth was every bit as proud and as dignified as her father had been, and if she once thought for a moment that the word 'released' had been politely used in place of 'dismissed' then John Dewar had no chance of ever being allowed into Beth's company again, no chance whatsoever.

And Mary hoped that would not be the outcome, because she liked John Dewar very much. She had secretly held high hopes for him and Beth, and she knew that George, also, would have approved.

Like herself, George would have seen that although John Dewar was not the laird of his own land and estate, he was the laird of his own mind and his own life; strong enough to fulfil his duty to his Navy and the freedom of the world's slaves when he would most probably have preferred to resign his commission and return to his sweetheart in Mull.

If only Lachlan could be that strong-minded, Mary wished. If only Lachlan could get a grip of the reins and start working to become a *real* laird of Jarvisfield, keeping it safe and protected from all harm and making it a good inheritance to pass on to his children.

'Time will give him wisdom,' Elizabeth had said, but with each week that passed, Mary was beginning to doubt that.

Chapter Thirty-Six

Having sold his racehorses, Lachlan put most of the proceeds into the Jarvisfield estate, keeping enough back to join William Drummond in another revelry down in London.

For all of Drummond's insistence that Lachlan should remain faithful and supportive to his wife, he had no hesitation in encouraging his friend to leave her for weeks on end while they endeavoured to have fun in the big bad city, on the excuse that they were 'attending to matters of business.'

Once again Mary was fretting about Lachlan's spendthrift ways, and she was now beginning to wonder if those ways were all due to his upbringing?

Treasured by his father and worshipped by his mother, Lachlan had been born into a life of great privilege in New South Wales. In the first eight years of his life he had wanted for nothing, and everywhere in Government House the servants were ready to attend to his every need. He was, after all, the son and namesake of His Majesty's Viceroy, Lachlan Macquarie.

Spoiled by his father and mother, spoiled by the servants, and even George and she, also, had spoiled him with affection, so likeable the boy had been.

And then as a young man William Drummond had come along to spoil him with his friendship, and was *still* spoiling him with handfuls of money to splash around and waste, taking him on revelries to London and allowing him to stay at Strathallan Castle for as long as he liked, despite the fact that he had a wife at home and an estate to run.

*

Isabella returned to Jarvisfield a few weeks later, and within a matter of days Lachlan also arrived back.

Once again Lachlan endeavoured to be a good husband, polite and attentive, and since his return he and Isabella seemed to be getting along quite nicely.

'Let's hope it lasts this time,' Mrs Keillor said, but Hector did not think so.

'Why?

'Well, the way she do walk round the garden,' Hector said, 'like a mettlesome filly who alus walks like she's got flies attacking her flanks.'

'There's nowt wrong with the way she walks!' Mrs Keillor defended. 'She walks like a lady as she should do. It's only when she sees *ye* lurking about that she gets all twitchy and jumpy.'

Mary put down her sewing and said, 'Well I think Lachlan is doing his best and trying very hard to make things right now. He has even assured me that he is going to spend more time on the estate and not leave Mull for weeks on end like he has done in the past. He assures me that he is ready at last to shoulder his responsibilities as both a husband and a laird.'

'Amen to that,' Mrs Keillor said with a sigh. 'And

about time too.'

*

It was like the years had never passed and they were both very young again.

In resuming his duties as a laird, Lachlan and Beth had also resumed their old friendship and both of them had never needed that friendship more.

Beth, because she was trying very hard to forget John Dewar and the easy way he had released her from their pledge in Calgary Bay to marry as soon as he had returned from Jamaica – or as she viewed it in her own heartbroken way – releasing *himself* from that pledge.

Lachlan, because he was trying very hard to spend as little time as possible with his wife. That way calmness at least would reign, if not happy contentment.

Once again the tenants and farmhands saw the fair young laird and the dark-haired girl riding everywhere together as they used to do in the old days, stopping to talk with the cottagers and farmhands and – once again – when the Christmas season arrived 'looking in' at the farm manager's house for a dram of seasonal cheer with some of the locals.

Robert Dewar was happy to welcome them, and old Jamie MacLaren the happiest of all; here today without his wife, and not yet with 'a load on.'

'By! If tis not young Captain Macquarie! Welcome sir, welcome!'

Beth gave Lachlan an enquiring look. 'Captain?'

Lachlan nodded, telling her he had left the 2nd Dragoons for a captaincy in the Scots Greys based in Lancashire, serving for only a few months before he had sold his commission. He had told Robert Dewar about it long ago. Had he not told her?

'No.' Beth shook her head, and then wondered if he had in fact told her, but her mind was too preoccupied at the time with thoughts of John to listen.

Kirsty Dewar was handing around a tray of her scones and not at all pleased to see the young laird and Beth sitting so friendly together, and he with a wife at home.

'How is John?' she asked Beth loudly. 'Ye remember, John Dewar? My cousin from Edinburgh?'

Beth stared at Kirsty, wondering why she had asked, and why she sounded so angry.

'John is away at sea,' Robert Dewar put in, 'and well ye know that Kirsty.'

'Aye, and Beth knows it too!' Kirsty replied sarcastically before flouncing with her tray out of the room.

'John?' asked Lachlan, frowning, looking from Robert Dewar to Beth, and asking again, 'John?'

'My cousin's son,' Robert Dewar answered. 'In the Navy and away at sea.'

'So how do *you* know him?' Lachlan asked Beth, still frowning.

'Och, he's been over here to Mull a few times in the last two years,' Robert Dewar answered. 'His father is looking to retire here one day, looking for a house in Tobermory?'

'So how well did you get to know him?' Lachlan asked Beth inquisitively.

Beth finally spoke. 'We ... became friends.'

'Friends?'

'Yes, good friends?'

'How good?' Lachlan demanded. 'Should I not have been told about this?'

Beth blinked at him. 'Why should you have been told?'

'Because I am your *laird.*'

Robert Dewar again intervened. 'Aye, John and Beth became good friends,' he said quickly, 'because they both enjoyed playing whist.'

'*Whist?*' Lachlan and Beth said together, both staring at the farm manager who shrugged.

'Tis not a card game I would bother with, and not many a man from around here would bother either, playing for a piece of rubber, but John says the lads on the ships play it a lot.'

Beth had not a clue what Robert Dewar was talking about, and she also wondered why he kept answering on her behalf.

'Of course they always played it in the company of your mother. The late and dear Mrs Macquarie, didn't ye, Beth?'

Beth nodded, not knowing why she was nodding or joining in this deception. It was nothing to do with Lachlan who she was friends with, laird or not.

'And this son of your cousin, Mr Dewar,' Lachlan asked politely, his mood returning to amiable. 'Where is he now? Where at sea?'

'Well, last I heard,' said Robert Dewar, walking

around the room refilling the glasses, 'was that he was going out with the West Africa Squadron, chasing slave-traders.'

'Now, isna that a strange subject for ye to be talking,' said Jamie MacLaren, sitting forward in his chair with more interest, 'because just there a while back, I was talking to a Navy man about the same squadron in West Africa.' Jamie made a grim face. 'Och, ye wouldna want to be going out there if ye were a Navy man, Captain Macquarie.'

Robert Dewar frowned. 'Why is that?'

'I had gone over to Craignure with the trap,' said Jamie, 'and my youngest son Aulay in it, and he was for catching the ferry over to Oban. So while we stood waiting, a man was sat down on the bench waiting for the ferry to come in also.'

Jamie sipped his drink. 'He was in the Navy uniform and soon as he saw me standing, and me so much older than him, he straights away gets up and offers for me to sit down.'

Robert Dewar nodded. 'An officer was he?'

'He was,' Jamie confirmed

'I thought so,' Robert answered. 'Politeness is one of the strict codes for officers of the Royal Navy. Even when they capture an enemy they have to question the enemy with politeness at all times. A strict code.'

'Oh, aye, he was polite enough. He was a man about thirty I'd say, but to me he looked as pale and sickly as a man waiting more for his coffin than a ferry. So I said to him, "I thank ye kindly for the offer, sir, but I'm thinking ye need the seat more than I."

Lachlan opened his mouth to speak but Beth quickly touched his arm to silence him, her face intent. 'What was wrong with him?'

'Well,' continued Jamie, holding his glass up to Robert Dewar for another refill. 'He stood up and insisted I take the seat, and when I did so, the three of us got to talking – my son Aulay asking him most of the questions, mind, not me. He told us he was not long back from two years out with the West Africa Squadron, and now he had been over in Mull, at a place near Fishnish, staying with a relative in an effort to get some rest and restoration before returning to the Navy.'

Jamie sat back, sipping his whisky and looking as if he had come to the end of his story.

'So what did he say about the West Africa Squadron?' Beth asked impatiently. 'Is that all he said, that he'd been out there with them? Nothing else?'

Jamie blinked at her, the whisky beginning to have an effect, and then he sat forward again, remembering the point of his story.

'Aye, he said it was one of the *worst* postings in the service, and most of the men hated it because so many fell ill with the diseases passed around by a flying insect called the *moskita,* and there was alus a large loss of lives of the white sailors. A ship going out with a full crew alus came back with only half a crew. And tis hard work sailing a Navy ship without the full complement of officers and sailors aboard.'

Robert Dewar's face was also looking pale now, his eyes filled with grave concern. 'And would my cousin's son John have known that? Before he went out?'

Jamie guzzled back the last of his whisky before answering.

'He woulda known it, and known it well, because the officer told Aulay it was a posting that every officer and sailor prayed no' to be given – the West Africa Squadron – and to keep that in mind if Aulay ever got a notion of joining the Navy. And aye, it made Aulay think, cos he's alus had a fancy to join the Navy and go fighting under sail – but not to get killed by a flying *insect*. Nay! Where's the honour in that?'

Lachlan had been silent with interest. 'I'm glad I chose the Army then,' he said. 'All I had to do was ride a horse and attend parades, and the only insects we had to contend with were flies, so not much danger in all that.'

Beth's mind was in a daze, realising now why John had released her from their pledge and set her free from any understanding of marriage they might have had.

She began to feel sick. 'I think I should not have drank so much whisky,' she said, rising to stand unsteadily, even though she had drunk only one small dram. 'I think I should go home.'

The ride back was done at a fairly slow and easy jogging pace, and with some relief Beth saw Lachlan blinking his eyelids to fend off a spell of sleepiness from drinking too many drams of the whisky.

Lachlan's sleepy ride home was done by instinct, and not by sight, with the help of a path known well to his horse.

Beth was silent throughout, and glad when she was finally able to dismount in the yard, rush into the house and whisper to her mother to come up to her bedroom.

Mary followed her up, concerned; and once inside the bedroom she asked, 'What is it? Did something happen out there today?'

Beth nodded, and told her about Mr MacLaren and the Navy man and all that he had said about the West Africa Squadron.

Mary dismissed all fears with a shrug. 'Are you forgetting, Beth, that John Dewar knows all about the hazards of Africa. On the first day he came here, did he not tell us that he had just returned from serving near Cape Town? And that is *South* Africa, just down the coastline.'

'Is it?'

'Yes, and your father and General Macquarie suffered no harm when they went out about in Cape Town, although I stayed in my cabin being pregnant with you and was within weeks of giving birth. And as well as that,' Mary continued encouragingly, 'there were mosquitoes galore in Australia and none of us suffered any harm.'

'No?'

'No. I think you will find that Navy man was a weakly type of man in the first place, probably not used to serving any further than the English Channel, but John is young and strong and the young and strong are always the hardest to knock down.'

'So ...' Beth asked, her mind now full of

confusion, 'why did he release me from our ... understanding?'

'Oh, I think that was more to do with the length of time he knew he would be away, two years, maybe longer. Time on the sea is not as definite as on land.'

'What do you mean?'

'Well, for example, when we were due to leave Portugal we were held back in port and unable to sail for over two weeks due to adverse winds. And before that, at St Salvadore, we were delayed there too, due to the amount of time it took to get fresh supplies on board. It was supposed to take no more than three days but in the end it took *nine* days.'

Beth was smiling, feeling so much better about it all. Impulsively she hugged her mother and gave her a kiss on the cheek.

'So you think he truly intends to come back to Mull – to me?'

Mary smiled. 'Of course he does. He struck me as being an honest young man who follows his own mind and only says what he wants when he *knows* what he wants. So when you two made this ... understanding ... did he *say* he wanted you?'

'Yes.' Beth was still smiling.

'Do you love him?'

'Oh, Mama, I would *die* for him!'

Mary laughed. 'Oh, I don't think he would want you to do that! I think all he is hoping is that you will *wait* for him.'

When the two of them descended the stairs together, they could hear Lachlan and Isabella quarrelling in the drawing-room.

'Poor Lachlan,' Beth whispered, 'I feel so sorry for him at times, being so unhappy, and trapped in a loveless marriage.'

Mary nodded. 'To be honest though, I feel more sorry for Isabella, because I believe she truly *does* love Lachlan, despite all his faults.'

'So there's hope?'

'Oh yes,' Mary said. 'In any situation there is always at least *hope* for better times to come. But for them, I believe the marriage will only settle down and become happier when Isabella gets pregnant and gives birth to Lachlan's child.'

The drawing-room door was half open, and Beth caught a glimpse of Isabella sitting in an armchair delicately dabbing her eyes with a handkerchief.

'As you say, Mama, there is always *hope*,' Beth said with a sigh, knowing that she too would be spending the next eighteen months doing a lot of *hoping* for the time ahead to fly past quickly, hoping for happier times to come.

Chapter Thirty-Seven

The time could not have moved slower, Christmas came and went. William Drummond and two of his friends arrived in Mull to spend the first few days of the new year at Jarvisfield with Lachlan and the house was full of merriment and laughter, but Beth avoided them, keeping to herself and spending much of her time over at the Dewar's house in Salen with Kirsty.

The winter months were full of frosts and the air was sharp. At the end of February Beth helped Robert Dewar with the birthing of the lambs and as always she beamed with joy at the delight of it, fussing over the tiny newborn lambs as if they were her pets.

Within weeks the lambs were up on the hills with their dams and Beth was elated when spring finally arrived and the frosts began to melt away.

One day in early April, Beth arrived at the Dewar's house to be greeted in the kitchen by Kirsty who had news she was eager to tell.

'We've had a letter from John,' said Kirsty. 'Father says I can write a letter back to him – but dinna worry, Beth, I'll no' be telling John that ye are back to spending so much of yer time now with the laird, always riding around in his company again.'

Beth stared at her friend. 'But, Kirsty, you don't know how to write, so how can you write a letter to John?'

'Ma father says he will write it for me. If I tell him the words I want to say, he will do the writing of it. And as I said – I'll no' be telling John about ye and yer bad ways, Beth, but only because ye are my friend as well as his.'

Beth digested this for a moment. 'I have no bad ways, Kirsty. I've done nothing bad.'

'Aye, ye have,' Kirsty said with a knowing glint. 'Ye've let the laird think he owns ye again, let him think ye are still his Beth, even though he's now wed and married to a wife. Least, that's what ma father says.'

Beth had no time to waste on such nonsense: all she wanted to know was – 'What did John say in his letter?'

'He said he didna know why ma father should be so worried about him. He said they all knew how to avoid the deadly mosquitoes and that was by not going ashore at night time, which he never does, and anyways, he said he spends all his time aboard his ship at sea, and rarely gets a chance to go ashore, day or night.'

'Was the letter from Africa?'

'Aye.' Kirsty frowned. 'Where else would it be from?'

Beth's heart was pounding. The last letter she had received from John was months ago, from Casablanca, so there was also undoubtedly a letter from Africa waiting for her at home too.

Kirsty was full of indignation when Beth ran out of the kitchen, out to her horse, jumping up on it as quickly and as lightly as a dancer and grabbing the reins to turn the horse around.

Kirsty ran out after her. 'Where are ye going? I told ye I wouldna tell John about ye and the laird!'

Beth was not listening so gave no answer, kneeing the horse into a fast gallop to get home as soon as possible.

Her excitement had built up to its height during the ride and her face was flushed with the thrill of anticipation as she ran into the house and bumped into her mother.

'Beth! Goodness – what is it?'

'A letter?' Beth gasped. 'Has a letter come for me?'

'No,' Mary said. 'No letters at all have come here today.'

'No?' Beth could scarcely believe it. 'Are you sure?'

'Of course I'm sure.'

'The Dewars at Salen received a letter from John today?'

'Ah ...' Mary said with understanding. 'Well, maybe your letter was put in a different batch and it will come tomorrow or in the next few days.'

'Yes,' Beth said despondently, knowing now that it would feel like an age before tomorrow came.

After a silence and a long deep breath, she said finally: 'At least ... at least I don't have to worry any longer about the African mosquitoes hurting him or even killing him. He told the Dewars in their letter that the mosquitoes were only a problem on shore and at night, and he never goes ashore at night.'

'There now,' Mary said, putting a comforting hand on Beth's arm. 'Didn't I tell you that John

Dewar knew all about the hazards of Africa and how to avoid them.'

Beth nodded, yet she could think of nothing else throughout the day but her coming letter, wondering what it would say, and certain it would be written in a different tone and in a different way to the letter he had written to the Dewars.

Because he loved her, and he didn't love them; they were just relatives. And when her own letter came she would stop feeling jealous about it all.

No letter came for her the following day, nor in the days and weeks or months that followed it. No letter from John at all. No words or love for her from Africa, only silence.

Beth was so hurt, so heartbroken, she stopped going to the Dewars for a time, and when she did, she was always in the company of Lachlan, so Kirsty had no chance of telling her about any other letters.

Whether any more letters from Africa had come or not, Beth did not want to know, not as long as no letter came from Africa addressed to her. And no letter came.

Towards the end of summer, Mary became so concerned about Beth, that on one of her regular visits to Tobermory, and her usual hour spent with Lizzie McLeod in the kitchen of the inn, she confided to Lizzie her worries about Beth.

'She's cheerful enough with me and Mrs Keillor, and even when she is with Lachlan, but Lizzie ...' Mary shook her head, 'most of the time she seems so separate from us all, so lonely within her own world. At least John Dewar helped her with that, helped to bring her out of herself during the time he was here, but now that he seems no longer interested in her, not even to write her a letter now and then, she's gone back to the way she was before.'

'Aye,' Lizzie agreed. 'I've noticed how she's gone back to her quiet ways and her shy manner. But I did warn her. I've warned her many times in the past, from as far back in her youth when she started developing breasts I have warned her.'

Mary frowned. 'About what?'

'About men!' Lizzie said. 'And most of all I've warned her about having nothing to do with any man that's also a sailor.'

'Why?'

Lizzie sighed and shook her head at the innocence and inexperience of these Jarvisfield females.

'Because, Mary, when it comes to sailors, who alus have a ship to jump back on, a female canna believe a word they do say.'

'No, no,' Mary insisted. 'John Dewar was not like that. He was a good and decent young man, a very nice young man.'

'Aye, he was,' Lizzie said, and then gave one of her saucy grins, 'verra nice indeed.'

'Lizzie!'

'Nay, to be serious though,' Lizzie said seriously. 'The best way to make a young woman forget about a man, is to settle her down with another young man.'

Mary could see some sense in that. 'But I doubt if Beth would even look at any other young man.

It's John Dewar she wants, so I can't see her showing any interest elsewhere.'

'Aye,' Lizzie agreed. 'But there's many a young man who would give up an eye to have a beautiful girl like our Beth. Aye, some might even give up a leg along with it if twould make a difference to sealing the match.'

Mary laughed. 'No, none of your matchmaking now, Lizzie, not for Beth, because she won't have it, and neither will I.'

'I know that young Ewan Macpherson is already mad about her.'

'And who is he?'

'He's the postmaster here in Tobermory. A very respectable young man if I may say so. Always reading books. He has a fine and cosy cottage up on one of the hills here, overlooking the harbour. And he has a good and well-paid job, and he's alus talking to me about Beth he is.'

'No!' Mary said again. 'I want you to have nothing to do with this Ewan Macpherson, not in any way that my Beth is concerned.'

'I canna stop him from being in love with her,' Lizzie insisted. 'I have no power to do that.'

'Just don't encourage him,' Mary said. 'Do you hear me, Lizzie, do not encourage him to pursue Beth, because all he will be doing is wasting his time.'

Chapter Thirty-Eight

At the same time that her mother was in Tobermory with Lizzie McLeod, Beth was sitting on a hill overlooking the sea. Her legs were drawn up and she sat with her hands around her knees. It was still summer and the afternoon sun was red and gleaming.

All around the land was quiet and peaceful, a tranquil haze from the hot sun misted over the horizon of the sea. White seagulls flapped their wings in the blue sky high above, but all else was calm, sleepily calm.

A time for dreaming ...

She dropped her head onto her knees and closed her eyes and allowed herself to dream ... the only escape from reality she had now ... to dream, to remember ... that long, long time of two summers ago ...

And it was all ... so beautiful ... that long ago summer ... from the long walks hand in hand, the laughter and the fun, the serious conversations, the silent kisses within the shade of the trees by the bubbling stream ... all ending on that dark night of stars on the dune in Calgary Bay ... experiencing what she had never before known, and all those wonderful feelings in her body, sending her mind reeling and spinning ... and then afterwards, lying in his arms, tranquil and blissful, she could still remember every word they had said afterwards ...

'We are lovers now,' she had said. 'When you are

away at sea, now I will always think of you in that way, as my lover.'

He did not answer, his eyes closed, but she knew he was not asleep.

'Will you think of me in that way too, as your lover?'

'No,' he said, opening his eyes, and smiling. She had waited while his fingers stroked the curve of her cheek. 'From now on, Beth, when I am away at sea, I will always think of you as ... my ecstasy.'

And he had been so loving, right up to the moment he had kissed her goodbye, a mist of sorrow in his eyes ... And he had promised, faithfully promised that he would keep in touch with her by letter, and he would come back as soon as he could and ...

She lifted her head and stared out to sea. No, no, she would not believe he had lied to her. She would not believe she had been a fool to believe him.

It was Lizzie McLeod who was the lying fool! It was Lizzie McLeod who thought that all sailors were alike. No difference betwixt one and another, all the same.

She jumped to her feet and began to walk in the direction of home, fast-paced and angry. No! She would not believe that he had deliberately fooled her. No, he was not like that!

By the time she neared home she had calmed down, her mind rational again. Any day now, a letter would come addressed to her, she was sure of it, and then sometime after that he would come back ... and then it would be Lizzie McLeod who would be seen as the foolish one.

As soon as she got indoors, she went straight up to her bedroom and then spent hours in solitude writing in her diary.

*

The evenings were drawing to a close, Mary noticed. Soon they would be gone altogether, and the afternoons would be followed immediately by the onset of night. Still, it was mid-October, so nothing unusual in that.

'The nights will soon be drawing in,' she said to Mrs Keillor, returning to her seat by the fire and lifting her sewing.

'Aye, and I need yer help with this list of provisions for the Christmas cooking,' Mrs Keillor said, looking at the list in her hand.

'Christmas cooking ... is it not a bit early to be thinking of that?' Mary asked.

'Early?' Mrs Keillor's eyes widened. 'How many Christmases have ye and me been together in this kitchen?'

'Quite a few.'

'More than a few. And have ye not learned yet, Mary, that I like to have the Christmas cake baked a good month or two before Christmas. And then the pudding done at least six weeks before so the flavours can blend. And then after that I have Hogmanay to think of, and ye know Master Lachlan will want a good table for the New Year that's coming along.'

Mary nodded. 'Yes, Hogmanay is an even bigger event for Lachlan than Christmas.'

'As it is for all Scots, ' said Mrs Keillor, looking at

her list. 'Now will ye take a look at this list, Mary, and tell me if I've left anything out.'

Mary put down her sewing and took the list, the business of running the household always foremost in her priorities, apart from Beth of course.

*

Beth was riding back from Salen with Lachlan. He had deliberately slowed their pace to a walk so he and Beth could do some personal talking together, his face friendly and smiling.

'Next year, you will be twenty-one, Beth. Mistress of your own life and able to do what you want.'

When Beth did not answer, he asked: 'Do you even know what you want?'

She looked at him, deflecting the question. 'Do you?'

'Do I what? Know what you want? Or know what I want?'

'Know what you want?'

He thought about it for some time, and then sighed. 'To be honest, I think I made a big mistake in getting married. If I hadn't of done that, I think all our lives would have been happier.'

'In what way?'

'Well, in the way it used to be before I went into the Army, in the days my mother was alive. It was all so happy and peaceful then. If I had one wish, it would be ... to go back to that time. Coming home every day to you instead of Isabella, not needing to drink so much, and all of us dining together like the family we truly are, and – '

'No!' Beth said, checking her horse and staring at him. 'You never came home to me. You just came home to the family house.'

'Yes, yes, that's what I mean,' he said quickly. 'And when I said coming home to you, I meant, as a member of the family, like a ... a sister, I suppose.'

Beth nodded, and began to ride on, thinking back to someone else who had said they would like to come home to her.

It was all lies. Now, with winter coming and still no sight of any letter from John Dewar, she was truly beginning to believe it had all been lies: all nothing more than a summer fling. A sailor's brief interlude with a stupid island girl from Mull who didn't have the sense or experience to know any better.

Lizzie McLeod had been right all along.

'And what about you, Beth?' Lachlan tugged at his horse's reins to make him walk slower. 'Have you any wish in the new year to find yourself a husband?'

'No!' Beth looked at him with annoyance. 'No!'

'No?' Lachlan smiled. 'A wise girl. After all, you do not need a husband, do you? You have everything you need at home, and I will always be here to take care of you.'

Beth looked at him. 'Is that what you want? For me to stay living at Jarvisfield for ever?'

'I think you would be happier in the long run. There's not many men on this island who could provide you with the comfortable life I do.'

'As a brother?'

'As a loving brother,' Lachlan clarified.

'I don't want any of that love nonsense. I don't want anything at all to do with men.'

Lachlan smiled again. 'That's my girl. Have nothing to do with them, Beth, just stay at home as always, and all will be well.'

*

The first snowflake fell, just three days before Christmas.

On Christmas Eve, Beth drove the trap up to Tobermory to collect the last of the provisions Mrs Keillor needed for Christmas Day and for Hogmanay after it.

The land was covered in snow, and snowflakes were still falling ... falling on her dark hair and wetting it. She pulled the hood of her cloak over her head but did not feel cold, the air always milder in the snow.

In Tobermory she collected the provisions, took them back to the trap, then remembered she had a letter from her mother to give to Lizzie McLeod.

As she turned back into Main Street, she suddenly stopped and stared at the scene in front of her ... and all around her. She had noticed a difference when she arrived in Tobermory, but gave it little attention, thinking it was because she had not been up to town for months.

But now she was looking at it ... Tobermory ... in a darkening December afternoon, so different to the quiet countryside. The streets and hills were covered in snow. Chimneys everywhere were puffing up smoke from the warm fires burning within: every window glowing with warm light. Clumps of red-berried holly were pinned on every door. Children were standing outside brightly-lit shop windows and peering in, jigging with excitement, and then merry laughter as they skipped by her ... and only then did she feel the enchantment of Christmas in the air, everywhere, in every smiling child's face that she saw.

And it was all ... so beautiful. The winter town covered in white, the lights, the laughter ...

And then she looked at the sea, and saw the snow was falling again, the snowflakes dissolving as soon as they touched the water.

Snowflakes were falling softly on her face, but her eyes were staring at the sea, staring far out to the horizon, and then her tears began to fall, slipping down her face with the snowflakes.

She turned and went into the Tobermory Inn. As soon as Lizzie saw her face she knew something was wrong.

'Still no letter?'

Beth shook her head.

'Then come.' Lizzie said quickly. 'Into my kitchen by the fire and I'll make ye some tea.'

Beth kept her cloak on as Lizzie sat her down in a chair by the fire.

'This has to end,' Lizzie said worriedly. 'Beth, ye will have to accept that he is never coming back, that he has no intentions of coming back, and he has proved that now – so long a time has passed, and still not a word in a letter from him.'

Beth was staring into the fire, her tears still falling. 'I can't forget him, Lizzie. I've tried, but I can't. Every time I see something beautiful, I think of him.'

'Then ye must try harder to forget him, my pet.' Lizzie looked at the girl's face, and felt sad for her, so sad.

'Oh, hen,' she said in distress, 'I'm no' meaning to hurt ye. I just want ye to stop picking at the scab all the time and allow the wound to finally heal. It's over, hen, and he's long gone.'

When Beth kept crying, Lizzie knew she had to be cruel now, if only to be kind in the long run.

'Listen now ... he has sent ye a message, Beth. Canna ye see that? He's sent ye the usual sailor's farewell – silence from a faraway place. In the end all lasses get the message. And so must ye, Beth, so must ye.'

Beth nodded, and drew on her breath painfully. 'I shared so much with him. I put all my dreams into his hand, and then he just threw them all into the sea.'

Lizzie put an arm around her and kissed the top of her head.

'Listen to me now, Beth ... ye will have other dreams, bigger and betterer dreams, and one day ye will meet a fine man, who will love ye truly, and will no' leave ye to go away on any ship. A land lover is what he'll be, aye, just like ye, Beth, just like ye.'

Beth nodded in silent agreement to everything Lizzie said from then on, and it pleased Lizzie, made her smile with some relief.

At the door of the inn, as they parted, Lizzie gave Beth one last reminder.

'He was not the man for ye, Beth, that's all. But it will serve ye good to remember that from time to time. He was not the man for ye.'

'No, not for me,' Beth agreed, pulling the hood of her cloak over her head.

And then she suddenly looked at Lizzie with her sensitive dark eyes. 'But I'll never stop loving him, only him. And when I die, I'll go to my grave unwed.'

'Beth!' Lizzie gasped in frustration, back at the beginning again.

'That's the truth, and that's all,' Beth said, and then she went out into the snow and left Lizzie staring after her.

'Oh, I don't know ...' Lizzie said to Angus later. 'I feel bad for her, but I'm at a loss now to try and know how to help her. She's beyond help.'

'Cock's life, Lizzie! She's only a young lass of twenty,' Angus said with irritable dismissal. 'And she's young in her knowledge and her thinking. What she's thinking and feeling now will have changed by next week. I don't know why ye women have to carry on so.'

'Aye, Angus, ye are right,' Lizzie said thoughtfully. 'She's much younger in her ways and thinking than any of the Tobermory lasses. Too sheltered a life, ye see, down there in that Jarvisfield. Too much protection. Not only from Mary, but the laird also.'

'Aye,' Angus replied. 'And see now what all their protection has done for her – the first man who comes along and kisses her and she thinks he must be the love of her life – now how young and foolish is that?'

'Aye,' Lizzie agreed again, 'and he a sailor, for heaven's sake!'

'An officer, Lizzie, an officer. Let's be fair now, he was no common sailor.'

'All sailors are common,' Lizzie argued. 'And all Tobermory lasses know not to take them seriously, not for one minute. But Beth ... poor Beth ...'

'There's nothing poor about Beth,' Angus said with increasing irritation. 'She may be young and inexperienced about life, but she's no fool.'

'Ye just said she was young and foolish!'

'Aye, in matters of the heart and the ways of romance and all that, but she's no fool in her mind. She's clever enough to learn a lesson from this in time, and a good lesson she will learn from it too.'

How d'y'know?'

Angus sighed. 'What ye have to remember, Lizzie, is that she's the daughter of George Jarvis. Now ye do remember George, don't ye?'

'Oh, aye, I do, ' Lizzie replied. 'I certainly do.'

'And was he stupid or foolish?'

'Not a bit stupid or foolish. George Jarvis was ... what's the word now ... oh, aye – gorgeous!'

'There ye go then,' Angus said. 'Like father like daughter. She has his good looks, and in time ye'll see that she also has, at least, some of his intelligence. So don't ye be worrying so much about her, Lizzie. It would serve ye better if ye spent more time worrying about me, and went now and made me some tea, like a good wife would.'

Lizzie laughed, and slapped his arm. 'I look after ye good and plenty!' she insisted, and then went like a good wife to fill up the kettle.

Book 4 – The concluding book in
The Macquarie Series

THE WAYWARD SON

Set in the mid 19th century, on the beautiful Island of Mull, on the estate of '*Jarvisfield*' owned by Lachlan Macquarie Junior – a young man deeply unhappy with his lot in life.

In love with Beth Jarvis – the young girl of mixed blood whom he believed would not be accepted in Scotland's high society, leading him to marry someone else, now much to his regret.

Beth – who has love for no other man but John Dewar, the young naval officer who loved her and left her.

John Dewar – tied to his duty in the slave prevention squadrons in West Africa – finally returning to Scotland.

A beautifully told dramatic and moving story of a young couple in love, and a young couple in hate, and the people around them who observe it all.

Based on the true story of the three families of Macquarie, Jarvis and Dewar, *The Wayward Son* is filled with wry humour and stirring drama as it tells their story leading to a tragedy that results in an unexpected and heartbreaking loss.

Thank You

Thank you for taking the time to read *'Jarvisfield'* the third book in The Macquarie Series. I hope you enjoyed it.
Please be nice and leave a review.

*

I occasionally send out newsletters with details of new releases, or discount offers, or any other news I may have, although not so regularly to be intrusive, so if you wish to sign up to for my newsletters – go to my Website and click on the "Subscribe" Tab.

*

If you would like to follow me on **BookBub** go to:-
www.bookbub.com/profile/gretta-curran-browne
and click on the "*Follow*" button.

Many thanks,

Gretta

www.grettacurranbrowne.com

Also by Gretta Curran Browne

MACQUARIE SERIES

BY EASTERN WINDOWS

THE FAR HORIZON

JARVISFIELD

THE WAYWARD SON

***

LORD BYRON SERIES

A STRANGE BEGINNING

A STRANGE WORLD

MAD, BAD, AND DELIGHTFUL TO KNOW

A RUNAWAY STAR

A MAN OF NO COUNTRY

ANOTHER KIND OF LIGHT

NO MOON AT MIDNIGHT

***

LIBERTY TRILOGY

TREAD SOFTLY ON MY DREAMS

FIRE ON THE HILL

A WORLD APART

***

ALL BECAUSE OF HER
A Novel
(Originally published as GHOSTS IN SUNLIGHT)

RELATIVE STRANGERS
(Tie-in Novel to TV series)

ORDINARY DECENT CRIMINAL
(Novel of Film starring Oscar-winner, Kevin Spacey)

Printed in Great Britain
by Amazon